D1521244

There's a Way

John Ingalls

Editor – Abigail L. Roeller

Cover Photo – Source ArtMan/Shutterstock.com

ISBN-13:978-1724791696

ISBN-10:1724791699

Available from Amazon.com

Cold-turkey Books

27167 engebretson road

Webster, Wisconsin 54893

www.coldturkeyleftovers.wordpress.com

For

Tammy

Over 40 years of marriage and never a boring day.

Preface

Writing has become an unresolved itch in the middle of my back. No matter how I rub against door posts and wall corners I can't quite satisfy it. It subsides for a moment and then another idea, another character or setting wedges its way into my mind and I find myself searching for a pencil to reach the spot and quiet the burning.

I started writing magazine articles when I was nineteen and was relentless enough to sell a few pages but Reader's Digest and The New Yorker never came calling. My young wife gave me a thesaurus and inside the cover is written; **To my wonderful husband on his 19ᵗʰ birthday. I Love You!** Forty years later I still thumb through its pages trying to stretch my vocabulary. I want to say I was inspired to literary greatness but I wasn't. I didn't sit still long enough for the seeds of youthful ambition to sprout and take root. I dabbled in homestead living, cleaning chimneys, selling bird feeders, raising cows and working in a sawmill, believing each would provide satisfaction and more importantly at that stage in my life, income.

Each of those activities played a part in shaping who I am and probably had more to do with writing than I realize. Because writing, at least my style of writing, comes from who I am, my thoughts, ideas, experiences, my pain and joys all rolled together. But its more than a sum of the parts - much more.

I believe my writing has matured a bit, but streaks of youthful irresponsibility still jump off the pages. When I wrote *If There's a Will,* I was compelled to tell a story and I did it with the recklessness of a novice. When I reread it, I find areas I want to change, confusing passages and wasted verbiage. I learned much in the process which I attempted to apply to this book. My readers will let me know if I succeeded or politely nod and change the subject.

My goal was simple; to write a story people wanted to read and leave them happy when the last page is turned. I harbor deep ideas that all things happen for a reason and I hang onto a hope that somewhere there's a lesson, a vein of gold amidst the rubble, a deep invisible undercurrent supporting the surface activity. Some have asked if there is a theme, an underlying purpose or thought I wanted to convey in my books. The simple answer is yes and no. Most of us don't set down and define a singular goal or purpose in life. It sounds wonderful but reality often proves differently.

There is a biblical command at the end of the book of Matthew to "Go..." but I tend to interpret this differently, not that I am trying to impose my own opinions on others. I think the command is "As you go...". There is a world of difference. "Go" implies a specific objective to accomplish or conquer, but "As you go" implies grabbing ahold of life's opportunities as they happen. Both are equally valid.

A quick review of our personal lives often reveals a strange and twisted course of events leading to our present situation. Very few establish a clear grand objective and then proceed through a series of steps to conquer that overall objective. Myself like many are a conglomerate of experiences, ideas, values, beliefs shaped and molded over time like an exposed cliff, eroded by wind and rain, freezing and thawing. Hardship and difficulties probably shape us more than good times but most would not seek that hardship as a way to achieve our goals. My life as well as Molly's life is better illustrated by an "As you go..." perspective.

If There's a Will is a story of a quirky family who finds their way in the face of death and danger. In *There's a Way,* the main character, Molly is the same Molly who hung from a rope, dangling over crocodiles, overcome by heat and dehydration. She's the same Molly who fed donuts to Petunia the 600-pound pig. She's the same Molly who loved to make sand castles at Papa and Grammy Ambrose's home on Lake Namukwa and play with her cousins. But now she's older. The storms of life have eroded some her childish façade and she doesn't quite know where she fits in. Like most of us, what she wants and what she gets aren't always the same. I like Molly. She's a little bit me and a little bit my children. She decisive and indecisive, strong and weak, rational and irrational, confident and worried. She has faith and doubts at the same time. She's knows where she's going but forgot where she left the map. You'll like her too.

My first novel was dedicated to my children. This novel is dedicated to Tammy, my loving wife of more than forty years. Like Molly, what she wanted in me and what she got are probably two different things, but it worked out anyway.

Happy reading.
John W. Ingalls

Table of Contents

Cast of Characters

Molly Mae Seymour- An eccentric genius looking for her place in the world; now 21, she's a graduate student at Penrose Christian University.

Dag Rasmussen-Retired DEA agent climbs out of retirement to help get Molly untangled from the FBI.

Bobby Smith-Chicago Cubs fan, English professor and big-time sports gambler.

Dutch Van Tassel-FBI Regional Director on the trail of Catch-22.

Lena Johnson-Tofu eating Minneapolis based FBI field agent tracking Molly and the Catch-22 conspiracy.

Dr. Lawrence Epstein-Cleveland based neurologist in charge of concussion studies through the NFL.

Elmore "Tuck" Riley-Executive for a division of Mork Industries, based in Chicago. They are major corporate sponsors for concussion prevention and treatment through the NFL.

Olivia and Harry Seymour-Parents of Molly and Libby

Libby Seymour-15-year-old sister of Molly

Charles "Chuck" Miller-Molly's fiancé. He's never around.

Gladys Keller-93-year-old widow, lives in 1710 Summit Avenue, St. Paul, Minnesota.

Vladimir Kalishnov-Russian crime boss.

Natasha Sokolov-Engaged to Viktor, she lives in St. Petersburg, Russia. She loves vodka and borscht and having dinner with Bobby Smith.

Chapter 1

Anyone who goes to a psychiatrist should have his head examined. – Samuel Goldwyn

November 1st, St Paul, Minnesota.

"I'm afraid of the dark," Molly said.

She sat on the edge of the lime green upholstered chair, awkward and straight, staring at nothing. The small sparsely furnished counseling room was beige, the ceiling tile was water stained and the window was streaked, but she noticed none of that.

"Don't you have a couch? Don't all psychiatrists have couches for crazy people to lie on?" Molly looked around, at the arrangement of the room.

The psychiatrist cleared his throat. He put down the file folder and checked his watch. 10:03. He tucked his narrow reading glasses into his shirt pocket next to his name tag. Dr. N. Simon, MD.

"No, I don't have a couch. That's a myth created by the media." He folded his hands together and leaned back into his own lime green chair. "Since you mentioned your fear of darkness, why don't we begin there?"

"This is dumb. I'm leaving." Molly abruptly stood and started toward the door. She muttered to herself, "I wish my mother would stop interfering in my life."

Dr. Simon made no moves to stop her. As she turned toward the door he asked another question. "Tell me about the tattoo on the back of your neck. Isn't a hangman's noose tattooed on the neck of an honor student out of character?"

She turned back and looked directly at his face. "How do you know this?"

"I can see the back of your neck." He replied. "You cut your hair." He reached for the file on the table next to him. "Your photo ID shows long hair." He flipped through several pages in her student file. "It says you are a grad student attending here at Penrose Christian University. Is that correct?"

Molly slowly returned to her seat and nodded. "I don't like bridges either."

Dr. Simon ignored her comments. He opened the file and reviewed her information. "Molly Mae Seymour is your full name?"

She nodded.

"You have a ring on your finger. Are you engaged?"

Molly looked down at the back of her left hand and nodded again. "Yes," she said quietly.

Dr. Simon paused, "Did you want to say something else?" The room was quiet.

"Your background is interesting. You had a full scholarship in mathematics and graduated from college when you were nineteen, but you changed your master's program to creative writing?" He raised his eyes from the page and peered over his reading glasses. "Do you want to tell me why?"

"No."

"According to your intake information, you started having panic attacks this summer. What happened?"

Molly was still for several minutes. She watched Dr. Simon check his watch three times. She saw the artery pulsing at the edge of his graying temples. She counted the rate, seventy-four beats per minute. Molly checked her own pulse, sixty-six. She pulled a small half-drunk water bottle from her hand bag and swallowed the rest in a couple gulps.

"Why should I trust you?"

"Ms. Seymour, I'm happy to listen to your story but you need to start somewhere." He checked his watch again.

"I was told to come here." Molly reached into the front pocket of her tattered backpack and pulled out an appointment card for the University Health Center. "According to this card I had an appointment with David Engel at 9:30. You aren't him and it's after 10 o'clock."

She put the card on the table between them and added, "I assume my mother made this appointment. She thinks I'm going crazy."

"Ms. Seymour, or may I call you Molly?" He paused. "David Engel isn't here today. I was assigned to meet with you. You intrigue me. You have some friends in very high places, or perhaps enemies." Dr. Simon reached over to his black leather attaché leaning against the leg of his chair and pulled out a large sealed unmarked envelope. He pushed it across the small coffee table toward Molly.

"I know why you're afraid of the dark." He folded his hands together in his lap, cracking his knuckles in the process. "Are you worried about anything else?"

Molly felt a flutter in her chest. She automatically counted her pulse, ninety-seven. Her eyes darted from the envelope to the dark unblinking eyes of Dr. Simon. She didn't move.

"Aren't you curious about the contents of the envelope?" He continued. "I bet you're curious about many things."

"I don't want to know."

"Tell me about your grandparents?"

Molly's eyes widened. She blinked twice. "They died 15 years ago, in an accident."

"Who is this in the photo." He pulled a photo from his folder and held it out. Two older people smiled at the camera. They were seated at a small worn wooden table with a carafe of wine and a plate of grapes, olives and cheese placed between them. "You took this photo, didn't you?"

"Yorrie and Anastasia Pappas." With a tissue from her bag she dabbed her eyes. "An old couple at the inn where we stayed in Greece."

He carefully laid the photo on top of the envelope. "Tell me about your Uncle Phineas." He checked his watch again: 10:17.

"Phineas?" Her eyes narrowed slightly. "He works with my dad as a cattle breeder back in Wisconsin. He plays the violin, he makes bluebird houses in his workshop. He eats raw sushi and drinks boxed red wine. Some people think he's crazy too. Why?"

"Is that all?"

She didn't answer.

"The honors paper you wrote in high school is impressive. That's how you got the scholarship for college isn't it?" He pulled his narrow reading glasses from his pocket and parked them on the end of his nose. Pulling a paper from his folder he skimmed the front and flipped it over. "Phineas was working on his PhD dissertation when he quit school, isn't that right? Something about music?"

Her mind raced trying to figure out his interest in Uncle Phineas. *Was he accusing her of plagiarism? Does he think she stole the data from Phineas?* She swallowed, her mouth was dry and her water was gone. Molly remained quiet. She turned her eyes from the envelope to the arm of her chair. The lime green color reminded her of puke. She felt nauseous and glanced toward the door.

"Who are you and why do you want to know this stuff?" Molly asked as she felt the hair bristle along the hangman's noose tattoo.

Standing up from his chair he took three steps and opened the door. Turning as he stepped out into the hallway, he said, "It's too bad about your academic advisor."

"Who? Professor Smith?"

"They found his car in the river." He closed the door behind him and walked down the hall. Dr. Simon took off his name tag and slipped Molly's file into a locked box containing documents intended for shredding. He punched in the access code for his phone and sent a text.

Package delivered.

Chapter 2

Life is not a problem to be solved, but a reality to be experienced. – Soren Kierkegaard

Molly walked briskly from the student center, heading along the walking path surrounding Love Lake. She ducked behind a large oak tree and glanced back to see if anyone was following. She didn't know who would be following but she felt uneasy, tense, confused. She stopped at a vacant bench along the path and pulled out the envelope and her phone.

After three rings there was an answer. "Oak Grove Dental Clinic. How may I help you?"

"Olivia Seymour please." Molly tried to control the wavering in her voice.

"One moment please. May I ask who is calling?"

"Molly, her daughter. Tell her it's urgent." Molly shifted the phone to her left hand as she gripped the unopened envelope in her right, holding it up to the light. She couldn't see through it.

"Molly...Is everything OK?" Olivia asked. "The receptionist said it was urgent."

Molly felt the tension is her neck relax when she heard her mother's voice. "Mom, something is really weird. I finally went to that shrink appointment you made for me at the health center. I thought I was crazy before but now..."

"Honey, I didn't make any appointments for you." Olivia said, "What are you talking about?"

"I had an appointment with a psychologist, David Engel at 9:30 today. I thought you made it. There was a reminder in my student mailbox. I just assumed it was you." Molly stuffed the envelope back into her backpack. Her eyes darted around.

"Your dad and I have been worried since you cut your hair and got tattoos and pierced your nose, but...well...I'm glad you're getting some counseling." Olivia paused for a minute. "Is everything OK on campus?"

"I think so. Why?" Molly slipped her right arm into the backpack straps and moved out of sight, further away from the walking path.

"Someone on Facebook just sent me a link to a news story. One of your professors is missing."

"Mom, this is getting really creepy. The doctor who talked with me today said something about Professor Smith."

"Molly...be careful." Olivia muffled her voice. "Your dad thinks some of those college professors are communist."

"That's stupid." Molly glanced about, staying out of sight. "Mom, I can't talk anymore, I have to go."

"Molly, are you in trouble?"

"Mom, just be quiet for a minute and let me talk, OK? I'm not pregnant if that's what you're thinking. The shrink, Dr. Simon, asked me about Papa and Grammy. He knew things...if you know what I mean. Anyway, he gave me an envelope with something in it, but I can't open it here. I think they're watching me."

"Molly, there you go with that conspiracy stuff again. I'm glad you're seeing the psychiatrist. Did he give you some medications?"

Molly's breathing quickened as she walked along the path away from campus. "Mom, you're the nutcase, not me. I'm going to disappear for a few days until I can make some sense of this. You can worry all you want but I'm not going to hurt myself or anyone else. Understand?"

"Molly, what are you saying?"

"There's only one person I trust right now."

"Are you talking about Chuck?" Olivia asked. "What about the wedding? Where are you going?"

"I can't tell you."

Molly terminated the call and opened the list of contacts on her phone directory. She jotted down some phone numbers and addresses on a scrap of paper and turned her phone off. She made her way toward a group of students waiting at a crosswalk and mingled with the crowd as they crossed the street. She dropped her phone through the grate of the storm sewer and went inside the Whole Foods market.

"Is there anything I can help you find?" The bubbly, shelf stocker seemed too eager.

Molly avoided eye contact keeping her head down facing away from any surveillance cameras. She continued down the aisle working her way toward the back of the store. In the gluten-free, lactose free, non-GMO cracker aisle she found her friend.

"Hi Gretta."

"Oh...hey Molly, what's up?" Gretta Benson had been Molly's friend since they started college together. Gretta quit stocking shelves and smiled at Molly. "What are you doing here? I haven't seen you since last semester."

"Listen Gretta. Can you help me?"

"Sure, what do you need?"

"Can I borrow your car tomorrow? I need to drive up north and get something. I'll make sure the gas tank is full."

"Yeah. No problem." Gretta walked into the back of the store and returned with her car keys.

Molly hesitated. "I changed my mind. Keep your keys," Molly said, "If I need the car I will stop by your dorm."

"Is something wrong?" Gretta asked.

"Just forget it. Don't tell anyone you saw me." Molly thanked Gretta and walked through the back of the store and out the delivery door.

Molly walked for seven blocks, ducking in and out of stores, always vigilant for followers. Finally, she reached a small coffee shop across from the Trailways bus station. She ordered a large French-press coffee and a turkey sandwich on a croissant and paid in cash. Finding a seat in the corner near the back she hid behind the daily newspaper while scanning the front entrance. After thirty minutes her coffee and sandwich were gone. It was time to move again.

Molly crossed the street and stepped into the bus station. Walking up to the ticket agent she looked up and smiled into the security camera. If Dr. Simon knew about her grandparents, then he had connections to people who could access security cameras at will.

"I want a one-way ticket to Denver."

"That will be $79 dollars plus tax." The agent took her debit card and completed the transaction. "Is there anything else?"

"Yes sir, is there an ATM nearby?"

"Just around the corner from the bus stop is a walk-up ATM."

"Thanks."

Molly took her one-way ticket and stopped at the ATM, withdrawing the maximum allowed. It might be the last time she could use her card. Three hundred dollars wouldn't get her far, but it was enough for now.

The city bus ride to the Union Gospel Mission took forty-five minutes and she changed busses twice. It was familiar to her. She had worked at the mission as a volunteer giving flu shots as part of an outreach through Penrose.

Slipping into the thrift store at the Mission, she traded her Eddie Bauer jacket and backpack for an oversized Army surplus coat, a faded Chicago Bulls cap and a scruffy stained Army rucksack. She transferred her personal belongings into the rucksack and boarded the next city bus heading north.

At the Rosedale mall, she bought two prepaid cellphones with cash and called an old friend, Gladys Keller.

"Hello?" The old voice of Gladys cracked as she answered the phone.

"Gladys. This is Molly Seymour. Do you remember me?"

"Of course, Molly. How are you?" Gladys seemed to light up as she spoke. "I haven't seen you lately. When are you going to stop over again?"

"Well I was hoping to stop over tonight. Are you alone?"

"I'm an old woman. I'm always alone."

"I need to ask you a favor. I am in the process of moving and I need a place to sleep tonight. Can I stay at your house?" Molly knew Gladys would insist on her staying, but it was always polite to ask.

"You're always welcome in my home. You know where I keep the key. Let yourself in the back and I'll have some supper for you."

#

Gladys looked hunched and crooked as she met Molly in the hall by the back door. Her thin gray hair was pulled back in a bun that hung at the back of her neck. Unruly wisps of gray framed her fissured and mottled face. She had some coarse hairs poking out from the end of her chin. In the dim light of the hall, Molly thought she appeared older than her years and she knew Gladys was somewhere past ninety.

"Molly, I'm so glad you called." Gladys reached out and gave Molly a hug. "It's been rather quiet since Otto died. It'll be seventeen years, next week." She took Molly's Army fatigue jacket and hung it on the hook in the hall. Gladys turned and walked into the kitchen with Molly in tow.

"Are you hungry?"

"I'm starved." Molly added, "It's been an interesting day."

"Well you can tell me all about it over soup." Over the phone she sounded weak and feeble but in person she was different. Despite her age, she sounded sharp and authoritative. "Have a seat." She motioned toward the small table in the corner of the big kitchen.

Big steaming bowls of potato soup sat between them on the table. A loaf of hot crusty bread was on the wooden cutting board and the teapot was ready.

"Gladys, thanks for letting me stay here."

"No worries." Gladys picked up her spoon and stirred the thick soup. Molly did the same. "Eat your soup and then tell me what's wrong."

"Why do you think something is wrong?"

"Molly, look at me. I wasn't born yesterday."

Chapter 3

If people concentrated on the really important things in life, there'd be a shortage of fishing poles. – Doug Larson

Early September; Richmond, Virginia.

"So, what's next? Knitting class?"

Dag Rasmussen lookup from his desk at his second in command. The only things remaining in the top desk drawer were a dozen paperclips, three pennies, a Mexican peso and a black government issue ballpoint pen that didn't write.

"Fishing." He grunted and looked away.

"Chief, you haven't been fishing in forty years. Old spooks don't retire. They just disappear. There's too much going on in your head." George Benson checked his watch.

"You're seventy-three years old. Why didn't you retire ten years ago? Has something changed?"

"Maybe...maybe not." Dag shrugged his shoulders.

He pulled out another drawer in his desk and emptied the contents into another government issue box. Over thirty years of work condensed into a couple of boxes. He didn't have regrets but he wasn't proud of everything either. The last drawer was opened and behind the ubiquitous files was his bottle of Scotch. It was nearly full. Pulling it out during office hours was bad form but it didn't matter anymore. *How much Scotch have I drunk over the years*? When he got his man he had a drink, but when he didn't, he drank more.

"Hey everyone." He looked over the office space at his coworkers, people he had shared countless hours of thankless duty. People who labored behind the scenes, putting themselves at risk to carry out risky, half-baked missions to save the world from itself. "It's 2:55, but it's time." He held up the bottle. "Get some of those Dixie cups and let's finish this." He opened the 25-year-old single malt scotch and gazed through the amber richness as he held it up to the fluorescent lights.

Cups were poured and lifted in salute. "Here's to Dag." George Benson raised his small red Dixie cup, "To a man who did more for this country than any elected politician. May he never be forgotten."

Grunts of approval arose from men and women accustomed to slaving in obscurity for paltry rewards. Dag grunted back and with his steely one-eyed stare, he nodded. It was reward enough. When the cups were drained they were refilled until the bottle was empty.

"Dag," one of the newer members of the team asked, "Of all the things you did over your career, what stands out the most?"

He tipped his cup back one more time and swallowed the last of his drink. He smacked his lips. Dag reflected on his tour of duty. It wasn't easy. Dealing with thieves and thugs and drug lords was easy. Dealing with politicians and the public was hard. Over the years he tangled with the Cubans, the Colombians, the Mexicans and the Chinese over imported, illegal drugs. He grew frustrated over the increasing use of meth and illicit drugs made in America, in kitchens and cottages and abandoned apartments. He didn't always follow the rules but he did get results. For him, the end justifies the means.

"One thing stands out the most." He said. "Getting El Chico was the best thing we did but we broke every rule in the book doing it. I have to credit old Roy Ambrose. Without him we couldn't have done it."

"Who is Roy Ambrose?" someone asked.

"I can't tell you," Dag said, "But let me put it this way. I have twisted many arms and forced many people to do things they didn't want to do. Old Roy was the toughest nut I ever cracked."

Someone found another bottle. "Here's to old Roy Ambrose, whomever he is." One of the agents raised his glass.

"George, when are you going to retire?" Dag looked at the second in command.

"I don't know." George hung his head and stared at the tile floor. "I thought about moving to Florida and living on a golf course, but...well...do you ever wonder if anything you do matters?"

"I think about it every day," Dag said. "We wouldn't do it if it didn't matter."

Dag stared at his life, reduced down to a couple of cardboard boxes filled with junk, a glass half-full of Scotch and a room full of people who lived every day with lies and deception. With sudden animation, he ripped open the boxes, dumped the contents into the garbage and poured out the remaining whisky.

As Dag reached for the office door handle, George asked, "Where are you going?"

Dag grunted, "Fishing."

Chapter 4

In Russia we only had two TV channels. Channel One was propaganda. Channel Two consisted of a KGB officer telling you: Turn back at once to Channel One.
- Yakov Smirnoff

Early October, Flight from Minneapolis to St. Petersburg, Russia

"Please have your passport and boarding pass ready. We will begin with our first-class passengers."

Bobby Ray Smith grunted as he pitched his body forward trying to get out of the low airport chair. It took three grunts and a wheeze before he was on his feet. He held his scuffed black plastic briefcase in his left hand and his carry-on luggage in his right. Most of the other first-class travelers were already standing. He took his place at the back of the line.

"Enjoy your flight." The tall, uniformed, blonde attendant smiled as she handed back his passport and boarding pass.

He nodded in response but said nothing.

Bobby checked his boarding pass three times. Seat 2-D, left side as he entered, by the window. They had provided him with a seat in coach, 37-E but there was no way he would survive a middle seat from Minneapolis to Helsinki, Finland and then St. Petersburg, Russia.

His eyes darted about as he entered the cabin. He wasn't sure who *they* were but he suspected *they* were watching. He maxed out his credit card upgrading from coach to first class but he didn't care. He had no plans of paying it back. He couldn't.

He cracked open the bottle of water waiting beside his seat and drank it. He handed the empty bottle to the flight attendant and she walked by and said, "Grey Goose on the rocks."

He hated traveling, flying most of all. He hated the meaningless chatter between passengers, useless drivel filling potholes on a road no one cared to travel. Bobby was intimidated by sharply dressed business executives continually surveying spreadsheets, punching numbers on their laptops or talking loudly on conference calls as if no one else existed. He was equally repulsed by slovenly dressed, rich college students hiding behind hoodies and head-phones; slouching in corners like piles of dirty laundry.

The man next to him made fleeting eye contact. "Ivan...Ivan Stalinkov."

"Hi, Bobby Smith." They shook hands. An awkward silence passed between them. Bobby asked, "Traveling for business?"

"Yes."

"Me too."

Ivan squinted at Bobby. The thick curled eyebrows screened his eyes from onlookers. "You are American. Why do you go to Russia?"

"Teacher." He cracked his knuckles. "To teach English as a second language in St. Petersburg."

The man nodded slightly and looked away. The pot-holes were filled; the conversation was over.

Bobby wanted to tell him he was excited to move to Russia. He wanted to feel anticipation at starting his new job, but he didn't. He wondered how it ever went this far. He blamed the goat, the curse, the Chicago Cubs. If it wasn't for the curse, none of this would have happened. Someday he was going to write a book about it. But not to-day.

When the attendant returned with his Grey Goose, he popped his briefcase open and pulled out his own set of Bose headphones. He gulped his vodka, he was in no mood for sipping. As he set his glass down he noticed the small writing on his napkin. *Channel 17.* Nothing else.

Bobby took the napkin and dabbed the sweat forming on his brow. His hand trembled as he tried to plug in the headphones into the seat jack. He struggled to bend forward, as he pushed the briefcase out of sight under the seat ahead of him.

He punched the digital channel selector, scrolling until channel 17 came into view. He was relieved to hear music. Bobby instantly recognized it as a composition by Igor Stravinsky. As the vodka began to work, the music flooded his brain. He began to doze. He thought to himself, maybe this is going to work out after all.

"Mr. Smith."

Bobby was jolted awake. He jerked his head around. The person sitting next to him was asleep. Other passengers were reading newspapers, watching movies or sleeping. He must have been dreaming. Embarrassed by his actions, he opened the window shade and lookout over the cloudscape below him.

"Mr. Smith." The words came through his headphones. He glanced about. No one gave any indication of recognizing him. He didn't know what to do or how to answer.

"Mr. Smith," the voice came for the third time. "If you can hear me, reach up and push the call button for the flight attendant. Ask for the English edition of the St. Petersburg daily newspaper."

His felt his pulse throbbing in his temples. His hand shook so much he missed the call button on the first poke.

"Yes sir, can I help you?"

"Do you have a newspaper?... St. Petersburg Daily?"

"Certainly. English or Russian?"

He cleared his throat. "English." He paused for a moment, "and another Grey Goose," as he handed her the empty glass.

He turned back toward the window as the voice returned. "I think you will find the front page interesting."

He gripped the glass in his right hand as she passed the newspaper to him. The ice in the glass clinked from shaking. It wasn't turbulence.

The front page was unfolded and a deep chill went through him. The photo showed a portly body lying in the street with several onlookers standing on the sidewalk. Even in the black and white photo, there was no mistaking the pool of red blood on the pavement.

The article was brief and to the point. *Professor David Budsenski accidently fell to his death while washing his fifth-floor apartment windows. Living in St. Petersburg, Russia on a foreign work visa, he was a well-liked teacher at the university.* Bobby checked the newspaper date, it was yesterday.

"Mr. Smith, enjoy your first-class seat. I doubt you will find your stay in Russia to be as comfortable."

Chapter 5

It's just a job. Grass grows, birds fly, waves pound the sand. I beat up people. – Muhammad Ali

Late October, Cleveland Ohio.

"Can someone tell me what happened?" Dr. Lawrence Epstein strode into the room with an entourage of medical residents and students in his wake. He reached into the breast pocket of his dark blue pinstripe, three-piece suit and pulled out a cheap penlight. He flashed it back and forth into the eyes of star quarterback, Rex Butterman.

"It was fourth down. The score was tied. We were mid-field, fourth quarter and we were going for it..."

"Not the game...him. What happened to him." Dr. Epstein rolled his eyes slightly as he waved his fingers in front of Butterman's face.

"He was dropping back to pass and someone hit him from the side. He collapsed." Assistant coach and athletic trainer, Walter Bungle checked his notes. "We reviewed the film, he wasn't hit hard and he didn't hit his head on the ground."

"What are you feeling?" Epstein asked Butterman, as he probed and manipulated the quarterback's neck.

"Dizzy, everything seems blurry." Rex blinked and shook his head slightly. "And my ears are ringing."

"Hold your arms out straight," Dr. Epstein continued his examination, "and close your eyes."

Rex Butterman held his arms out straight and Epstein watched the right-hand shake as it drifted off course, down and to the side.

"Do you recall feeling anything before you were hit?"

"Not really," he said. "But I was concentrating on the game and the crowd noise was loud." Rex rubbed his eyes and back of his neck. "It was like...my eyes suddenly went blurry...like they were vibrating. I don't know, I can't really explain it."

"Have you ever had this happen before?"

"Maybe...once at a rock concert...but..."

"But what?"

"There was plenty of smoke in the crowd, if you know what I mean."

Dr. Epstein completed his examination and turned to the athletic trainer. "He needs an MRI and he should be kept in the hospital at least, twenty-four hours for observation."

"We initiated the concussion protocol immediately," Bungle said.

"It might be a concussion but I doubt it." Epstein scribbled the orders for an MRI of the head and neck. With a nod of his head, the sea of lab-coated trainees parted and he left the emergency room. He stopped for a minute in front of the waiting room television to watch the final seconds of Big-10 conference football. Wisconsin edged out a win over Ohio State 27-25. He didn't care about the score, or the game for that matter. He was a neurologist and as a neurologist he liked brains, not sports. Football was the enemy of the brain, but if it provided plenty of lucrative work for the neurology department, he didn't mind. Over the years he had come to appreciate football because it provided a laboratory of sorts for head trauma.

The television announcer addressed the Wisconsin head coach, "Coach, can you give us an update on Rex Butterman?"

"He was taken to the hospital for further tests. That's all I know. When he was carted off, he was moving his arms and legs, so that's a good sign."

"As we replay the film, it didn't appear too serious. Do you have any comments?"

"Football is a violent sport. We take precautions but anything can happen." The coach bent his head lower to better hear the questions.

"You've got a week off before the next game, do you think Rex Butterman will be ready to go?"

"It's too early to tell. We'll wait and see what the medical staff has to say."

Epstein leaned forward as the television replayed the hit to Butterman. In slow motion you could see the quarterback's eyes close and he shook his head side to side, well before the defender collided with him. In real time, you couldn't see anything unusual but in slow motion Rex acted abnormal. He wondered what the MRI would show.

#

Tuck Riley's hand shook as he poured another drink and tipped it back. One wasn't enough anymore. He entered the password on his laptop and pulled up the spreadsheet. A high six-figure loss on the day. It wasn't supposed to happen. He had guaranteed an Ohio State victory in the Big-10 conference. The boy's downtown and in New York weren't going to be happy. Before he could log out of his computer, his phone rang.

"Yes?"

"Riley, let's meet for coffee. Maybe you can explain some things to me." The icy monotone voice did little to comfort him. Tuck didn't like coffee. The phone went silent. He didn't need directions to the coffee shop. He knew where and he knew when.

Riley needed more information before the meeting. Skimming through the list of contacts on his phone he came to "H" and pushed the phone icon. Riley could hear someone pick up the phone but there was no friendly greeting.

"It didn't work. Tell me why." It was Tuck's turn to sound ominous.

"You know it works. You saw the demonstration."

"I saw the Governor of Minnesota collapse when giving a speech. He was old and weak. He wasn't an athlete." Riley wiped sweat from his forehead.

"Tuck, I guarantee it works." There was a pause on the end of the line. "You can tell the syndicate in New York to double down on the next one. They'll get everything back and a profit to boot."

Riley wasn't sure he wanted to make the bet. If he won, he might be off the hook. If he lost, he might not see Monday. "If this doesn't work, I'll make sure your name and address is all over social media, because after they take me out, you and your family will be next. Understand?"

"Don't worry. Just tell me who you want to win. I'll make it happen."

"USC...and it better not be close." Riley clicked off his phone and headed out the door. He hated coffee.

#

Dr. Epstein retreated to the physician on-call lounge as he waited for the lab and MRI results on Rex Butterman. The television was on, showing the PAC-12 conference contest between the two championship contenders. Midway through the first quarter, USC was already ahead 14-0 over Stanford.

"Hey Larry," one of the staff surgeons seated in front of the television turned as he walked in. "Plenty of work for you out in Stanford."

"What's up?"

"Two of their starters are already out with concussions, and their best linebacker just went down."

"Good for business." Epstein replied. He stopped to watch the game for a few minutes. "Do you mind if I replay it?"

He picked up the DirecTV remote and skipped back to the first injury. Stanford's starting quarterback stepped in behind the center, calling out signals. Suddenly he stopped and reached up with both hands clutching his helmet, he shook his head. The center hiked the ball unexpectedly and it bounced free as the opposing team collapsed on the offensive line. The quarterback was pushed to the ground but as far as Epstein could determine there was no direct blow to the quarterback's helmet, nor did anyone fall on him.

Once the play was whistled dead, players began shuffling on and off the field, everyone except the Stanford quarterback. He staggered in a disoriented fashion toward the opposing team's sideline. Dr. Epstein replayed the event several times going forward and back in slow motion. When he exhausted his curiosity on that event he fast-forwarded to the next injury time-out.

This time Stanford was on defense and their all-conference linebacker yelled out signals to his teammates. As if on cue, suddenly the linebacker clutched his helmet with both hands and shook his head. The play ensued and the linebacker was knocked to the ground but there was no clear evidence of foul play or any severe collision. He displayed the same disorientation as the quarterback as he stumbled off the field, assisted by the trainers.

"What do you think of this?" Dr. Epstein asked his surgical colleague.

"Looks like he got his bell rung, if you ask me." Dr. Olson got up from the chair and headed toward the door. "You can deal with the noggin, I only fix the breaks." And he left the room.

Seven times he played the event, forward and back, and never witnessed anything to explain the sudden change in behavior. Something unusual was happening but he couldn't make any sense of it.

Chapter 6

The mind, once stretched by a new idea, never returns
to its original dimensions. – Ralph Waldo Emerson

Molly finished her soup and pushed the heavy bowl back
from the edge. She pulled apart another slice of bread and
inhaled the warmth as the butter melted and soaked into
the cracks. "Gladys, you once told me about leaving Austria
during the war. What was that like?"

"Are the Nazis after you too?" Gladys sipped her tea
and looked at Molly. Molly smiled back.

"Otto was an architect. He was out of school and starting to work when Hitler started rattling his sword. We had
our little boy then, Ezra..." Gladys paused and turned toward the credenza. A faded, cracked black and white photo
was carefully preserved and displayed. "You know, after all
these years, it still hurts." She wiped her eyes.

"Ezra was a good boy and he was always so happy. He was four when the baby came." Gladys sipped her tea and was quiet for several minutes. "Then came measles and diphtheria. I lost both of my babies five days before Hanukkah."

Molly watched her staring off into the dark corners of the room. Gladys was somewhere else and Molly dared not follow. Molly followed her gaze, surveying the room. The house had the feel of a museum. Old furniture, old photos, and old faded drapes hung over drafty windows.

"Otto was a very wise man, at least I let him think he was." Gladys smiled as she turned back to Molly. "After we lost the children, he almost lost his will to live. But we heard news about the Jews in Poland and Otto decided it was time to leave. His parents were old and didn't want to leave but they encouraged us to go because of the uncertainty we all faced in Austria."

Gladys got up from the table and walked to the credenza, returning with several photos. "Kurt and Helga. They were Otto's parents." She held the yellowed, creased photo under the light for Molly to see. "Kurt was a jeweler in Vienna. When we were ready to leave, Helga sewed diamonds into the hems of our coats, to smuggle them out of the country, so we had something to sell and get American money."

"Were you able to sell them when you got to America?"

"We were processed at Ellis Island. I fell asleep in the big room where we waited. Someone stole my coat." Gladys laughed. "Otto was furious about losing the diamonds, but I wanted my coat back. I was cold. I suppose they used the coat not realizing the value in the hem."

"When did you move to the Midwest?"

"There were many people coming into New York back then. We found some people who sponsored us, but Otto couldn't get work. We did anything we could to make some money." Gladys sat the photos back on the table. "Otto somehow heard about a job for an architect in Chicago. We barely saved enough for the train. It was a one-way ticket. We lived in Chicago for about twenty years and then Otto took another position in St. Paul and we have been here ever since. He died 17 years ago. I've been alone since then."

"Gladys, I'm so sorry for what you went through. It makes my troubles seem very small."

"Don't feel sorry for me. Otto and I were the lucky ones." Gladys thought for a moment. "You know... I think if the children hadn't died, we would have stayed. Then all of us would have gone to the gas chamber."

It was quiet in the old house. The monotonous clicking of the dark grandfather clock in the hall was enough to drown out the distant traffic sounds from Summit avenue. Molly fidgeted in her chair, wondering what Gladys was thinking. As if reading her mind, Gladys abruptly stood up and started clearing the table.

"When we get the dishes washed, it's your turn to start talking." Gladys turned and marched into the kitchen.

Molly was impressed at the quickness and dexterity of the ninety-three-year-old woman. The dishes were washed and dried before Molly had time to gather her thoughts. Gladys put on another pot of water for tea and directed Molly to the front room.

The old woman pulled back the sheet used as a dust cover on the sofa and patted the cushion. "You have a seat." She took her own seat in a faded overstuffed chair in the corner and pulled the chain on her reading light.

"Now... what do you know, for sure?"

Molly was silent for a few minutes, gathering her thoughts. She didn't want to appear paranoid but she was. She didn't think she was frightened, but every shadow, every sound outside, made her jump on the inside. She wondered about the envelope but she didn't want to open it. She had no idea what was in it.

"Gladys, do you trust the government?"

"That's a silly question coming from a young woman," Gladys replied. "The government from my country gassed and burned my family. What do you think?"

"I mean our government, here."

"I want to trust, but I harbor doubts. Do you think the government is trying to do something it shouldn't?" Gladys looked puzzled.

"Let me tell you what happened today." Molly sipped her green tea which was starting to cool and summarized the events of the day. For fifteen minutes she shared details of the discussion in the Student Health office, the envelope and her efforts to avoid being followed.

"And I have a one-way bus ticket for Denver, if you want to take a trip," Molly said as she wrapped up her story. "I'm sorry I lied to you on the phone. I'm hiding until I can figure out what to do."

The grandfather clock clanged nine times in the hall. Molly glanced at her watch wondering what to do next. Four hours ago, she felt confident in her actions, evading detection, buying a bus ticket to divert followers, calling her mom, but now she was in the sitting room with an elderly holocaust survivor asking for advice.

"Molly, you're smarter than I will ever be. The only thing you lack is experience," Gladys said. "You can figure out the next step without my help." She put her bony feet up on the hassock and leaned back. "You can start by opening the envelope."

"I'm not sure I want to know what's inside."

"Why not?"

"What if it's bad…something about my family that I don't want to know?"

"Alright then. If you don't want to open the envelope, then tell me about your Uncle Phineas. Why would the doctor know anything about him?"

"I don't know." Molly thought for a minute. "He quit school when my cousin Beatrice was born. She's fifteen now."

"What did he do?"

Molly looked toward the grand piano in the shadows of the front room. The lights from the street reflected on the angled top. "He played music. He knew things about music that most of us will never know."

"Otto loved music," Gladys said. "He took me to concerts in Vienna before we came to America."

"Phineas knew about the power of music. I once heard him say 'Music is the thread binding the soul to eternity.'" Molly thought for a minute. "He could play music that quieted us or stirred us or made us want to do things. I can't explain it, but he understood it."

"Why did he quit?"

"Babies and love." Molly knew he loved music but his love for his family drove him to find work which paid for food and shelter. "He never completed his dissertation because he was busy caring for his family. With the passing of time, it was harder to go back."

"Why did you quit?"

"What do you mean?"

"When you first came to visit, you sat at the piano for hours playing Chopin and Beethoven. When I opened the windows, birds sat on the ledge, listening. Now you're quiet." Gladys looked at Molly. "What's wrong, Molly?"

There was a long silence. Molly didn't want to make eye contact with Gladys. There was something piercing about her old eyes staring out from their hiding place among the wrinkles and the gray wisps of hair framing her face. Despite her frailty, Molly sensed an indomitable spirit forged in the fires of hardship and betrayal. Molly's own inconsistencies and failures seemed exposed.

"Molly, it's time to open that envelope." Gladys went to the kitchen and returned with a long sharp knife. "Here, don't cut yourself."

Molly's hand shook slightly as she reached into the tattered Army rucksack and pulled out the unmarked envelope. She slipped the shiny narrow blade into the corner of the envelope and with a quick motion, slit the edge wide open.

A single tri-folded letter slipped out onto her lap. Molly unfolded the creased paper and stared at the letterhead. She sucked in a quick breath.

"What is it?" Gladys asked.

"I don't understand."

"Who wrote the letter?"

"The FBI."

Chapter 7

Rather than love, than money, than fame, give me
truth. – Henry David Thoreau

Early November, Minneapolis.

"OK, everyone, listen up." The speaker stepped behind
the gray metallic podium at the front left of the conference
room.

FBI field officers gripped paper cups of lukewarm coffee as they settled into their assigned metal folding chairs
in the conference room. Yellow legal pads and cheap, black,
government issue pens were already distributed, ready for
notes and doodling. A briefing packet of information, en-
closed in a bland manila envelope sat atop the legal pad.

"Hi, I'm Lena Johnson, Minneapolis." Her short blonde
hair bobbed as she shook hands.

"Hi, Melvin Pitts, St. Louis. Call me Mel." The tall lanky agent flipped his comb-over hair into place after shaking hands and settled into his chair. "Have you heard what this meeting is all about?"

"Not yet, but we'll find out." Lena clicked her pen open and turned her attention to the front.

"I'm Dutch Van Tassel, Director of the regional field office in Chicago," The speaker began. "We have a lot to go over today and I'm going to try and make it brief."

Lena groaned inwardly. She knew getting 'briefed' was an oxymoron like Military Intelligence, jumbo shrimp, and true lies. She checked her watch, 10:45. The meeting was supposed to start at 10:00. *Typical.*

Dutch Van Tassel continued, "I'm skipping to item three on the agenda, *Catch-22*. There has been an increase in social media chatter with references to *Catch-22*. Homeland security has been monitoring this and is sharing some info with us. We believe this is code for something. None of our sources link this with terrorist organizations, more likely organized crime. However, there has been some increased activity with known Russian links. We are intercepting more messages but we haven't determined their significance yet. In the past, when there was increased social media activity with these groups, something happened."

"Are there any persons of interest we need to be aware of?"

Dutch clicked the button on his computer and a face appeared on the screen at the front of the conference room. "*Catch-22,* as some of you may know, is a book written by Joseph Heller, published in 1961. It is synonymous with a no-win situation. This book was frequently used in the classroom of this individual, Robert Smith, professor of English at Penrose Christian University in St. Paul, MN."

"But, there's no law against using the book in a class-room." Lena spoke up. "Does Professor Smith have a history of fringe political involvement?"

Dutch unscrewed a bottle of government issue water and took a long drink. "No, he doesn't, at least not that we're aware of. There was nothing suspicious or unusual about Smith until last year. He is an avid baseball fan and based on his social media posts, his favorite team is the Chicago Cubs. From information we have gathered, he believes in the Billy-goat curse against the Cubs. If you don't know what that is, look it up. Anyway, he made a hand-some fortune betting large amounts against the Cubs for many years. Even when the Chicago Cubs made it to post-season play, he doubled down on his bets and he won."

"What does this have to do with *Catch-22*?" Mel asked.

"We aren't sure, maybe nothing." Dutch clicked his computer and another picture appeared. "This is Vladimir Kalishnov, a well-known figure in Russian organized crime. He has several aliases and has traveled to and from the United States under various names. Here is a photo of Kalishnov with Robert Smith at a Starbucks in the Mall of America."

Lena squirmed in her seat. Mall of America was in her backyard. A Russian crime boss meeting with a small college professor was curious. She felt a small wave of nausea and took another swallow of cold coffee.

Smith's photo reappeared on the screen. "Professor Smith bet heavily against the Cubs, the year they won the World Series. Despite being an avid Cubs fan, he gambled against them because of the curse. Well, the curse was broken and he lost big. His debt to bookies here in Chicago was somewhere around $4-$500,000."

"Is the Mob trying to collect?" Someone asked.

"No. Here's the interesting part. Vladimir bailed him out. Dr. Smith accepted a position teaching English as a second language in St. Petersburg, Russia. He left Minneapolis a month ago on Icelandair going through Helsinki, Finland. Because of the international scope of events, we shared information with the CIA and they had one of their operatives follow him. No news on any contacts yet."

Dutch flashed several more photos on the screen. "We overheard Smith use the phrase, *Catch-22* during his visit with Kalishnov. We realize this could have been used as an idiom, but we don't think so."

"Are we hearing about this anywhere else, outside of Minneapolis?" Mel asked.

"Yes, we are, but I'm not done yet." Dutch returned to his laptop. A smiling girl's face flickered into place. "This is Molly Seymour a grad student at Penrose Christian University. She was a student in Smith's creative writing class. A couple years ago she wrote a science fiction paper which held some very interesting concepts. It came to our attention after part of it was posted on her blog."

The front page of the story replaced Molly's face on the screen. *Man of War, Weaponizing Barry Manilow by Molly Seymour*. A soft chuckle rippled throughout the agents in the room.

"You may laugh but there is truth to this. In Australia, broadcasting Barry Manilow's music has been used to combat loitering and gang activity. Mr. Manilow wasn't too pleased with it but you can't argue with success. Miss Seymour took this concept a bit further, designing an acoustic weapon. In her story, it was used against politicians to influence elections."

"But isn't this just fiction? How many fictional accounts can you find in bookstores about killing politicians? There must be thousands." Someone in the back of the room asked.

"I agree." Dutch continued, "But we are interested for a few reasons. First...the connection to Dr. Robert Smith. Second, because she is a genius with an IQ somewhere in the neighborhood of 200. What she thinks about before breakfast is more than I can understand in a year."

Lena spoke up. "So, she's a girl Einstein with an interest in creative writing, why should that concern us?"

"Kalishnov thought the paper was worth something. We think Smith sold the girl's plans to Kalishnov to satisfy his gambling debt."

"That's a lot of coin for a school paper." Someone said.

"That's what I thought, too. We had an agent give her a note with a very simple encrypted reference to *Catch-22* to see what would happen." He stopped and looked around the room. "She dropped her cell phone down a sewer drain, bought a one-way bus ticket to Denver and disappeared."

"Why Denver?"

"She never got on the bus."

Chapter 8

Life is simple, but we insist on making it complicated. - Confucius

"**Harry**, I'm worried about Molly."

Olivia Seymour paced back and forth in the kitchen, going from the pantry to the refrigerator to the stove but accomplishing nothing. She washed her hands at the kitchen sink, dried them on the towel and held the towel to her face and cried.

Harry stood silent before the door entering into the garage. He was late for work but Olivia's words held him back. "Molly has always been a free spirit, she'll be alright...I think." He put his lunch box down on the floor and turned toward Olivia. "Has she tried to call anymore?"

"No. It's not like her to be this way." Olivia wiped her eyes with the towel and slumped down into one of the kitchen chairs. "First, she cut her hair, then the tattoo, then she changed her college major and forfeited her scholarship. I just don't understand."

"Tell me again what she last said."

"She called and said she went to the psychiatrist and then she went all paranoid and claimed they 'knew things' about my dad and about Phineas. She said she was going to disappear until she could figure things out." Olivia stood up and reached out to Harry for a hug. "We need to do something. Do you think she is going schizo or something? I'm going to call Luella, maybe she knows what to do."

"I'll ask Phineas if he's heard anything." Harry opened the door to leave. The cold November air rushed in, sending a chill across the floor. "I'll let you know if I learn anything." Harry gave her a quick kiss and pulled the door shut behind him.

Olivia tapped speed dial on her phone, hoping for a live voice at the end. Nothing. It was the fifth time in two days. No answer. Olivia ended the call and dialed her sister, Luella.

"Hello?"

"Hi Lu...this is Olivia. Have you heard from Molly anytime over the past couple days?"

"No...why?"

"She told me she was going to disappear for a couple of days until she could figure things out." Olivia sniffed and swallowed the tears running down the back of her throat. "I'm scared something happened."

"What do you mean...disappear?"

Olivia sat down on her living room couch and spent the next hour trying to explain everything to Luella. Talking to her older sister helped clear her mind but she was no closer to finding any answers.

"Olivia?" Luella asked, "Do you think she is depressed or might hurt herself?"

"One side of me that believes she could and the other side of me would never believe it," Olivia said. "I don't know what to believe."

"If you think she's in some type of trouble, you might want to call the campus mental health hotline and explain the situation. Because she's in Minnesota, they can call the police and file a missing person report."

"I think I will. At least it makes me feel like I'm doing something. I'm going to call Vera as well. I doubt she has heard anything, but she would want to know."

Olivia called the campus mental health hotline and did her best to explain what she knew. The office was sympathetic but reminded her that Molly was an adult and situations like this weren't unusual. However, they would notify appropriate authorities especially about a student who might be suffering from depression or other mental health issues.

Olivia called everyone she knew and when she couldn't think of anything else to do she dropped to her knees beside the couch and bowed her head. She voiced no words, she had no thoughts, she shed no tears. She was a mom with empty fear gripping her heart.

Her phone rang.

Chapter 9

The man who does not read books has no advantage
over the man that cannot read them. – Mark Twain

October, St. Petersburg, Russia

"In English, a proper greeting is 'Hello, good morning,
good evening and so on...' But most of the time people
greet each other informally such as 'Hi, what's up, how are
you, what's happening...'"

Bobby Smith stood before his English as a second language class on the first morning of his second week in St.
Petersburg. Seventeen students stared at him without expression. Bobby knew some were successful business executives with international connections. Some were teachers
looking to further their language skills and some had ties to
the government. To Bobby that meant KGB. He suspected

one or two of them were probably there to watch him and report back to someone. But he couldn't separate one from the other.

The faces were no different than the surroundings. Bland, blank architecture existing only for utilitarian purpose. No flare, no color, no life. Bobby moved his eyes from the faces to the floor and then around the classroom. Concrete with paint- white and gray. The windows were dirty, one was cracked. The gargantuan iron heat register creaked and clanked and hissed as the steam rushed through its bowels dispensing warmth at the benevolence of the motherland.

The first week was difficult. He was still rattled by the message on the plane. He had no further contacts and after a few sleepless nights, fatigue took over and dulled his jumpiness. Cheap Russian vodka helped. But, as his father used to say, "he was more nervous than a cat in a room full of rocking chairs".

"Can us speak as real Americans?" One of the students in the third row asked.

"No. I don't mean to discourage you but if you go to the United States, everyone will know you are foreign. However, America is a very big country. Even Americans don't speak like Americans."

"What mean you by that?"

"Different regions speak differently. They have different words, different accents, different slang or common language. Someone from Maine or New York may have trouble understanding someone from Alabama or South Carolina."

"Why we do this then?" The young man shrugged his shoulders and raised his hands.

"I mean no disrespect to Russia or any other country, but English has become the universal business language. If you hope to succeed in business, especially on an international level, learning English will benefit you very much."

A man in the back raised his hand.

"Yes?" Bobby nodded toward the student.

"So, if we no learn English...we lose... but if we learn-speak English...it no matter? Like...as you say...catch-22".

#

When the FBI regional briefing was over, special agent Dutch Van Tassel walked directly to agent Lena Johnson, blocking her access to the outside.

"Here's a file on the girl." He said as he extended his hand. "See what you can find out. We doubt she is a criminal type but she's probably tangled in this without realizing it."

"How much do we know about her family?"

"There's a top-secret file on her grandparents which was recently declassified. They disappeared fifteen years ago in a staged hot air ballooning accident in the Canary Islands, off the coast of Africa."

"Top-secret? What's that all about?"

"Witness protection program. Related to Espinosa and the Sinaloa drug cartel. Roy and Lola Ambrose were the grandparents. He testified in a military tribunal and received millions in reward money. They disappeared with the help of Dag Rasmussen, head of DEA counterintelligence. Last I heard, Dag was thinking about retiring." Dutch looked around the room. Most of the other agents had already filed out. He and Lena were alone. Even when talking with a low voice it seemed, their voices echoed in the large empty room. "If you can find Dag, he might shed some light on Molly and the rest of the family."

"You said millions...do they act like rich people?"

"No..." Dutch scratched his head. "Ambrose split the reward money with his cousin, Earl. The rest of the reward money was divided between four families, Molly's aunts and uncles. Based on tax records, it appears they have donated much of the money."

"Where do you want me to start?" Lena felt the file and thought it was much thicker and heavier than she would expect on a twenty-something college student at a small private midwestern college.

"See if you can find the girl. I would start with her family in Oak Grove, Wisconsin. Also, she has a younger sister in high school. Maybe she knows something if the parents don't." Dutch checked his watch and turned toward the door. "I want updates every twenty-four hours."

"Why the high priority?" Lena asked.

Dutch stopped and looked directly into her eyes. "This kid knows something and the Russians don't play games.

"But this is all over a science fiction story? It doesn't make sense."

"The weapon she designed...it works."

#

"Hello?" Olivia picked up her phone. No caller ID.

"Olivia Seymour please," said the voice.

"I'm Olivia."

"Ms. Seymour, this is officer Mark Stafford with the St. Paul police department. We received a phone call from Penrose Christian University about Molly Mae Seymour. Is she your daughter?"

"Yes. Have you found her?"

"No ma'am. I just calling to get more information." Olivia could hear Officer Stafford shuffling papers on his desk. "Does she have any close friends we could contact?"

"She's engaged. Chuck Miller is his name." Olivia rattled off his contact information from memory.

"Are there any reasons to suspect Mr. Miller of foul play?"

"No reasons that we are aware of," She said. "He's a great kid, a bit nerdy, but nice."

"Do you think she might be getting cold feet about the engagement or wedding?"

"I don't know. The wedding is scheduled in February, that's more than 4 months away." Olivia said. "Well anyway, she disappeared and I think she's depressed and she keeps talking about conspiracy things, like she's paranoid or something?"

"Does she have a mental health diagnosis?" Officer Stafford gave a deep sigh into the phone. "I understand your concerns but the streets and shelters are full of homeless people with mental health issues. I can file a missing person report, but it's doubtful this will get priority."

"Mr. Stafford," Olivia said, "anything you can do is appreciated. Thank you."

"OK, here's what we need..." Mike Stafford went through a list of questions about Molly. Physical descriptions, clothes, habits, friends, background and education.

Before they finished the phone call, Olivia said, "Officer, one more thing you should know."

"What's that?"

"She's a genius, an IQ around 200. You won't outsmart her."

Chapter 10

No one can make you feel inferior without your permission. – Eleanor Roosevelt

Molly stared at the letter, confused. It didn't make sense.

"What does it say?" Gladys leaned forward from her worn rocking chair.

"I think there is a hidden message in here." Molly said.

"Why do you think that?"

"The words, the order of sentences...it doesn't flow like a normal letter," Molly said. "Besides, if the FBI wanted to talk to me, they could have just sent an officer or agent or whatever they call themselves. I don't have anything to hide."

"Why would the FBI want to send you a letter with a secret message?" Gladys asked. "Don't you find that rather strange?"

"I think it is very strange. And they reference a college paper from a long time ago," she said. "Gladys, do you mind if I read it aloud? I want to know what you think."

Molly Mae Seymour,

Because of past academic activities and current academic interests, your name became a source of interest to our office. Letters of recommendation for your scholarship were reviewed as part of our investigation. We believe you may know something of importance.

One of your professors, Mr. Robert Smith recently left the country, with the expressed intent to just teach English as a second language in St. Petersburg, Russia. In one of his conversations with superiors in Russia, your name was mentioned.

Mr. Robert Smith was accused of illegal sports betting. When he left, he had significant gambling debt to several organized crime groups in Chicago and New York. His debt was settled by Vladimir Kalishnov a Russian crime boss and FSB operative.

I'm sure you are also familiar with Captain John Yossarian.

We would most enjoy a visit with you to discuss this information.

When Molly finished reading the letter she handed it over to Gladys and reached for her cup of green tea gone cold. She gulped what was left and rubbed her eyes.

Gladys reread the letter and handed it back without comment. Molly looked at the eyes of Gladys, staring ahead into the corner of the sitting room. The cogs of experience and curiosity were grinding together and Molly didn't want to impede the progress. After minutes of silence, marred only by the ticking clock and distant street sounds, Gladys stood abruptly and started out of the room.

"Are you leaving?" Molly asked.

"I'm going to sleep on it. Everything looks clearer after a good sleep." She shuffled out of the room and turned right by the kitchen and headed down the dimly lit hall. In the shadows at the end of the hall she stopped and raised her voice, "You know your way around, I'll see you in the morning."

Molly heard the bedroom door close and the old skeleton key rattle in the latch. Gladys always locked herself in. She once told Molly it was a *force of habit*, brought about by years of discrimination and distrust. Fellow citizens and neighbors publicly campaigned for diversity but privately threw stones. Molly would never know the extent of her life's experience and she felt guilty bringing her own problems to Gladys' door.

Molly returned her attention to the letter. It was addressed to Molly Mae Seymour and signed by Special Agent, James Olson. No phone numbers, emails or contacts listed. Molly wondered if James Olson was a real person or some contrived generic name, plucked out of a small-town phone book. The only address was the official letterhead for the regional office of the FBI in Minneapolis, Minnesota.

She walked over to the old writing desk in the corner of the sitting room next to the credenza. The hinges on the desk creaked a bit as she pulled the cover open. In the back of the desk were several small drawers and cubby-holes containing pens, pencils, letter openers, paper clips and various normal contents of a writing desk. Molly pulled the chain on the reading lamp. It illuminated the desktop but sent the nooks and crannies into mysterious shadows, lurking with secrets. Molly opened one drawer. A folded letter poked its margins out from the dog-eared recesses of a worn book by Josef Heller. Molly pulled the yellowed paper out and carefully unfolded it. An unfinished letter to President Harry S. Truman, dated May, 1947. It was a thank you note, nothing more, signed by Gladys' husband, Otto. It was never sent. Molly wanted to read further but she felt as though she were intruding into the private life of Otto and

Gladys Keller. She returned the letter to its resting place in the book and sat down at the desk.

Molly took a blank sheet of paper and began to jot down items of interest from the letter. It was printed in a normal font on 20# bond paper. The letterhead appeared official. Several of the letters were bold print and she doubted they were random. The flow of the letter seemed awkward as if trying to confuse or convey information, but she didn't know which. And who was Captain John Yossarian?

> Sentence 1- bold letters; **B-m-a-n-i**
> Sentence 2-bold letters; **l-o**
> Sentence 3-bold letters; **W**
> Sentence 4-bold letters; **p-R-o-j-e-c-t**
> **Captain John Yossarian??**

Molly saw the obvious; **B Manilow Project**. It was her freshman English paper at Penrose Christian University. It was a creative writing class under Professor Robert Smith; a science fiction story. *Why was the FBI interested? What did they want? What did Dr. Neil Simon know? Was he James Olson? What was happening? Why me?* She put her pen down and leaned back in the chair. She knew Gladys had no computer or internet access. Molly's phone was in the street sewer drain. *Who is John Yossarian?*

Molly stood up from the desk and stretched. The clock chimed in the hall. She had been sitting at the desk for nearly an hour and all she had for her effort was **B Manilow Project** and more questions. The kitchen light was on and she wandered toward the pantry, checking for a bedtime snack. A slice of crusty bread with marmalade was enough and she returned to the desk.

She reviewed the letter again but discovered nothing new. Molly set it aside and searched the desk again. The drawers were archives, preserving history, news clippings, and letters from the past sixty years. She picked up the book again and pulled out the Truman letter. She flipped open the book, *Catch-22.*

Opening to page one she read,

It was love at first sight.

The first time Yossarian saw the Chaplain it was...

Chapter 11

The whole problem with the world is that fools and fanatics are always so certain of themselves, and wiser people so full of doubts. – Bertrand Russell

Molly slept fitfully. She last remembered hearing the clock chime twice before she lapsed into a troubled sleep. She was awakened by noise in the kitchen in the early dawn; Gladys opening and closing cupboards and drawers. The gray light of an early November day filtered through the gaps in the dark curtains. The heavy quilts pressed around her and she didn't want to get out of bed. She felt safe and warm in her little cocoon, but thoughts of the letter pierced her bubble.

After a quick shower she combed out her short, wet hair, got dressed and walked down the hall, into the bright warm kitchen. Gladys had a platter of warm cranberry-walnut scones and carafe of steaming black coffee ready.

"Good morning, Gladys."

"Good morning to you, too. I hope you slept well." Gladys pointed toward the small kitchen table and they sat down together.

Molly broke open a hot scone and watched the butter melt into the cracks. She breathed deeply, inhaling the steam from her coffee mug. She knew it was Lavazza, Italian roast. It was her favorite and Gladys always had it ready when Molly stayed over. Molly felt at home in the big old kitchen. Gladys was the grandmother she didn't have. Her own grandmother was "killed off and given a new identity" as part of the witness protection program. She loved her Papa and Grammy but Icaria, Greece was far away. Gladys filled in, admirably.

"Well? What do you know for sure?" Gladys asked.

Molly smiled to herself. Gladys always said that when there were quiet gaps in their conversation.

"I know a bit more but I have questions."

Gladys poured herself some hot green tea and took a bite of a scone, without the butter. "Are you going to tell me or do I have to guess?"

"My first question has to do with the book you have in your desk; Catch-22. Who is Captain John Yossarian? And is he the same Yossarian mentioned in the letter?"

"What do you think?"

"Catch-22 has come to mean: there is no good solution or you lose either way. But what does that have to do with me? Or my college paper? Or Professor Smith? This is all crazy. It isn't rational."

"Do you think the letter is legitimate?"

"If it's from the FBI, then we have to assume it's rational and done for a reason. If the FBI didn't send it, then who? And why go through the charade? For what purpose?"

"Let's start with what we know." Gladys bit off another corner of scone. "Tell me about this B. Manilow Project. What's that all about?"

"It's a science fiction story about the government developing and using an acoustic weapon; a weapon based on the use of sound waves. In the story, the weapon was used to disable government leaders, spies, and influence outcomes like elections." Molly was quiet for a few minutes, reflecting on her storyline. "I got the name 'Manilow Project' from an interesting news story. In an Australian city, the music of Barry Manilow was broadcast on outdoor speakers to discourage loitering by groups of young people.

69

It worked but Mr. Manilow wasn't pleased with the type of publicity he received."

"So, your weapon played Barry Manilow music at congressional hearings and balloting places?"

Molly laughed at the absurdity of the idea. "I wish it was that simple," she said. "I designed a device I dubbed the Cossack weapon, after the Russian-Ukrainian ethnic groups known for their military prowess. It's also an acronym based on its working name; Coordinated Operational Sub-Sonic Acoustic Concentrator."

"Is it real?"

"No. It was science fiction but the weapon was based on real math. It's basic physics, using the interaction of concentrated acoustic energy or sound waves, on biological systems." She thought for a minute. "The Cossack weapon could be easily developed but I doubt it would be practical."

"I'm an old Jewish woman. Explain it in terms I can understand." Her tea was cold, she poured another cup and leaned back in her chair.

Molly spent the next hour drawing diagrams, explaining parabolas and sound wave theory to the old woman. Gladys asked more questions and Molly did her best to offer simple explanations. At the end of an hour, Gladys took off her scratched bifocals and cleaned them with her napkin.

"I think the FBI believes something that you don't believe."

"What's that?" Molly asked.

"They think your weapon is real. Somebody took your plans and made the Cossack weapon. Why else would they come sneaking around with funny letters and code words." Gladys leaned forward. "Molly, look at the obvious. They must believe this thing is real and a threat to someone. I would be willing to bet a pocket full of diamonds, your professor, Mr. Smith is behind this."

"Are you serious?" Molly asked.

"You may be a genius, but sometimes you don't see the obvious," Gladys said. "Anyway, do you have a better idea?"

"Yes," she thought for a minute. "I'm going to find Dag Rasmussen and Papa Roy."

"I thought your grandfather was dead?"

"He is. Sort of..."

#

The Harry's Happy Heifer Breeding Service truck pulled to a rolling stop at the mailbox. Harry reached into the black dented box and retrieved the mail. He shuffled quickly through the junk, the bills and the catalogs. He mentally sorted the stack into garbage, maybe garbage, and maybe worth opening. *No one sends letters anymore.* Then he saw the envelope and his heart fluttered. A letter from Michael's Bridal Emporium.

Harry coughed from the cold November air rushing in through the open truck window. He dropped the pile of delivered mail into the vacant truck seat and pulled into his driveway. He was home early, worried about Molly. Olivia had worked herself into a modified panic, calling everyone she knew, searching for Molly. It had only been 24 hours since Molly called but even he felt angst. He hoped it was nothing more than pre-wedding jitters. *This isn't like Molly. It's more than cold feet. Something's different.*

"I'm home." Harry pushed open the side door between the garage and mudroom and stepped inside, out of the cold.

"Honey? Is that you?" Olivia appeared from the kitchen. She stopped when she saw it was Harry. "I was hoping it was Molly. Did you learn anything from Phineas?"

"Nope."

"I'm going to call the police again to see what they might have learned."

"Olivia, don't bother them. If they learn something they'll call."

"Aren't you worried?"

Harry sat in the entry room chair and bent forward to take his boots off. *Of course, he was worried, any normal father would worry.* "No, I'm not worried. Molly is very capable and a bit eccentric with a strong independent streak. I'm sure she's OK. Just cold feet, that's all."

"Cold feet? Do you mean about the wedding?"

"Here," He handed Olivia the envelope from Michael's Wedding Emporium. Olivia ripped open the envelope. "I almost forgot. Molly organized a wedding dress shopping day and all my sisters and her cousins were coming. That's next week."

"Do you think there's something between her and Chuck?"

"I don't think so, but I haven't talked to him since we were all together at the lake on Labor Day." Olivia brushed her hair back from her face. "Why? Do you suspect something?"

"I guess not. I like Chuck but...he's a bit odd...if you ask me."

"Well no one asked you."

Harry put his boots and coat into the closet and stepped into the kitchen, dropping the mail on the table. He reached into the pantry and pulled out a bottle of Louis Martini Sonoma Valley, Cabernet, 2014, and cut the foil away.

"Harry, what are you doing?"

"What does it look like I'm doing?"

"But, it's only 3:30."

"Close enough."

Chapter 12

My father gave me the greatest gift anyone could give another person. He believed in me. – Jim Valvano

Early November, St. Paul, Minnesota

"Mom, the FBI is looking for me."

"Molly? Is that you?" Olivia sounded worried. "Whose phone are you using? It isn't your usual number. Your father and I are worried sick."

"I'm fine but I'm not sure what's going on. I'll tell you later."

"I think you owe us an explanation now. What did the psychiatrist say to you?"

"He said I'm crazy and I might have a worm in my brain."

"Don't talk like that. I don't think he really meant it."

"Mom? Do you really think he said that? You're loonier than he is."

"Molly, here's your father."

"Molly, this is Dad."

"I know who you are, Dad," Molly sighed. She felt frustrated. "Dad, listen to me. I'm not crazy and I'm not running away. I need something important."

"What?"

"You're gonna think I'm crazy for asking."

"What now?"

"Contact Papa Roy, I need the unlisted phone number for Dag Rasmussen, the DEA agent."

"Are you crazy?" Molly could hear muffled mumbling in the background. "Molly, I'm not doing anything until you tell us what's happening."

"You won't believe me if I tell you."

"Try me."

"OK... The FBI thinks I'm involved with some conspiracy involving acoustic weapons, Barry Manilow and some guy named Captain John Youssarian."

There was a long pause. "You're right, I don't believe you."

"OK, listen...Get me Dag's number and I promise I will tell you everything I know."

Chapter 13

A life lived in fear is a life half-lived. – Spanish Proverb

Early November, St. Petersburg, Russia

Bobby Smith's hand trembled just a bit as he folded the note and slipped it into his shirt pocket. The directions were clear; 9:00 pm, Friday, bus stop corner of Prospekt and Pribrezhnaya street. Smith knew the bus stop well. It was six blocks from the school. It's where he got off the bus every morning and on every evening. There was night club across the street from the bus stop. On Friday night the street corner would be busy.

Bobby wrapped his scarf around his bare neck and put on his gray wool overcoat. Early November had been mild for St. Petersburg but there was a new chill in the forecast. The coat offered little comfort.

The writing assignments were scattered across his desk. It was a simple task for his students; write a short narrative giving directions to a location or event. Not unlike a task they might encounter in the real world. *Go here, stop there, turn right or left, take the red bus to the intersection of...* What he didn't anticipate was the note in clear, concise English, he held in his hand. Bobby knew this demanded more than a letter grade. He intended to follow the directions.

In St. Petersburg, Russia the sun sets early in November. A cold rain coming off the Baltic Sea to the west further dampened his enthusiasm. He didn't have an umbrella and a thin rivulet of ice water leaked under his collar and down the center of his back. He shuddered. The city clock on the street corner said 6:32 pm. Too late to ride the city bus to his apartment and back to Prospekt and Pribrezhnaya in time for the 9:00 pm meeting.

Two blocks from the arranged meeting place was a coffee shop frequented by academics and students. It was always busy, a place to discuss philosophy, religion, politics, the latest books or anything you wanted. Only the naive believed their conversations were safe from eavesdropping. In Russia, everyone listened, everyone watched and some reported to others. One could never tell if the radical student or the old professor hiding behind thick lens was a dissident or KGB. Most couldn't define KGB. It represented everything they didn't understand and didn't trust. The true power of the KGB rested in that very fact, it was undefinable and ubiquitous.

Bobby Smith was a good American at heart. He believed in government but only to a point. He liked freedom and he didn't like interference. He always believed government was established to protect its citizens but not to dictate their actions or decisions. He also knew he couldn't have it both ways. After a few weeks in Russia he was slowly assimilating into Russian life. But unlike Russians, he still trusted others.

The doors to the coffee shop opened and smoke from a dozen cigarettes billowed out as the belch of diesel exhaust from city busses rushed in. Bobby found a seat in the corner, sharing a table with a young couple who appeared to argue above the table but clutched hands under the table. They ignored him. He preferred it.

The waiter also ignored him. After nearly thirty minutes had passed, Bobby caught his arm as he passed. Bobby felt the waiter was rude but decided not to make a scene. Everyone was rude. He ordered as quickly as possible. He wouldn't get another chance. Coffee, soup and bread.

The animated conversations ebbed and flowed, rising in volume when the city busses stopped outside at the corner and quieting a bit when they drove off. Bobby coughed from the smoke. No surgeon general warnings about second-hand smoke here. No one seemed to care. Anyone self-righteous enough to give a health warning would have been laughed out of the room. The lukewarm soup tasted good after a long day. The crusty bread was just that. At home if he ordered crusty bread at a restaurant it was fresh with a crunchy crust. Here it was literally crusty bread, day old was considered fresh. The coffee was hot and black with an acidic aftertaste. He took a big gulp. The coffee grounds stuck to his teeth.

Across the room, three tables away, he noticed a fat old woman with a fur cap and a ragged wool coat, open at the front. Her simple print dress was stained over her ample bosom. Coffee or grease, Bobby couldn't tell which, probably both. She munched on the same crust of bread and crumbs came to rest on the stains. But it was the book she was reading which interested him more: *Animal Farm by George Orwell.* She looked up from her reading and her eyes met his. She smiled. Her left front tooth was missing. She didn't seem to mind.

Bobby politely nodded in her direction and smiled back.

He returned his attention to the soup, slurping it down before its remaining warmth escaped into the smoky room. He wiped the bottom of the bowl with the end of his bread, letting the last drops of soup absorb into the crust. He raised his head when a shadow passed over his table. The fat woman squeezed into the space across from him. The young couple at the end of the table abruptly stood and left.

"I'm Natasha Sokolov," she said. "You're the American? Yes?" She burped and wiped bread crumbs from the bristly hair on her chin.

"Bobby Smith," he said and nodded yes.

"Do you come here often?"

"To St. Petersburg?"

"To coffee shop."

"Sometimes, after my class."

"You like to read?"

"Yes," he said. "I teach English at the University."

"I know."

A long awkward silence passed between them. She smiled. He nodded. She burped. He coughed. She scratched. He yawned. Finally, she reached into her handbag and pulled out a copy of Josef Heller's book, *Catch-22*. He swallowed. She noticed.

"You have meeting at bus stop? Yes?"

He said nothing.

She left a couple rubles on the table and stood as gracefully as she could in the tight space between tables. She buttoned the tattered woolen coat over her stained bosom and smiled.

"Don't be late."

#

Tuck Riley opened his laptop and checked the latest news release. He scrolled through the sports headlines until he found what he was looking for. Mork Engineering in partnership with Cleveland Clinic, the NCAA and the NFL made a grant of five million dollars to retrofit all football helmets with a gel-based helmet liner. In concussion studies, gel combined with air cells demonstrated better dissipation of impact force when compared to foam or air cells alone. Efforts were made to replace all protective helmet padding as soon as possible. It was estimated to reduce concussion frequency and severity by 50%.

He posted a link to the news release into another email and thumped the enter key to send his message.

Everything was on schedule.

#

Bobby walked down Prospekt for thirty minutes, until his legs were tired. He rested at a bus stop then turned around and walked back. He checked the clock on the corner. 8:43 pm. He rested again and watched the night club.

Young people with money came and went. Slim, tall and well dressed. He didn't fit in. Everyone smoked. He checked the clock again. 8:49 pm.

He didn't want to appear anxious or worried so he went to the bus stop and pulled out a newspaper. His mind was elsewhere. He stared at the front page for three minutes before he realized it was upside down. When he flipped it over, four more people joined him in the small bus shelter. The rain intensified. It was dark and the glow of the weak street lights in the mist added to his sense of gloom.

The busses came and went. People got on and off. Some lingered, some left. One person sat close to him on the bench but said nothing. He appeared to be a college student with a backpack. He set the backpack under the bench out of the rain as he waited for the next bus.

Bobby looked down the street at the clock. 9:13 pm. No contact, no words, no signals. He didn't even know why he was here. *Why did the fat lady have the book, Catch-22? What does it mean? Who wants to meet with him? Why?* A hundred questions bounded in and out of his mind.

The next city bus splashed through the puddles collecting on the side of the road. The door opened and the young man perched at his right elbow bounded up and got on the bus. Just as the bus pulled away from the side of the road, Bobby noticed the backpack under the bench. He picked it up and jumped toward the bus, but it was gone. He was the only one left in the shelter.

There was plenty of noise across the street at the night-club. Bobby looked down at the backpack. It had a Chicago Cubs logo embroidered into the side. He set the bag down on the bench and turned to look at the clock one more time. 9:19 pm. The fat lady was standing under the clock looking at him.

She waved.

He didn't wave back.

Chapter 14

Whenever you find yourself on the side of the majority,
it is time to pause and reflect.   – Mark Twain

"**So**, what are you going to do?" Gladys asked.

She swept the last crumb from under the table and put
her broom and dustpan into the hall closet. She took off her
apron and hung it beside the broom on a hook and turned
back toward the kitchen. Gladys sat down opposite Molly
and waited.

Molly thought for several minutes. The ticking of the
clock in the hall helped her think. It gave her brain a
rhythm, a pace, to contemplate, to calculate, to guess.

"Gladys, I'm not sure what to do. I don't know what
this means."

"Take a piece of paper and divide it into three columns.
In the first column write everything you know. In the third

column write all the questions you have or the things you don't understand."

"And the middle?"

"That's where you fill in the blanks."

Molly did as Gladys suggested. Over the next two hours, she wrote every detail she thought was fact on the left and every possible question or unknown possibility on the right. She knew she did nothing wrong so the only possible conclusion was suspicion of wrongdoing or she was being framed. Connecting the dots wasn't going to be easy. And she was supposed to be planning her wedding.

After two pots of tea she was little closer to understanding the situation than when she started. But she understood the questions a bit more.

#

Dutch Van Tassel went over the details of the morning briefing. There were the usual white-collar crimes, concerns about terrorism, threats to politicians on social media and countless other items certain to usher in the apocalypse. One phrase kept coming up on social media and he didn't like it: Catch-22. Everyone knew about the book and the vernacular meaning. It had shown up in emails, Facebook, even news articles about unrelated items. Dutch knew there was a team at the national level searching for connections to organized crime or terrorism but no conclusions were drawn. So far, no one had been able to fill in the blanks.

Molly Mae Seymour was an enigma. She was a bright kid, came from a good family, went to a conservative private college, had no connections to subversive groups as far as he could tell and yet her name was connected to Bobby Smith who was tied to the Russians. The only logical link was her creative writing class.

He pulled out the diagrams from her paper, *Man of War, Weaponizing Barry Manilow*. The Coordinated Output Synchronized-Sonic Acoustic Concentrator or Cossack device was simple by design. A parabolic listening device in reverse. The transducer emitted computer generated acoustic waves, with wavelengths of exact multiples. The crest of each sound wave added to the crest of other frequencies causing a pressure pulse. The parabolic dish concentrated the acoustic waves and allowed for directional output. A coordinated use of three or more devices aimed and intersecting at a particular location or person resulted in disorientation, confusion, seizure-like activities and, at times, unconsciousness. *Interesting idea, dumb story. She should stick to math and leave the writing to others.*

#

Bobby Smith entered his apartment and hit the light switch. The fluorescent lights flickered and buzzed and finally committed to lighting up the room. He looked around, but he could see nothing amiss. He lived in a studio apartment, there were no other rooms except the bathroom. The door was open, the toilet seat was up, just as he left it.

The Chicago Cubs backpack dripped onto his floor. He took off his wet woolen coat and hung it on the hook behind the door. It stunk, like the sheep was still in it. His shoes were wet and squished when he walked. He took them off and his socks, leaving them on a stack of old newspapers on the floor under his coat. The floor was cold and creaked as he went to the wardrobe beside his rollaway cot and pulled out dry clothes. He hung his wet clothes on the retracting clothesline strung across his bathroom. Finally, he sat on the edge of the bed and looked at the backpack.

No identification on the backpack except the Chicago Cubs emblem. No names written or luggage tags. He cautiously unzipped the bag and looked inside. One book, *Catch-22,* a plastic toy gun and a cellphone. Nothing else.

He unzipped the side pockets. Nothing.

The book kept showing up and he had no idea what it all meant. *Was someone sending him a message? What did it mean?* He opened the book. Two envelopes fell out.

The first held airline tickets. The tickets had his name on the top. Leaving in less than forty-eight hours. The itinerary was Helsinki-London-Madrid-Toronto-New York-Chicago. Coach. According to the departure times, he had a layover of four or five hours in each city. In addition to the tickets he found a list.

H 750K €

L 1,200K £

M 650K €

T 800K $

NY 3,000K $

Ch-Codename-Yossarian; Speed Dial #6-instructions.

It didn't make sense. He understood the places and the money but he couldn't link them with any common denominator. Bobby picked up the phone and pushed the power button. It was a typical unlisted, prepaid cellphone. The screen flickered on but it was blank. He found the button for contacts. There were six listed, identified only by initials, correlating with the cities.

He opened the second. *Meet the girl, Mall of America, Michael's Wedding Emporium.* The date and time were listed. *Who? Wedding shop? I have to get from Chicago to Minneapolis on my own...on a weekend. I hate the Mall of America on weekends.*

My teaching days are over.

Chapter 15

The mass of men lead lives of quiet desperation.
– Henry David Thoreau

October; On the road.

In the days and weeks following Dag's final days in office, he lurched about, distracted, disoriented and without focus. He still arose at five AM and challenged his body with strenuous exercise designed to strengthen the muscles and test the soul. When his hour of testing was over, he was aimless. He missed the camaraderie and challenge. He loved the test of wits against ruthless opponents. He felt alive when he fought evil and let good triumph. The Times crossword puzzle didn't measure up.

Within a week of his retirement, he was lost. He tried going back to the office to catch up on the latest dirt but his security clearance was terminated. He could only enter his old office under the watchful eyes of former subordinates. It was amusing at first but soon became frustrating and humiliating. He didn't belong anymore. Not at the office, not anywhere.

He had no family and no long-term friends to welcome him for a long visit. His son was dead, killed by El Chico the Sinaloa drug lord and his common law wife was long gone, married or living with someone else. He hadn't heard from her in over twenty years. So, he did what any red-blooded American male would do. He called his friend and fellow Dane, Terry Larsen and paid cash for a new blue 1500 Chevy Silverado pickup. Next, he bought a twenty-two-foot shiny silver Airstream travel trailer and a fishing rod. He never owned a house and had few personal possessions other than a gun collection and several poetry books and Jack Reacher novels. He left on a Sunday morning just as the first early risers were making coffee.

It was the 9th of October when he left his home near Fredericksburg, Virginia. He headed southeast toward the Atlantic coast and eventually turned inland stopping at Fort Benning, Georgia to visit with old friends still working with the military. He rekindled old relationships but they quickly flamed out. Their bonds of friendship were forged under the auspices of duty until death. Friendships were bound by shared adversity not good times. Even Dag tired of the same old war stories day after day and night after night.

His customary shot of aged and expensive Scotch whisky, to celebrate victory, became a daily ritual to dull his defeat. Though he was a decorated American hero, his heroics were done in secret and he had no one left to share his exploits.

He tried bass fishing in Georgia and Florida and he hired a guide to catch redfish along the coast of Alabama but he soon tired of the chase. He wandered toward New Orleans, stopping at diners and redneck hangouts along the way. When he reached the Mississippi delta, he hired someone to take him out in the bayou on an airboat, hunting gators. He put the crosshairs of his rifle scope on the walnut-sized brain of an alligator sunning himself in the Louisiana swamp but he couldn't pull the trigger. The thrill was gone.

As his disciplined will faded, his taut and lean waistline grew. Within a few weeks of leaving Virginia he let his belt out two notches. Cheap scotch replaced the good stuff. A bottle lasted a month or more in his previous life, it now barely stretched a week.

From New Orleans, he took the on-ramp for Interstate 10 to Baton Rouge but he was uncomfortable with the speed and heavy traffic. If Laser guided, high-tech weaponry was a metaphor for his work life, he was now a Civil War musket pointed randomly at a noise in the dark. He plodded northward, keeping Old Man River to his left, the grill of his blue Chevy Silverado ahead of him and the Silver Bullet behind.

He didn't know how many days he had been traveling. It didn't matter. His closely cropped hair, thinning and gray was now disheveled and unruly, almost long enough for a ponytail. His beard had grown in, full and bristly. One morning he glanced in the mirror when brushing his teeth. He laughed to himself, thinking he could be an undercover agent for Mother Earth News.

One night he was camped in a small county park on the shore of an oxbow lake along the Mississippi. As usual, he had a small campfire going. He liked to sip his scotch and watch the flames. It filled the empty spots in his brain with peace. It was quiet until a group of young thugs pulled in and started making noise.

Three scruffy guys with dirty clothes and dirtier language. It could have been him in another life. He did his best to ignore them. But they didn't want to be ignored.

"Hey girls, mind if we sit by your fire?" They approached a small blue and gray tent pitched under pines, about 50 yards from Dag. Two college age girls huddled by the fire, keeping warm in the cold autumn air.

"No thanks," they said. "Our boyfriends went to town and should be back any minute."

"Now, little girls, don't be lyin' to us. That little pink Prius and your cute little tent couldn't hold more than two people."

"We aren't lying to you," the girls answered. "They have another car." One girl inched closer to the other.

In the flickering firelight Dag could see worry on their faces. He watched the drama unfold. The thugs encircled the girls and walked slowly into the firelight. Dag assessed the situation. The biggest was easily six-feet-tall with the start of a beer gut. His faded green plaid flannel shirt was half untucked with black grease stains, probably from stripping car parts in a backyard. The sleeves were rolled up to the elbows. Dag could see tattoos or grease, he wasn't sure which. The other two were subordinate flunkies, with greasy hair and rotten tobacco stained teeth, grinning and nodding in agreement with their slob leader.

Dag had seen their ilk before. Probably high on meth and weed. Like a bad rash, he knew they weren't going away without some serious scratching.

"What you girls got in the tent? Beer? Girly wine coolers? Soft, warm sleeping bags? Maybe we could spend the night with you, huh?"

"Let's see what you got." One of the grease balls opened his knife and slit the side of the tent wide open and pulled two sleeping bags outside onto the ground, around the fire.

One of the girls punched 911 on her phone but before it was answered, the big-shot grabbed her phone and tossed it into the fire. "Ain't no police gonna help you now," he said. "Since you don't wanna share with us, we're gonna take it anyway." He grabbed the first girl by her long hair and yanked her toward the sleeping bag. She screamed.

"Leave her alone."

The three garage rats turned to see Dag standing in the edge of the flickering firelight. "Well, lookie here. Grandpa's gonna save the world."

The big one dropped his grip on the girl's hair and stepped toward Dag. His friends stepped in behind.

"You boys get back in your truck and go home to mama," Dag warned. He didn't have his eye patch on and his glass eye pointed sideways toward the river like an angry iguana caught in a cold rain. But his good eye was focused on the thug in front of him. That's all that mattered.

"Maybe we put you in the river and take the girls home to mama. How's that sound, old man?" The guy with the knife flicked it open. Dag saw the honed edge flash in the firelight. From three feet away, the six-inch blade waved menacingly. Dag never flinched.

In unison they stepped closer. The girls retreated back from the group.

"This is your last chance boys, I don't want to hurt you. Get in your truck and drive away now." His cold steely voice had no effect on the drugged-up backyard mechanics.

The guy with the knife jumped forward, the blade tip angled toward Dag's throat. Dag reflexively stepped aside grabbing the right wrist. With a hard twist, he wrenched the arm up and back. The right shoulder dislocated with a sickening pop. The thug collapsed to the ground screaming in pain, his right arm immobilized at an awkward angle.

The other two rushed toward Dag. Dag grabbed one by the arm. Twisting it around he sent the thug headlong into the side of the Prius. Simultaneously, at a downward angle, he kicked the side of the knee of the third guy. The ligaments snapped and the knee buckled. He joined his friend on the ground writhing in pain.

Dag picked up the knife from the dirt and calmly walked over to the rusty pickup truck with Missouri plates. He slashed all four tires and as the last hissing rim settled to the ground, he turned to the girls.

"I would recommend you get your stuff and get out of here." His voice was low and even with an edge, like a father assessing a daughter's prom date for the first time.

Too shook to answer, they frantically grabbed their belongings. Stuffing them into the open hatch of the Prius, they breathed out a "Thanks for saving us" toward Dag.

The dirt bags were still flopping about in the dirt, yelling murderous threats toward Dag and anyone else who could hear them. Once the Prius was out of the campground and onto the highway, Dag knelt next to the guy with the dislocated arm. He grabbed him by the front of his greasy red flannel shirt and with his other hand he twisted the guy's good wrist and elbow to the breaking point. Dag leaned down, inches from his face and spoke in a hoarse whisper.

"I've killed garbage better than you. If you even think about doing this to anyone else, I'll gut you and throw you in the river. You'll be 'gator bait in the delta before your mama knows you're missing. Understand?"

The thug spit into Dag's face.

Dag never blinked. With a twist, the left arm popped like the first.

The one unconscious from his collision with the Prius regained his awareness and came at Dag. He kicked Dag's ribs, just under the arm on the left side. The blow made

Dag wince but he caught the boot under his arm and gave a vicious inward twist to the right leg. The hip snapped and he laid between his friends, three ugly flapping carp, each wishing they had never climbed out of the river.

Dag took their cell phones and tossed them into the fire. As a final act of defiance against the three, Dag reached under the dash of their truck and ripped out all of the wiring. He locked the door to his Airstream, poured water on his fire and started his truck. He knew someone would find the boys in the morning when they didn't report for work or school or probation.

As he pulled out of the campground and onto the county road his phone beeped. No one had called him in three weeks. The screen indicated he had a voicemail. He entered his security code and turned on the speaker.

"Mr. Rasmussen, this is Molly Seymour. Are you the same Mr. Rasmussen who knew Roy and Lola Ambrose...?"

Chapter 16

Life's tragedy is that we get old too soon and wise too late. – Benjamin Franklin

"**Hello**? Molly?" Olivia asked as she picked up her phone.

"Olivia...this Luella Tinker, your sister. Remember me?"

"I'm sorry, Lu. I've been expecting Molly. She worries me."

"Wedding problems?"

"No...yeah...well no...I don't know."

"Sounds like you need to get out more," Luella said, "Anyway...I'm calling about this weekend. I thought we were getting together in Minneapolis for Molly's final wedding dress fitting, but I haven't heard from you."

"Oh, the wedding," Olivia groaned. "I forgot about that."

"What?" Luella raised her voice. "Your oldest daughter is getting married in a few months and you forgot about the wedding? Hello...anybody home?"

Olivia blew her nose and wiped tears from her cheeks before responding. "I think something is wrong with Molly. She's talking weird conspiracy things about the FBI and Barry Manilow."

"That sounds weird. I worked on a psych ward right after school. Do you want me to talk to her? Sounds like she's going schizo...or something like that. It's probably just wedding jitters."

"I know...it scares me." Olivia coughed. "She's not at her dorm anymore. She won't tell me where she is."

"Have you and Harry considered calling the police?"

"I did...but they weren't any help." She paused for a few seconds then continued. "They said they had plenty of homeless people with mental health concerns. Unless there was something urgent they likely wouldn't be able to do anything...oh God...I don't know what to do."

"Let me do this. I'll call Emma and Vera and let them know what's happening. We'll plan to meet in Bloomington at the Embassy Suites unless we hear differently. OK?"

"I guess that sounds good. Thanks Lu..."

"Bye."

Olivia glanced out the window. A cold wind moved the bare tree branches and a few snowflakes drifted about in the air currents. It was gray and lifeless. She stared at the empty bird feeder hanging from a rope in the backyard. Olivia pulled her sweater close around her as she felt a chill. She could never erase the memory of six-year-old Molly hanging from a rope, lifeless with flies buzzing around her and crocodiles gathering in the water under her dangling feet. Molly died that day, she was certain. Only a miracle brought her back. Olivia couldn't explain it but she felt every minute. She felt it all the way to the core of her being. Tears streamed down her face. She made no move to dry them.

#

Dutch Van Tassel stared at the Chicago Tribune Saturday edition and ran his fingers through his thinning hair. He didn't consider himself an avid reader but he was interested in this week's bestseller list. He glanced through the top listings with the usual popular authors. James Patterson, Lee Child, John Grisham, Dan Brown and others. He didn't care about them. He stared at number seven on the list. Catch-22 by Josef Heller. He cared about that one. Seventeen agents working on it and they still didn't know the significance of Catch-22. Calls to the editor compounded the puzzle. They weren't aware of the book being in the bestseller list. Their explanation was equally puzzling. Someone must have hacked their computers and inserted the name into the list. According to their records, number seven should have been a book by C J Lyons not *Catch-22*.

His phone rang.

"Van Tassel."

"Dutch...Blake Carlson here. Some interesting information just came through NSA. Bobby Smith, the professor linked to the girl, went through customs. He flew out of St. Petersburg, Russia and made five stops including Helsinki, Madrid, London, New York and Chicago. He landed in Chicago early this morning."

"Do you think it has anything to do with Catch-22?"

"Don't know. But Smith was implicated in some serious gambling debt with the mob last year...settled by Kalishnov. An English teacher from Russia doesn't travel the world on his own dime. This isn't a holiday."

"Did he make contact with anyone?"

"We don't know." Blake paused a minute. "There's one more thing. He chartered a private plane from Midway up to Minneapolis."

"Call Lena Johnson in Minneapolis. Have someone tail him and get photos of any contacts. Keep me updated."

Dutch terminated the call and went back to the paper.

There was the usual drivel about politics, the economy, "fake news", celebrity divorce and the latest movies. He tossed those sections aside and picked up the sports section.

He read through a piece about concussions in NCAA and NFL players. An interview with renown concussion expert, neurologist Dr. Lawrence Epstein, followed. He had a theory that concussions were more severe today compared to twenty or thirty years ago, in part due to noise. Modern stadiums are almost parabolic in shape and the noise generated by fans and sound systems concentrates on the field resulting in further disorientation. He was an outspoken critic against new helmet liners donated by Mork Engineering. In direct contact studies the gel dissipated energy but when exposed to loud noise, the gel was much more efficient at transmitting sound directly to the head of the athlete, which aggravated ringing of the ears, blurred vision and increased confusion. *Interesting.*

Dutch turned to the crossword puzzle. It was Saturday.

#

Dag looked at Molly's phone number on his screen and poked it with his thumb. Her phone rang.

"Hello, this is Molly."

"Molly, I'm Dag Rasmussen. You left a message on my phone."

"Mr. Rasmussen, thank you for returning my call."

Dag pushed the speaker button on his phone and set it on the center console of his truck. "Why are you calling me?"

"You helped my grandparents about fifteen or twenty years ago. You probably don't remember…"

"Molly, I remember you and your family…did something happen to your grandparents?"

"No…I don't think so. I have a strange situation and I don't know who I can trust. My grandpa Roy trusted you. I got your private number from him."

Dag turned left onto the highway from Garage Rat campground and turned his metallic blue Silverado north. He glanced into the driver side mirror and saw the three punks writhing on the ground. "Give me a quick summary but don't say too much on the phone. All phone conversations can be overheard. Understand?"

"The FBI…"

"Stop there. Don't say another word. Where are you?"

"St. Paul, Minnesota."

"I'll be there in twelve hours. I'll call when I get close."

"Thank you, Mr. Rasmussen."

"Call me Dag and don't thank me yet." The phone call ended. His truck speedometer registered 77 mph and the airstream swayed slightly in his wake.

Molly spent two days hiding in the shelter of the big brick house on Summit avenue. Gladys was a good hostess, offering everything she had and asking nothing in return. Molly was grateful, but she had to move on. Hiding behind a ninety-three-year-old woman wasn't kosher.

Molly was engaged to be married to Charles Miller, her high school sweetheart. The wedding was scheduled for the first weekend of February. Her heart fluttered at the thought of getting married but she had to try on the dress first. Molly checked the clock in the hall. She was due to meet her mother at the Mall of America for lunch with her aunts and cousins and then go to Michael's Wedding Emporium on the second level for the final fitting. She was anxious and excited and scared to death.

"Gladys, I can't thank you enough. You're so kind."

"You're always welcome here. You are the only family I have left."

"I need to go to my dorm and change clothes, but I don't know if the FBI is watching."

"Just go. If you haven't done anything wrong, you don't have anything to fear."

"I know you're right. I just don't know who to trust."

"Trust God and trust yourself."

Molly left 1710 Summit Avenue and walked downhill to Grand Avenue. She loved the pastries from Café Latte. After a pecan caramel roll and black coffee, she caught a cab which took her down Grand Avenue to Snelling Avenue and then turned north all the way to Penrose. She paid cash and pulled the baseball cap low over her eyes as she stepped out of the cab, onto the sidewalk. Saturday mornings on campus were usually quiet. However, today visitors were taking over the parking lot, with their blue and gold shirts, waiting for the basketball game against conference rivals, St. James University.

With plenty of different faces, it was hard to know who belonged and who didn't. She slipped through the commons area, out the back door and took the narrow sidewalk over the hill to her dorm on the north side of campus.

Molly hopped into the shower. It was good to wash her hair and get rid of the old house smell clinging to her clothes. She toweled off, ran a comb through her short hair and decided to wear something nice, so her mom wouldn't suspect she was going bonkers. She picked a blue dress, simple but elegant enough for a nice dinner on the town. It was knee length and tied in the back. She pulled on a nice light-colored cardigan to complement the dress and shoes, low heels, something she could run in, if necessary.

Molly debated calling Gretta, her roommate, to see if she could borrow her car but decided against it. If the FBI wanted to find her, then let them come. She took the keys to her own car and slipped out the back side of the dormitory into the student parking area. Her Subaru Outback was parked facing out, ready for a quick getaway. Out of habit she checked the trunk. Her bug-out bag was packed.

She was ready to play dress-up.

Chapter 17

Some people think football is a matter of life and death.
I assure you, it's much more serious than that. – Bill
Shankly

Dr. Epstein yawned and stretched. He had been in the film
room of the Cleveland Browns training facility for 7 hours
and all he learned was something he didn't understand.

As the leader in concussion evaluation and treatment,
he had unfettered access to all training films and coaches
tape. Dubbed *All-22*, it was the tape most utilized by
coaches because it located and identified all twenty-two ac-
tive players on the field during any play. He could zoom in
or out and rotate the field of play to evaluate any given situation from any angle.

His yellow legal pad was full of names, dates, notes and
questions. He reviewed every documented concussion from

the beginning of the season, including the most recent games played last week. Most were simple and straightforward. A running back or wide receiver collided with a defender, helmet to helmet and a concussion resulted. Sometimes it was a quarterback being knocked down and his helmet struck the ground and bounced. In each of these instances the results were predictable.

He had 7 concussions on his list that didn't make sense. He typed in the necessary letters and numbers and the first play on his list was displayed. It was 2nd and 17 on the 36 yard line of Philadelphia. Atlanta had the ball. The score was 31-24 in favor of Philadelphia. The clock showed 5:22 to play in regulation. The quarterback dropped back to pass and the defenders rushed the quarterback. He passed the ball. It was caught but one of the defenders knocked the quarterback to the ground. No head to head or head to ground contact was visible from any angle. The defending Philadelphia Eagles did their usual victory contortions on the field. When the quarterback stood up, he appeared to act normal. He stood in one place staring up at the big screen getting his own assessment of the instant replay.

Suddenly he grabbed his helmet and seemed to stagger. He bent forward as if he was going to vomit. Without warning he slumped to the ground and appeared to shake or twitch as if having a seizure.

Epstein played and replayed that segment of film but couldn't determine what happened. The audio was equally as puzzling. As a concussion investigator, Epstein appreciated having as much information as possible. Parabolic microphones recorded sounds and voice detail that was otherwise unavailable several years ago. Film crews were instructed to focus the microphones on key players, usually quarterbacks so signals and conversations could be broadcast to enhance the viewers experience.

The audio signal was clear. The voice of Mitch Regan, the Atlanta Falcons quarterback was also clear and distinct. No wavering, no evidence of weakness, grunts or groans. Immediately after the quarterback was knocked to the ground the signal was distorted. The background noise was garbled and there was a clicking and buzzing noise, but it lasted only for a few seconds, then the audio was clear again. However, the clicking and buzzing correlated exactly with the abnormal quarterback behavior.

Regan was carried off the field on a cart with careful attention to NFL concussion protocols. He didn't return to the game.

Epstein played the postgame interview of Mitch Regan. Epstein did a fast forward through the usual questions until he was asked about his injury.

"Not sure what happened. I didn't feel hurt when I got knocked down but when I stood up everything was distorted, fuzzy-like. I couldn't see straight and it felt like my eyes were vibrating...you know...buzzing...like...it was weird." He paused as if to think a minute. "Then I think I blacked out. I don't remember much after that until I was on the sidelines and coach was waving his fingers in front of my face."

"How do you feel now, and do you think you will be able to play next week?"

"I still have a headache and ringing in my ears, but as far as playing next week, that's up to the medical staff and the coaches."

Epstein watched Regan step off the podium and vomit on one of the reporters.

The second concussion in question was Philadelphia Eagles against New Orleans Saints in New Orleans Superdome. New Orleans had the ball at midfield. It was early 4th quarter, 1st and 10 on the 43-yard line of Philly. Running back Ja'quon Mellon took the ball and ran around the right side for an eleven-yard gain. A simple tackle around the legs, nothing violent, no helmet to helmet contact. Mellon jumped up from the ground as if nothing was unusual, but like Mitch Regan, Mellon suddenly grabbed his helmet and spun around staggering toward the sideline. He fell to the ground and as he attempted to regain his footing he fell again and lay still. Medical staff attended to him immediately and he also was carted off. There was no postgame interview, Mellon was taken to the hospital by ambulance.

Epstein turned up the audio. Clear recordings of the signal callers, clear sounds of contact between players. The usual grunts and groans and trash talk. Then garbled transmission, clicking and buzzing for a few seconds. The clicking and buzzing again correlated with the collapse of running back, Ja'quon Mellon. No one else appeared affected.

Using his computer, it was easy to review the stats from each player. Ja'quon Mellon was a stable reliable player without any missed games over the past 3 years, due to injury. He was having a stand-out year with talk of NFL MVP.

Dr. Epstein went through every other questionable concussion, jotting down similarities and differences. The similarities were startling. Minimal contact, sudden symptoms always to a key player. Usually offense but two of the events were against disruptive defensive players, one was linebacker Clayton Marlow of the Green Bay Packers and one was linebacker Ben Harris of the Pittsburgh Steelers. In every event the players were disoriented and carted off the field.

It was the audio recordings which concerned him the most. Every time there was clear and distinct audio followed by garbled noise with buzzing and clicking. Each time lasting only seconds. And every time it was followed by a player being carted off the field.

Looking for a common thread with the broadcast team, he checked each game but found nothing. ESPN, FOX, NBC, Sunday Night Football, Monday Night Football, AFC, NFC , home team, away team, he cross checked everything but found nothing.

Lawrence Epstein logged out of the Cleveland Browns computer system and slipped on his coat. It had been a long day. Nothing made sense. He checked his watch and pulled out his phone.

"Hi Elaine. Sorry I'm running late."

"Where are you?"

"Just leaving the Browns training facility."

"It's after seven. Did you already eat?"

"No, I'm starved. Let's meet at that Italian place we went to last month, Bella Sera, on the east side. I'll be there in fifteen minutes."

"Larry, you need to spend some time with your daughter. She's got a geometry test next week and I don't know anything about polygons. You need to explain it to her."

"No problem," he took a deep breath, "I have some questions but I want dinner and a glass of wine first."

#

Chicago, the next day.

"Mr. Riley...a call for you on line three."

Tuck picked up his phone. "Who's calling?"

"It's Dr. Epstein from Cleveland Clinic. He called three times today."

"What does he want?"

"He is the lead investigator for concussion studies through the NFL."

"Why does he want to talk to me?"

"Mr. Riley...he seems very insistent."

Tuck stood up from his desk and closed the door to the front office area. When he returned to his desk he casually rearranged a few things and took a deep breath. "Tuck Riley here."

"Mr. Riley, thank you for taking my call."

"Hello Dr. Epstein...what can I do for you?"

"I'm the lead investigator for..."

"Yes, I know all about you. Our parent company, Mork Industries is a contributing partner in the work you are doing."

"Yes...your contributions are appreciated. Thanks...but that isn't the reason I called."

Tuck leaned forward and reached into the right lower file drawer. Behind the last file was a bottle of Jameson. He poured a generous portion into his coffee cup. He cleared his throat. "Is something wrong?"

"I'm not sure. I don't want to raise an alarm but I found some interesting things as I was reviewing some concussion cases."

"What kind of interesting things?" Tuck leaned forward and grabbed a pen, ready to make notes.

"When I replayed the audio feed just before the players displayed concussion like behavior, there was a clicking noise and a buzzing noise, as if something was interfering with the transmission."

"What could that be?"

"I'm not sure, and it may not be important but..."

"Have you shared your concerns with anyone else?"

"No...why?"

"What do you suspect?"

"I really don't know. Nothing makes logical sense."

"What do you want Mork Industries to do?"

"Well...nothing really."

"Then why are you calling me?"

"Would you be willing to send me the schematics for the parabolic microphones used by the broadcasting team?" Dr. Epstein asked. "They're made by your division in Mork Industries."

"The parabolic microphones? That's a strange request."

"I asked your secretary but she told me I needed you to approve this."

"Now doctor...we want to cooperate with you and the concussion studies but I can't authorize your request."

"Oh...Why not?"

"That's proprietary information." Riley paused for a minute. "You see...competitors might get our plans and make a similar model. They could undercut our cost and supply cheaper models...and we lose."

"I assure you, we will exercise caution to respect your property."

"I have no doubt you will but...well...I can't release the plans." Then Tuck added, "We also supply similar devices to the government for military surveillance purposes. The plans are classified."

"It's a parabolic listening device. I can buy one at Walmart."

"Then I suggest you do that but I can't release our plans. I'm sorry." Tuck clicked his phone to terminate the call. He took a gulp of Jameson and swallowed hard.

Tuck finished his Irish whiskey and leaned back in his chair. From his downtown Chicago office on the fourteenth floor he could lookout over Lake Michigan. It was rippled and gray, like cold corrugated steel. A white pigeon sat on the ledge outside his office window. He could hear the soft cooing through the glass.

He stood at the window, unmoving for several minutes, before he took his phone from his pocket. He opened the list of contacts and dialed.

"Yes?"

"Riley here."

"I know."

"Who has our parabolic sideline mics?"

"Every network that broadcasts sports. ESPN, NBC, FOX...all of them. Why?"

"I was just wondering...that's all."

"You called me for that?"

"Sorry to bother you. Thanks." He ended the call and turned his chair toward the lake. Tuck stood and paced back and forth in front of the large windows. *What does Epstein want with the parabolics? What does he suspect? What does he know?*

He returned to his desk and logged into his computer. He opened his email account and typed in an address.

Watch Epstein.

Tuck hesitated for nearly a minute before hitting send. But he did.

Chapter 18

Happiness is a perfume you cannot pour on others without getting some on yourself. – Ralph Waldo Emerson

Saturday, Bloomington, Minnesota

Molly found a parking spot in the east ramp at Mall of America. She checked her watch as she locked her car door, 12:04 PM. She was late.

She slipped into a gray wool blazer and wrapped a light blue scarf around her neck to ward off the cold of the early November afternoon. Her heels clicked on the floor as she hurried toward the skywalk and entrance into the second level of Mall of America. For the first time in days she felt light and happy. She was getting married.

She imagined Chuck's face when he would see her for the first time in her wedding dress, all buttons and lace, smiles and flowers. *Dreamboat Charlie* was her pet name for him. He hated it or at least pretended to, but she loved it. She secretly wanted to slip the name *Dreamboat Charlie* into her vows but...she didn't want to offend him. But she might do it anyway.

"Molly!" She lookup from her daydream to see her family waiting her arrival.

"Mom, I am so glad to see you. It's been a long week." Molly reached out to Olivia and gave her a warm hug.

"Molly, I've been worried sick. But we can talk later?" She whispered into Molly's ear. Molly simply nodded as she let go of her mom.

"Daisy, Oh, my gosh...I haven't seen you since last Christmas." Molly held out her arms and embraced her cousin Daisy. "You look great. When is the baby due?"

"Not till spring. I will still be able to fit into the bridesmaid dress. I promise." Daisy stepped back from the hug and turned for everyone to see her profile.

"When did you all get here? I'm sorry I'm late." Molly surveyed the group. Aunt Luella, cousins Maddie and Zoe, Aunt Emma and Beatrice, Aunt Vera and Daisy. Finally, she looked directly at Olivia and her little sister, Libby. Despite her quirks and eccentricities, Molly knew everyone loved her and she loved them right back. "I made reservations at the California Grille," She said. "We have plenty of time before the dress thing. Is that alright?"

Everyone agreed, and the group shuffled toward the restaurant, chatting about old memories and new plans.

#

Agent Lena Johnson sat at a table in the food court on the third level. She was dressed in a plain maroon jogging suit with a Minnesota Gophers emblem on the front. Her government issue 9mm Glock was safely hidden in the side holster under her baggy zipped up sweatshirt. A Nordstrom shopping bag was at her side with a jacket loosely tucked in the opening. Under the jacket was a Nikon d5500 camera with a Nikkor 70-300mm zoom lens.

She checked her phone for updates. Nothing new. She reviewed what she knew. It wasn't much. Tuck Riley and Robert Smith flew into the Humphrey Terminal. Lena tailed them, staying two cars back. They turned into the west parking ramp of Mall of America. She followed them into the ramp but when they stopped at the second level she continued up to the third level and parked. She slipped into the food court and found a spot offering a good view of the second level west entrance.

She was there to watch Professor Smith and she had little knowledge about Tuck Riley. A Google search on her phone was informative. He was executive Vice President of

Engineering a subsidiary of Mork Industries. He was recently promoted. His previous position was chief engineer in the broadcast audio equipment design and manufacturing division. According to Google, he was 43 years old and graduated from Kansas State University with a degree in electrical engineering.

What was he doing with Bobby Smith? And why were they here?

#

Dag stretched from his morning nap. He made it to Minneapolis by 6 AM and left a text message with Molly. She had replied almost immediately. She outlined her schedule for the day. Dag agreed to try and meet her briefly at the mall. He would watch the dress shop for activity and be discreet, or at least as discreet as a scruffy old man with a ponytail could be in a wedding dress shop filled with women.

After receiving Molly's message, he followed interstate 494 to the Mall of America exit and found a double-parking spot in the back of the Ikea lot. He turned the truck off, locked the door and climbed into his Airstream. After an all-night drive from Missouri he was tired. He was asleep before the first workers arrived to open Ikea.

#

Bobby's stomach made an uneasy rumble. He had been traveling for 36 hours, eating airline food, brushing his teeth in airport restrooms and sleeping in narrow, upright coach seats, rocked by turbulence and serenaded with safety announcements and crying babies.

At each scheduled stop he dialed the numbers he had been given. It led into an automated data entry link. He gave his name and entered the numbers as instructed. Then the phone connection ended; no further directions and no explanation. This was repeated at each location until he got to Midway Airport in Chicago.

At Midway he called the number and entered the data and codename *Yossarian*. He was given instructions and a combination to a locker in the United Airlines Sky Lounge. In the locker was a package wrapped in shiny silver paper with a white bow, addressed to Molly Seymour at Michael's Wedding Emporium.

A private charter flight was waiting to take him to Minneapolis. He was joined by a man who identified himself as Tuck. Bobby thought Tuck was pleasant enough, but Bobby knew this didn't have anything to do with teaching English. The forty-minute flight was awkwardly quiet.

When Riley stood up to exit the plane a small notebook and a zip drive fell out of his pocket into the aisle. He inadvertently kicked it across the aisle and under Bobby's seat.

Bobby bent down and discreetly stuffed them into the top of his sock before walking out of the plane and into the terminal.

A driver met them at the airport in a black suburban with dark tinted windows. *Who is this guy? CIA? FBI? Secret Service? James Bond? KGB? Why do they always drive black Suburbans with dark windows? What am I doing?*

"Can I ask you a question?" Bobby shifted uneasily in his seat.

"Sure."

"Do you know where we are going?" Bobby asked.

"Mall of America."

"I'm supposed to meet a former student. I have a package for her. It looks like a wedding gift."

"I know." Tuck turned and looked out the dark tinted window at a Boeing 737 descending toward the airport runway.

"What else do you know?"

Tuck shook his head.

"So...you don't know what I'm doing either?"

Tuck said nothing.

The GPS screen in the Suburban showed the time: 2:37 PM. The outside temperature was 39 degrees. Bobby stared out the tinted window. It was cloudy.

They parked in the Mall of America lot. As Bobby opened the passenger door a cold wind struck him. It reminded him of St. Petersburg Russia, only colder. They entered the main west entrance and checked the lighted kiosk for the location of Michael's. It was on the second level. It was 2:49 PM.

#

"I'll have the lobster tortellini, a house salad and...a glass of a nice buttery chardonnay." Molly glanced back at her menu and then at her family. "On second thought...why don't you bring a couple bottles. We're here to celebrate."

"Amen," someone said.

Molly overheard her mother mutter something about wedding costs but there was no open dissent. Olivia reached across the table and turned off Libby's iPhone. Molly wished she hadn't because now instead of an annoying fifteen-year-old addicted to social media, they were forced to embrace her ever-present indifference and sarcastic eye rolling.

The waiter took the orders from everyone else and returned with appetizers of bacon-wrapped scallops and bruschetta with a hot cheesy artichoke spread. The wine was perfect. Molly reviewed the label, a three-year old Dolly Hill Vineyard chardonnay from Carneros. She poured a glass for her little sister, ignoring the disapproving eye from her mother. Molly stood and raised her glass.

"To my family, I love you all, more than life itself. May we live with ecstasy, laugh with exuberance and love with extravagance." A unanimous cheer arose as they touched glasses together. They sipped their wine in unison.

Then Daisy stood. "To Molly and Chuck, we wish you a lifetime of happiness together." Again, wine glasses were clinked and savored.

After the toasts to good health and a good life, the mood of the group relaxed considerably. Chatter about husbands, life, children, and wedding plans flowed gently back and forth across the table. Molly knew her mother had been worried but when she appeared at the mall, healthy, happy and well groomed, Olivia seemed to relax. The chardonnay helped.

"So...Molly...What are you and Charles planning for the honeymoon?" Maddie asked.

"Top secret." Molly said.

"Aw...come on. Give us a hint." Libby said. The chardonnay was working wonders on her mood, too.

"Chuck won't be done with grad school until May, so we're not going anywhere until after he graduates."

"Where are you going?"

"All I know is this…when I asked him if I would like it, he said 'Oui'." Molly smiled.

"France? I bet it's a cruise, isn't it?" Libby asked. Molly shrugged her shoulders.

Another bottle of wine, this time a nice French Pinot Gris was ordered along with cheesecake and crème brulee'. The time slipped quickly.

#

Dag ate a meatball sub and drank a blue Gatorade as he checked news highlights on his phone. From his perch on the third-floor food court he could look down on the central amusement park commons area of the Mall of America. He could also look directly across the mall, to the entrance of Michael's Wedding Emporium on the second mezzanine. It was a long way across, and his eyes didn't see as clearly as when he was young, but he had a small pair of binoculars in his coat pocket. He didn't want to look like a stalker, so he limited his use of the binoculars to a few seconds and only when people were entering or exiting the dress shop.

Dag hadn't seen Molly in several years. He pulled up a profile photo of her from Facebook, dated last year. She had long hair and straight teeth. He hoped it was enough. His watch said 2:56. He expected Molly any minute.

Years of covert activity and constant vigilance, left him with deeply ingrained habits. He surveyed the people to his right. Mostly young people, texting emojis and social drivel to friends. Some were engaged in games on phones and iPads. Tables were littered with slices of pizza, sandwiches and soft drinks. Nothing suspicious.

He looked to his left. More of the same except one person was out of place. A thirty-something young woman with short blonde hair. It reminded him of military or law enforcement. She seemed to be more alert than the other shoppers. She wasn't eating. She also glanced around, looking from her phone to her surroundings but quickly returning her attention to the second level directly across; the dress shop. Suddenly she leaned forward, intent on someone or something. Dag followed her gaze.

Two men with scarves wrapped around their necks and knee length trench coats sat down on a bench outside Michael's. *Am I in a James Bond flick?* Dag lifted his binoculars trying to identify them.

#

Lena Johnson pulled her jacket aside and pulled out her Nikon. She set the camera to burst mode and focused on the men. With their backs toward her she clicked the shutter. They turned. *Click.* They picked up the gift. *Click.* They sat back down. *Click.* In a matter of a few minutes she had enough photos to fill a high school yearbook. She watched.

She sent a text to Dutch Van Tassel. *Visual contact with Smith, Riley-package in hand.*

As she was waiting for a reply she saw a group of women laughing and talking as they made their way slowly from the California Grille on the west end along the railing of the second floor toward Michaels Wedding Emporium. The men turned their attention toward the group as they approached the dress shop.

She swung her camera toward the group. *Click.* They turned the corner and Lena could see their faces. Click. They all seemed jovial and relaxed, centered around the leader. Click. Lena zoomed her camera lens to its maximum-click. There was something about this girl which seemed familiar. *Click. Click. Click.*

As the ladies entered the store, they were greeted by a clerk. *Click.*

#

Dag instantly recalled the first words out of Molly's mouth 'The FBI...'. He didn't know what was happening, but he didn't like it. He didn't trust the FBI any more than he trusted his ex-common-law wife, and he hadn't seen her in 23 years. The woman to his left was no wedding photographer. He knew she was looking for something, but he didn't know if it was Molly or the men...or both.

He hurried from his food court lookout toward the stairs leading down to the second level. As he approached Michael's he slowed his approach. He looked across toward the photographer. He waved. *Smile for the camera. Let's have some fun.* He watched her turn toward him and imagined the shutter gleefully capturing his image.

The girls were inside. He overheard giggles and chatter. Dag took a position on a different bench next to the men and pretended to stretch and rub his back. He bent and tied his shoe. As he was hunched forward he used his phone to take as many photos of the men as he could. He didn't know them, but something was up. He sat back and crossed his legs. He could see most of the way to the back of the store. One of the dress shop workers appeared from the back of the store with a long wedding dress in hand. Assisted by a co-worker they held it out for approval. Molly held her hands to her face and wiped a tear from her right cheek. Dag figured it was her dress.

The men on the bench fidgeted, craning their necks to see into the store. *Who are they? Why are they interested in Molly? If the photographer was FBI, who was this?*

Molly disappeared into a changing room. Everyone waited. The young girls ran their fingers over every silky lacy dress within reach. They laughed, they pointed, they pulled out dresses and shawls, holding them up for inspection. *Oh to be young again.*

A collective cheer went out from the group as Molly reappeared, gliding into view, adorned in lace and pearls and yards of brilliant white satin. *She's beautiful.* At that moment the two men stood up from their bench and walked into the store toward Molly. The chubby one had a package, gift wrapped in silver with a white bow.

As they approached Molly, Dag heard her say, "Professor Smith? What are you doing here?"

"Molly we have a gift for you." He held out the package. Dag watched the other guy take out his phone and snap some pictures of them together.

"You don't need to give me a gift," she paused. "I thought something happened to you. Are you OK?"

"Congratulations" was all he said, and they left the store, heading toward the west exit.

Dag turned and looked at the photographer. She was gone.

He debated walking into the store but decided to hold back. It wasn't appropriate to intrude. His presence was sure to bring confusion and worry. He watched Molly stand and turn and smile for her family. Olivia was all tears and full of joy.

"Hey Molly, open the present from your professor."
Libby said.

"Right now?"

"Do it." The rest chimed in.

Molly pulled the ribbon off and tore open the paper. It
was a box about the size that would fit a pair of gloves, but
heavier. She lifted the lid. Ten bundles of hundred-dollar
bills fell out onto the floor.

From Dag's position he could see the shock on their
faces. No one spoke. Everyone turned toward Molly. The
life had gone out of her smile. Libby and Olivia quickly bent
down and picked up the cash. Molly turned and went into
the changing room. It was quiet in the store.

Ten minutes passed, fifteen minutes passed, nothing
happened. Dag could hear murmuring in the group. It was
time for Dag to go in. Everyone turned as he approached.

Olivia gasped, "Mr. Rasmussen?" Despite his beard and
long hair, his patched right eye and stern approach gave
him away. "What are you doing here?"

Luella, Olivia, Vera and Emma all approached him. The
younger girls held back.

"I'm sorry. I didn't mean to intrude. Molly called me.
She was worried about something."

"Called you? Worried...about what?"

"I don't know."

Olivia turned to Libby, "go see what's keeping her. Tell her to hurry up."

Libby went into the back to the changing area. She came running out with fear in her eyes.

"Molly's gone."

Chapter 19

It is far better to be alone than in bad company. – George Washington

Dutch Van Tassel's gut told him something was wrong. But his gut didn't tell him what, or when, or why. He chewed another antacid tablet as he waited for Lena Johnson. He took a commuter flight out of Chicago and landed in Minneapolis in less than an hour. He was frustrated. The big boys in the national headquarters got the private jets, he got coach on the commercial flights. But his position was high enough to be blamed for everything that went wrong.

He saw the black suburban with the tinted windows approaching. *Why do we always drive black Suburbans with tinted windows? The bad guys can spot us a mile away.* He stepped outside into the cold air and waited by the curb.

Lena pulled up. He opened the passenger side door and climbed in.

"How was your flight?"

"Don't ask."

"Let me bring you up to date..."

"Save it for the meeting."

Lena shut up. She reached forward and turned on her radio to something easy listening. Dutch turned it off. It was a tense, quiet, thirty-minute ride to the downtown office.

The conference room was small. The table allowed for twelve people comfortably, with fifteen present it was uncomfortable, and the room was warm. Dutch took a deep breath, trying to block out the smells of body odor, bad cologne, garlic and flatulence. He was a Chicago Bears fan and he had a headache. He didn't expect it to get better anytime soon.

He unwrapped another Tums and chewed it slowly before he started the meeting.

"This is it people." He slapped his hand down on the manila envelope, resting on the table in front of him. "The people in D.C. are getting nervous. They need something to calm their nerves and we need to give it to them."

No one spoke. Someone in the back of the room burped. Dutch glared at him. If he didn't know *Catch-22,* at least he could identify the source of the garlic and the flatulence. Maybe the cologne and the body odor too.

"Catch-22, what is it?"

"A no-win situation."

"Who said that?" Dutch glared over the table.

"I did."

"What's your name, genius?"

"Ben."

"Ben what?"

"Ben Dover."

"Is this a joke? And, I suppose your partner is C. Howitt Feels?"

"No sir, my partner is..."

"I don't give a rip who your partner is. D.C. has given us five days to have solid information on *Catch-22*. I need you to pool your collective wits and give me something tangible to report. Lena Johnson is going to take over the rest of this meeting. And the next time you move your lips I expect something intelligent to come out. Understand?"

Lena got up cautiously from her chair and moved to the whiteboard at the front of the conference room. She opened her laptop. Faces appeared on the screen, as she began.

"This was 48 hours ago," she started. "Robert Smith, former professor at Penrose Christian University. He's the one on the left. The other guy is Elmore "Tuck" Riley. They left Terminal 2 and their destination was Michael's Wedding Emporium on the second level of Mall of America." She paused, clicking through several photos showing the two together at the airport and in the Mall.

"The background on Smith is in your packets. We believe he is linked to organized crime because of this man, Vladimir Kalishnov." She clicked through several more photos. "Kalishnov has several aliases and many international connections. Here he is a year ago, in Minneapolis meeting with Smith. He entered the US from Bulgaria on a fake passport under the name of Alexander Sokolov."

"Do they have any other confirmed contacts here in the states?"

Lena looked at an old man with fissured skin and thin hair. "What's your name?"

"Maynard Ford" He scratched his head as he spoke. "From Minot, North Dakota."

"Thanks for asking, Maynard. So far, we have linked these three men together; Smith, Kalishnov, Riley. We don't know the exact nature of their relationship, but it isn't Boy Scout camp. The wild card is this..."

She changed the photos. Smith and Riley appeared side by side in front of the wedding emporium with a beautiful young woman in a wedding gown. "This is Molly Mae Seymour. She is scheduled to be married February 1st at a resort in northern Wisconsin." She changed the photo. "This is her fiancé, Charles L. Miller. He's a grad student at the University of Wisconsin, Madison. He's working on a master's degree in actuary science. We don't think he's involved."

"So, why is she the wild card?" Ben asked.

"Because we don't know what her involvement is. She's a genius, she's pretty and she's got a history of international travel."

"If Smith is a former teacher, maybe he's just giving her a wedding gift."

"Ten thousand dollars? And he didn't even receive an invitation to the wedding."

Dutch Van Tassel spoke up. "There's another fly in the ointment which doesn't make any sense. Lena, put up the next photo."

A photo of a scruffy old man with a North Face jacket, leather hunting boots and a ponytail flashed onto the screen. He didn't look like he was shopping for a wedding dress.

Lena said, "This is Dag Rasmussen. Some of you may have heard of him. He's the guy responsible for bringing down 'El Chico' the drug lord. It was Molly's grandfather, Roy Ambrose, who testified at the trial."

"So...what's Rasmussen doing in Minneapolis?"

"Good question," she said. "He recently retired."

"Hey, maybe he's helping Molly pick out a dress?" There was a flurry of subdued snickering until Dutch looked around.

"Dag's a national hero among law enforcement. But he didn't get there by following the rules. He has more secrets than the CIA," Dutch added, "Dag has one good eye, he drinks scotch and he doesn't waltz, so I doubt he's here for the wedding."

Lena flipped the screen back to show Molly and her family with Dag in the edge of the photo. "Molly went into the changing room right after this photo. She never came out. No one saw her leave. And she left ten thousand dollars on the floor of the wedding store."

"Was she abducted?"

Lena said, "Good question, we don't know." She clicked through the remaining photos of Molly and her family.

"What do you want us to do?" One of the agents asked.

Dutch said, "Riley returned to Chicago, Bobby Smith returned to St. Petersburg, Russia on a flight out of Minneapolis that same afternoon but he was identified on a security camera dropping a package into a mailbox in the airport terminal. We don't know what it was or it's intended destination. The girl is missing but she's the only person left to question. I want her found yesterday, understand?"

"Do you want us to arrest her?"

"The federal judge won't issue an arrest warrant without probable cause, but under the Patriot Act we can pick her up and hold her for questioning."

"Patriot Act?" Ford looked at the faces of the other agents. "That means you are treating her as a potential terrorist."

"I have a room full of agents assigned to *Catch-22* and they still don't know what it is. We are working with the assumption it is a potential terrorist act." Dutch stood up from his chair.

"What if we don't find her?" Ben asked.

Dutch said, "Then...I'll invite myself to the wedding."

Chapter 20

Be kind, for everyone you meet is fighting
a harder battle. - Plato

"**Harry**, listen to me." Olivia rubbed her temples as she talked into her phone. The rest of the girls stood close by. "She's gone."

"Who?"

"Molly...She disappeared from the wedding store while we were waiting."

"Did you call the police?"

"Not yet. Something's weird. Dag Rasmussen showed up. Molly called him."

#

Molly's mind raced. *It's not supposed to be like this.* It was her day. Today she was the princess living out the fairy tale. *The wedding dress...her mom...her sister...her family...Dreamboat Charlie waiting for her as she and her dad made that long slow walk...and Professor Smith?* It didn't make sense.

She saw the money fall to the floor. Everything seemed to be in slow motion. In a blink, she counted seven-eight-nine-ten bundles of cash. $100 bills. Franklins. $10,000. *He wasn't paying for lunch...he wanted something...but what? Who was the other guy? I need to call Charlie.*

She dropped the cash and turned toward the changing area in the back of Michael's Wedding Emporium. The store attendant stepped aside as she passed. For a few moments everyone seemed paralyzed by the cash. Molly went into the changing room and realized she couldn't get the back of the dress undone without help. She cracked open the door and motioned toward the attendant who helped unbutton the back.

Molly left the dress in a heap on the floor. It was her wedding dress now, her dream wedding gown and it fit to perfection. It had been her grandmother's wedding dress, restored and altered. Molly thought they would save some money but the restoration cost more than two thousand. *So, what.*

She put on her blue dress and jacket, grabbed her handbag and opened the door just a crack to peek out. The opening to the changing area was not exposed to the main part of the store. Molly slipped out the back of the store into a common hallway used for storage and deliveries. She grabbed an empty box, and carried it in front of her face, allowing just enough room to see down the hall. Except for a couple of shops receiving deliveries, the back hall was empty.

Her heels clicked on the tile floor and she went as quick as she could, counting the back doors as she passed them. *6...7...8...9, Glamour Shots.* She set the box down and opened the back door. She remembered being in the back of the photography studio last year. The room with props and costumes was just on the right near the back entrance. She carefully looked toward the front of the store. *Lots of people...good.* Molly ducked into the costume room and did a quick search through the selection. *No dancing girl...no movie star...no princess...here.* She found a section of uniforms and pulled out a UPS uniform and checked the label. Small. And a baseball cap. *Perfect.*

One of the changing rooms was open. She clicked the lock on the door as she closed it behind her. The blue dress went into the box. The gray jacket followed. She pulled on the UPS uniform and looked in the mirror. It was meant for a man but she made it fit. The inseam was thirty-four inches, six inches too long. Molly rolled the pant legs high enough to avoid dragging on the floor and stuffed her belongings into the empty box and slipped out the door into the studio.

"Do you want me to sign something?" One of the workers asked, as Molly approached the desk.

"No. This is a return package. Have a good day." Molly left a twenty-dollar bill on the counter to cover the cost of the uniform. She slipped out the front door into the crowded commons area and headed to the parking ramp.

As she neared her car, she cautiously surveyed the cars around her, watching for anyone who might be waiting for her. She saw none. Molly put her box in the back seat and started the car but before she backed out of the parking spot she sent a text from her tracfone to Dag.

#

"Mom, what should we do with this money?" Libby held the bundles of cash, counting and recounting, always coming up with $10,000.

Olivia was silent. The only color remaining in her face was makeup and even that was fading fast. The others stood in the middle of Michael's Wedding Emporium, lost in a wilderness of fabrics and frills without a map.

Luella was the first to turn to Dag and ask, "Can you tell us what is happening? Why are you here?"

Dag was a man of action. He won staring contests with congressmen, drug lords and crime bosses. He survived hand-to-hand combat with knife wielding thugs. He could fire a sniper rifle 1000 meters and hit his target. But now he found himself drowning in a rising tide of estrogen and he forgot how to swim.

"I'm not sure."

"Not sure of what? Molly? The money? Professor Smith? The other guy? What are we doing here? What are you doing here?" Luella asked.

"Can we go find a place to sit down. I have some questions." Dag studied each face searching for information. Hearing nothing, he turned toward the entrance, expecting people to follow.

"Ma'am?"

Olivia turned.

"Mrs. Seymour. Here's Molly's dress. She left it in the changing room on the floor." The attendant placed the dress on the counter. It was protected by a large zippered fabric bag with gold imprinted letters on the front, *Michael's Wedding Emporium*. "The invoice is attached to the hanger."

Olivia glanced at the invoice and dropped two bundles of hundred-dollar bills on the counter and walked out after Dag. The other women followed.

Dag walked without talking until he came to Starbucks. He ordered a large coffee of the day, Guatemalan, black and found two tables side by side. They pushed them together and talked.

Dag looked at Olivia and Luella and the others. He had fleeting thoughts of Roy and Lola Ambrose with El Chico and Mexico. He remembered the problems Molly and her parents faced in Costa Rica. He recalled the national attention they received about the will. *Ten million dollars divided between Roy and Earl. And they gave most of it away.* He smiled to himself.

"What's so funny?" Emma asked.

"Nothing...I was just thinking about your family. That's all."

"We're just a normal family."

"No...you're different."

"I'm sorry to interrupt your little chat but what about Molly?" Olivia said. "What do you know and what can you tell us?"

Dag took a long slurp from his coffee and set it back on the table. Everyone leaned forward. The din of mall traffic faded behind them.

He said, "There's something strange going on." And then he was quiet.

#

Molly took her phone and dialed Chuck. *Dreamboat Charlie. Let's elope and run away to Fiji.* The phone kept ringing.

"This is Chuck Miller. Leave a message." Click.

"Chuck, I need to talk to you. The FBI is after me. Call me back at this number. I threw my other phone away because they could track me. I love you. Call me."

As she ended the call it occurred to her how stupid this must sound, especially to Chuck. He was like an accountant. Black-white. Right-wrong. Stop-go. Yes-no. If she told him she was afraid of global warming, he quoted the statistical probability of an asteroid hitting your house on a Friday night. If she told him how he made her feel, all warm on the inside, he adjusted the thermostat. He was brilliant but concrete. An anchor in their relationship. She was Ben Franklin's kite in a thunderstorm, wild with ideas. He analyzed things. She felt things.

Her car was still idling in the Mall of America parking ramp. Just before she put her car into reverse, her phone rang.

"Hello?"

"Molly, this is Chuck. What's going on?"

"Chuck..." She started to cry. She just wanted to be with him, away from all this craziness. "...something's wrong and I don't know where to start."

"Start at the beginning," he said.

She did. She condensed the previous eight days into ten minutes. The meeting with Dr. Simon, her family, the FBI letter, Gladys, Bobby Smith, the money, Dag Rasmussen. She blurted it all out and there it was, like a plate of goulash placed in front of Chuck.

"Did your mother make the doctor appointment for you?"

"What? You're missing the point."

"What point?"

"Someone is after me. The FBI doesn't send letters for fun. Nobody drops off ten thousand dollars at a dress shop and leaves."

"Molly, listen to me. The probability of the FBI coming after you is less than 0.0025%. The idea is preposterous. There is a much higher probability of you making this up in your mind and getting others to believe it." He was quiet for a couple seconds. "Don't you agree?"

"Agree with what? That you think I'm crazy?"

"I'm sorry, Molly. Crazy is a poor choice of words. Maybe psychotic or paranoid."

"Chuck...don't treat me like this. I have never lied to you."

"I didn't accuse you of lying. But I wonder if you know the truth even if it's staring back at you from the mirror."

"What do you want me to do? Turn myself in to the FBI?"

"There you go again. The FBI isn't after you."

"That's not what Dag said."

"Who is Dag?"

"He's was with the DEA..."

"What? Now you have the DEA involved. You've been watching too many James Bond movies. Molly...hang up your phone and get some help."

"My phone...if they can track me they're probably tracking your phone as well. So, they know this phone and where I'm at. I need to go. I love you."

"Molly...." The phone went dead.

#

"Mr. Rasmussen. I'm Vera, the third sister." Vera glanced around at the others before continuing. "Did Molly call you?"

"Yes."

"Why and how did she get your number?"

"Your father, Roy had my number." He slurped his coffee. "She got it from him."

"But why?" Olivia added.

"She called me last night as I was leaving a campground in Missouri. She sounded worried and she mentioned *FBI*. I told her to stop talking. Any mobile phone conversation can be intercepted."

"Now you sound paranoid."

"If you live long enough, doing what I'm doing, you're always suspicious."

Emma cut in, "What about this money? Doesn't that confirm something is odd?"

"Maybe, but it could be unrelated."

"So now we have two issues? FBI and a crazy professor?" Luella said.

Dag thought for a moment, "you might have two things but I bet these are connected in some way."

"Please tell us what you think." Emma said.

"When I can't figure out a situation, I always start with the questions and the facts, as we know them."

"And then?"

"Connect the dots." Dag pulled out a small notebook from his pocket. "Tell me all about Molly. Facts first, opinions second."

Over the next hour Olivia and everyone else described Molly. She was a brilliant student. She started college at 16 and graduated at 19 with honors in mathematics. She was accepted into a graduate program in mathematics but quit and went back to an undergraduate program in creative writing. She had professor Robert Smith as a professor during her first round as a freshman. She loved to volunteer and frequently participated in community action programs sponsored through Penrose Christian University. She liked working with the elderly and would visit many of them even after the programs were over.

She was engaged to Charles Miller, a graduate student at the University of Wisconsin.

Dag scribbled notes on the left side of the paper and drew lines to make three columns. "Now tell me your opinions."

"Chuck's a nerd," Libby said.

"We're talking about Molly," Olivia said. She gave a disapproving glance toward Libby.

"But she's engaged to him. I think he's a dork."

"Okay, tell me about Chuck Miller," Dag said. He flipped his notebook to a fresh page and turned toward Libby. "Tell me one reason you think he's a nerd."

"When Molly cut her hair and dyed it black, he told her, she was 13.9 times more likely to get into trouble with the law and when she got a tattoo on the back of her neck he said, she was 73.7 times more likely to get a hidden tattoo somewhere else."

"Did she?"

"Did she, what?"

"Get a tattoo somewhere else?"

"Yes." Libby glanced to her left at Olivia. "But, she made me promise not to tell anyone."

"So now you're telling everyone?" Dag asked.

Olivia rubbed her eyes and shook her head. "What does this have to do with the FBI and Molly's behavior?"

"Nothing...and everything."

Chapter 21

To die is poignantly bitter, but the idea of having to die without having lived is unbearable. – Erich Fromm

Molly's mind was well mixed. A dozen scenarios flashed through her thoughts. Nothing was clear. *Who was the other guy? Why the money? What do they want?*

She left ten thousand dollars on the floor and now she needed money. What she got from the last ATM withdrawal before staying at Gladys' house was nearly gone. Molly was already identified at the Mall of America so it made sense to get cash here rather than somewhere else. She also knew her family would be in no mood for shopping after the strange wedding shop meeting so they wouldn't interfere with her desire to escape and hide.

Molly turned the key and shut off her car. She emptied out the box holding her dress and other personal things and carried it back into the second floor of the mall. *UPS drivers carry boxes. No one cares about a UPS driver. They're invisible.* Coming to an ATM she put in her card and pin number. She withdrew $300 in twenties, folded them in half and stuffed them into her left front pants pocket. She picked up her empty box and returned to the exit. She left the box near the door and hurried to her car.

Think Molly...keep focused. She drove out of the parking ramp and headed toward interstate 494 west. It was Saturday and the traffic moved along without problems. She took the exit ramp turning north on interstate 35w. She frequently glanced into her rearview mirror. She changed lanes often and took an unusual route hoping to identify followers. From there she turned east on highway 36, then south on Cedar avenue until she finally came to one of the remote parking areas for the University of Minnesota. She parked her car and hopped the University bus to the St. Paul campus, then another bus to the University Hospital system. *People can get lost in here for weeks.*

Blend in, don't stand out. She found one of the surgical locker rooms, shared by students, interns, residents and staff. It was simple to find a set of surgical scrubs, with booties, a surgical hat and mask completed her ensemble. She was again invisible. Hundreds of students and staff all dressed alike. No one gave her a second glance.

Every doctor-on-call room had a refrigerator stocked with sandwiches, juice, bottled water and eat-on-the-run food options for surgeons and residents. She entered on-call rooms with confidence and helped herself. Computer terminals in these rooms, intended for surgeon use, had open access for internet use but password protection for medical records. She could access the internet without logging in as a user.

I need to talk with Dag. Fearing her first phone was compromised because of her call to Chuck, she refused to use it unless absolutely necessary. Taking her second pre-paid cellphone out of the package she entered Dag's number from memory and sent a text. *U of M hospital cafeteria 8pm.* She turned her focus back to the computer.

Who was with Professor Smith? Molly tried to recall any recognizable features to help her identify the man. Her mind was blank. He wasn't someone she had seen before. She closed her eyes and carefully reconstructed the picture of him and them together in her mind. *His coat had a logo. What was it?* She tried to focus. She saw him in her mind, about six-feet-tall, average build, dark hair parted on the right side, slightly gray at the temples. Natural hair color, not dyed. A wedding ring, two diamonds and another ring on the right hand. *Fraternity ring? College ring? Society ring? Freemason? Gold?* She couldn't see it. Too many things were happening at once. *What did Bobby Smith call him? Rick? Tick? Tuck? The logo on his coat started with M.* She did a Google search with the basic information she knew and found Rick's clothing for women and Rick's Dry Dock in Michigan. No familiar images showed up on the computer screen.

Did they say something about Chicago? Was he FBI? She entered FBI, Chicago, Tuck, Freemason into Google and hit search. 183,000 hits. Nothing was familiar. *Let's try Tuck, Chicago, Freemason, M.* 3,247,591 hits. Nothing. *He looked like a business leader, executive. Tuck, Chicago, Executive, Freemason, M...* Bingo. On the second page she saw him. Elmore "Tuck" Riley, Executive Vice President of Mork Engineering, a wholly owned subsidiary of Mork Industries International. He was on Facebook and Linkedin. He was a Master Mason. He was married to Julia (Anderson) Riley and they had two children. *What was he doing with Bobby Smith?* She was going to find out.

She knew calling him directly wasn't going to work. Someone at his level never answered the phone and they didn't talk to strangers. But they might call a stranger with their private phone if they were curious, or frightened.

It took Molly twenty-three minutes to hack the Chicago Tribune. It would go to print sometime after midnight and be on the streets before the first Sunday morning church services. She entered an obituary notice. *Elmore "Tuck" Yossarian. Died November 13th of suspicious causes. His death is still under investigation. He is survived by his wife Julia (Anderson) and their two children. Anyone with information about this should call 1-952-447-1357.* She copied the photo from the Google search and inserted it into the Tribune obituary section. The Tribune security team would connect this back to the University of Minnesota, Hospitals and Clinics, 3th floor surgical suite. But Molly would be long gone. This would get someone's attention.

She expected a call tomorrow. She had no intention of answering the phone call but it would provide a private number to follow. She was tired of hiding and acting defensive. It was her turn to call the plays and make something happen. But first she had to meet Dag in the cafeteria.

Chapter 22

It is not what you gather but what you scatter that tells what kind of life you have lived. – Helen Walton

Dag parked on a side street a block south of Washington Avenue and walked to the main entrance of the University Hospital. He took off his eye patch and pulled a Minnesota Twins baseball cap over his chaotic mop of hair. It was second nature to look for surveillance cameras. He kept his head down and followed the signs and arrows toward the cafeteria. He looked over the food selections and picked a cup of blueberry-pomegranate yogurt, a banana and a cup of coffee.

The cashier said nothing as he totaled the items and pointed to the total on the monitor. $5.79. Dag handed over six one-dollar bills and walked into the main seating area. He picked a small table near the corner of the room, giving him a clear view of the entrance and exit. He watched and waited.

Medical people were all the same to him. Blue surgical scrubs, blue booties on their feet, paper hats and face masks. Short white lab coats, long white lab coats, no lab coats. He couldn't distinguish one from the other but, he could identify the higher-ups, the hoity-toity professors with tweed jackets and bowties. The ivory tower elite. Dag ranked them with lawmakers and congressmen. They were the know-it-alls who did nothing but write textbooks and heavy-handed policies for the people in the trenches to follow.

Dag peeled back the foil on his yogurt cup and glanced around. No one looked his way. He appeared to be a homeless person, seeking refuge from the cold November evening. Without a ponytail his gray hair stuck out in many directions from under his baseball cap. He let some of it cover his glass eye. He couldn't see out of it anyway. He thought he resembled the beer commercial guy who said, 'Stay thirsty my friend'. But that was his opinion, he never asked anyone else.

He counted eleven tables with people seated. A group of young medical people, the short lab coat kind, came out of the food area carrying trays of pizza, sandwiches and diet coke. *Probably students.* They talked and moved together like a school of fish or a medical amoeba. He didn't recognize Molly among them.

Dag dipped his spoon one last time into the yogurt cup and scraped the edges. As he licked the spoon he looked up to see a short, spry old woman walk briskly across the room and sit down at his table. *I hope she isn't looking for a husband. Probably has dementia and got lost.*

"Can I help you?" He asked.

The old woman smiled. "Molly said you would be surprised."

"You know Molly?" Dag pushed his hair back and raised his shaggy eyebrows.

"I've known Molly since she was sixteen years old. How long have you known her?"

"Since she was six." Dag couldn't help but smile. Very few things surprised him but this did. "I was supposed to meet her tonight."

"I know."

"I'm Dag Rasmussen." He extended his hand in greeting.

"I know that too." She took his hand and gave it a squeeze. Dag smiled again. "I'm Gladys."

"Are you involved in...whatever Molly's involved in?"

Gladys didn't answer. She reached into her handbag and shuffled around before pulling out an envelope. She opened the envelope and placed a black and white photo on the table in front of Dag. "Who are they?"

Dag looked from the photo to the face of Gladys and back to the photo. *Where did she get that photo?* He looked back at her face. Eye to eye, his laser vision was losing its effect on people, at least on old women.

"Why do you want to know?" he asked.

"If you won't tell me who they are then you aren't the person Molly needs." Gladys started to get up from the chair. "It was nice to meet you Mr. Dag." She started to put her coat back on.

"Some people call them Yorrie and Anastasia," he said.

"What do you call them?"

"Some of the bravest people I've ever met, but the world will never know, will they?"

Gladys paused and sat back down. She pulled out the FBI letter and slid it across the table toward Dag. "Is this for real?"

Dag studied the paper. "It's a stupid way to send a message. It must be real." He thought for a minute. "Is this why she called me?"

"Why don't you ask her?"

"Where is she?"

"She's right there." Gladys pointed toward a table a short distance from them.

He turned to see a young woman in surgical scrubs, reading a newspaper, seated three tables away. Molly walked over to the table in the corner and gave Gladys a gentle hug around the shoulders and extended her hand toward Dag.

"Thank you for coming," Molly said.

Very few people catch him by surprise. He almost smiled again. "You're welcome," He said

#

Olivia and Libby walked into the side door from their garage. Olivia's mood went from crying to anger to frustration and then back to crying. She had grown used to Molly's disappearing acts since she started college. Molly was one of those precocious kids who always knew where they were going but no one else did. Molly spent one semester abroad, in Europe, bouncing from city to city, and country to country. Harry and Olivia never knew what to expect and they never felt comfortable with it. They just paid the cell-phone bills when they came due. In January that same year, at Penrose Christian they had what was called *J-term*. Harry called it a paid vacation for rich kids. Olivia didn't have an opinion, or didn't share it, at the time. Molly volunteered for a short-term mission project, teaching something in Ethiopia. While she was in Africa, she climbed Mt. Kilimanjaro and rafted the Zambezi river.

As Olivia came in the side door she heard Harry get up from his chair and turn off the television. "How was the dress shopping?"

"She's gone again." Olivia dropped her coat and purse on the floor and reached out for support.

"Who's gone?" He asked.

"Molly." Olivia let go of Harry and bent toward her purse. "Here." She handed him eight thousand dollars in cash.

"What's this all about?"

"I don't know. It's either the KGB, or the DEA or the FBI or the CIA or somebody else."

"You're not making any sense."

"I know."

"Where's Libby?"

"Sleeping in the car. Molly gave her too much wine at lunch."

Harry went out to the garage and looked in the car. Libby was sound asleep in the back seat. Her shoes were off and she appeared comfortable. He left her alone. She was too big to carry inside.

When he went back inside, Olivia said, "Harry, there's something weird happening. It's hard for me to understand but I think Molly's right.

"More weird than usual?"

"Dag Rasmussen was there." Olivia said.

"At the dress shop? Why? Does he have a girl getting married too?"

"Don't be stupid...Molly called him. And then two guys showed up, out of nowhere, and gave her ten thousand dollars...in cash." She rolled her eyes and held her arms straight up in the air. "Ten thousand dollars, Harry. Normal people don't do that..."

Harry stood there with a blank look for a few minutes, then he said, "Chuck called."

"What did he say?"

"He thinks Molly needs help."

"He doesn't believe her?" Olivia asked.

"Do you?"

"No...yes...I want to, but I'm not sure...What else did Chuck say?"

"Did you already pay for the dress?" Harry asked.

"Yes

"Oh."

Chapter 23

Only the wisest and stupidest of men never change. - Confucius

Bobby Smith stared into the face of every student in his class and he didn't see what he wanted to see. No nervous sideways glance, no one looking down at the floor, no twitch, no tic, no scratch, nothing.

"KGB," he said. "Who is KGB?"

There was no answer. The only classroom noise was the hiss and clank from the heat register. The dull rumble of the traffic outside was like a persistent migraine inside of his head. He rubbed his temples and shook his head. He had ringing in both of his ears. His eyes were red and his eyelids were puffy from lack of sleep.

"Not KGB."

Bobby looked at the man in the second row. Graying at the temples, creases in his face, Bobby thought he was probably younger than he appeared.

"No KGB. KGB is no more." He said.

"What is your name?" Bobby asked.

"Viktor."

"Viktor, tell me about the KGB."

"KGB is old Soviet Union. We are free country now." He smiled at Bobby and was quiet. Everyone sat silent and impassive.

Bobby conducted the class with waning enthusiasm. He asked few questions and read from his lesson plan. His first two weeks he was excited to teach but day by day the weight of his situation pressed on him. He wasn't sure when he realized the truth that he wasn't in St. Petersburg to teach English as a second language. He was here because of the goat, the curse on the Cubs. He was here because Vladimir Kalishnov bailed him out. He was here because Kalishnov kept him from being fitted with cement shoes by the mob. And now he would do whatever Kalishnov wanted, he didn't have a choice.

As the last of his students filed out of the classroom, Bobby sat with his head in his hands and his elbows on the desk. If he had a sense of elation at being bailed out from his gambling debt, he didn't have it now. He reflected on the past week. Multiple international stops, coded messages, numbers...and Molly. *What did it mean? She's a good kid. What does she have to do with me? And the KGB...or whatever they're called?*

He felt listless as he gathered his stuff. He wrapped his scarf around his neck and slipped his arms into his long wool coat. He buttoned every button and folded the collar up around his neck. Minneapolis was cold but St. Petersburg felt colder. His sense of doom did nothing to warm his spirits. *I need a drink and food.*

He stepped from the building onto the damp sidewalk. The fog cloaked the flickering street lights. He felt like a character in an Edgar Allen Poe story. Bobby counted the blocks from the school to the coffee shop. Five blocks from Pervomaiskaya Ulitsa to Prospekt. Two street lights on each block. The third one didn't work. He counted the diesel belching busses along the way. Three. When he couldn't sleep, he counted. When he was nervous, he counted. When he didn't know what else to do, he counted. As he opened the door to the coffee shop, he counted seventeen people smoking, ten tables with four people to a table and only one empty spot. Next to the fat lady, Natasha Sokolov. Their eyes made contact. He counted to seven hoping she didn't recognize him. She did.

"Mr. Smith." She waved as she stood, brushing crumbs from her chest. "Mr. Smith, I have a seat for you."

He nodded politely. He looked around hoping against hope for another empty spot at a different table. There were none. He waved at the clouds of smoke and considered retreating into the foggy street. A man at his left gripped his arm and pointed toward Natasha. He couldn't avoid her any longer.

Bobby squeezed carefully between two tables and zigzagged his way to the back corner.

"Remember me? I'm Natasha."

"Yes...I remember."

"I saved a place for you."

"You were saving this place for me? How did you know I was going to be here?"

"My friend Viktor was in your class," she said. "He thinks you're funny."

"Funny?"

"Yes, you asked about KGB but KGB is gone many years. Now is FSB."

"A rose by any other name would smell as sweet."

"What you say about roses?"

"Nothing, just talking to myself."

"The borscht is good. You want some?" She slurped the remaining soup on her spoon. Some drizzled down her lower lip and clung to one of her chin whiskers like a trapeze artist. She dipped her spoon back into the borscht and offered it to him. He glanced around the room, looking for watchful eyes.

"No thanks. I have a cold."

"Taste it." She pushed the dripping spoon closer until it nearly touched his lips. He couldn't lean back any further. Finally, sensing defeat, he opened his mouth and accepted a spoonful of salty, greasy, lukewarm cabbage soup. He chewed a couple times and swallowed quickly. The cabbage slipped down like a raw oyster. He wiped his chin with the back of his hand and smiled.

"You want to know about KGB?"

"Why do you ask?"

"Viktor told me."

"Oh." Bobby waved a hand toward the waiter. He was ignored as usual.

Natasha whistled and the waiter turned and came to the table almost immediately. She said some things to him in Russian and he made notes. The waiter avoided looking at Bobby, as if he didn't exist. He tried to understand what was said but could only interpret 'vodka'. When Natasha was finished the waiter headed toward the kitchen, leaving Bobby wondering what Natasha ordered.

"Viktor asked me to tell you something."

"Viktor?" Bobby asked, "Is he FSB or KGB or whatever you call it?"

"Ha! My Viktor?"

"Yes, your Viktor."

"He delivers bread from the bakery." She smiled. "We're getting married in spring."

"Does he tell you everything we talk about in the class?" It seemed, Viktor told her everything

"I know what you talk about."

"How much do you know?"

She shrugged her broad shoulder and smiled. The gap from her missing front tooth was like a black hole in the universe. Bobby wanted to ask her more but his greasy borscht arrived with a crust of bread and a glass of vodka for each.

He tried to ignore her as he slurped the soup with his own spoon. It reminded him of old dishwater with floating chunks of cabbage, but it was supper. It was all he had. The vodka improved the flavor of the borscht immensely. After he soaked up the last of the soup with his crust, and took a gulp from his glass, he returned to his engaging conversation with Natasha.

"How much to you know?" he asked again.

"Here is your assignment." She reached into her handbag and handed him another phone and a package of airline tickets. She raised her glass and clinked against Bobby's glass.

"What am I doing?"

"You don't need to know."

"I don't need to know or you won't tell me?" Bobby raised his voice but no one around him seemed to care. Everyone else just talked louder.

"Both."

"What do you know about the girl?"

She handed him a photo of Molly in her wedding dress, standing beside himself at Michael's Wedding Emporium. "Molly?"

"You know her?"

She smiled again. The gap from the missing tooth was partially filled with a chunk of bleached cabbage. She sneezed and the cabbage flew out and hit the table next to them.

"Why am I doing this?" He asked. Bobby thought the cabbage helped her appearance.

She shrugged again. "You don't want to know."

"What if I call the FBI or the CIA on my next trip?"

She said nothing. Natasha pulled a long metal finger-nail file from her bag and stabbed it through the middle of Molly's photo, pinning her to the worn wooden table.

Bobby swallowed his vodka and slowly set his glass down. He asked no more questions.

Chapter 24

Rare is the person who can weigh the faults of others
without putting his thumb on the scales.
— Byron Langenfeld

"**Neurology** office. How can I help you?"

"Natalie, this is Dr. Epstein. I have an urgent meeting
and I won't be in the office until later today." He sorted
through the papers on his home desktop as he spoke.

"No problem, doctor. I'll let the staff know."

"Thanks. I'm working on the concussion study, in case
anyone needs to know. I'll be at the practice facility for the
Browns. You have my cell number." He ended the call and
checked his watch. 8:23, Tuesday.

He rechecked his notes from yesterday's conversation
with Tuck Riley. He made a list;

1.   *Parabolic mics clicked before player demonstrated symptoms.*

2.   *Parabolic mics made by Mork Engineering, division of Mork Industries Inc.*

3.   *Elmore "Tuck" Riley head of division.*

4.   *Riley is reluctant to release schematics*

5.   *Mork Industries are major corporate sponsors for the project he is directing.*

Questions

1.   *Is Riley hiding something?*

2.   *If so – what?*

3.   *Is there really something fishy or am I imagining this?*

He put his notes in a folder and his laptop on the passenger seat of the silver Volvo and backed out of the garage. It was an easy forty-minute drive to the Cleveland Browns practice facility and it gave him time to think. Normally he drove quiet, no music, no talk radio, no audiobooks, nothing. But today he turned on XM7 and listened to music from the 1970's. He was a 70's kind of guy.

It took him back to bellbottoms, long hair and Three Dog Night. He loved the Eagles and Fleetwood Mac. The Eagles were his favorite and when *Take It Easy* came on the radio he turned up the volume and sang along. He could sing most of their top hits from memory. After the last notes of *Take It Easy* faded, Led Zeppelin took over. The loud jarring music and lyrics were a stark contrast to the relatively easy listening Eagles. He thumbed the volume controls on his steering wheel and turned it down to a tolerable level. He remembered his first Pink Floyd concert. It was so loud his eyeballs vibrated, his head hurt and his ears had continuous ringing for nearly a week. *Like a concussion.*

He turned onto Interstate 275 and picked up his phone. He kept glancing at traffic and his screen. He texted his project assistant. "Search NFL interview database. Keywords-*noise, headache, dizziness.* Send results to email." He swerved slightly into the adjacent lane. *I know, I know. Don't text and drive.*

It said 9:17 on his dash screen when he pulled into the staff parking area. He didn't expect any players to be onsite after last night's game. New England Patriots played the Cleveland Browns on Monday Night Football and there was another strange concussion last night. He saw it on television and replayed it a dozen times trying to see something, anything to explain it. He couldn't, but today he was going to review that tape and try to find a link.

Two years ago, the NFL granted Epstein access to players and training staff because of the seriousness of head injuries and the risk of lawsuits. Concussions became a household conversation after Junior Seau took his life in 2012. A life filled with promise but cut short by the consequences of repetitive head injuries, of concussions. Epstein hated concussions but as long as society paid millions of dollars to aging boys, expecting them to smash their heads into one another, he would have plenty of work.

Dr. Epstein held the magnetic strip on his access key to the card reader and the monitor flashed his name as the door unlocked. There were plenty of support staff wandering the halls. They ignored him. No household names here today. *Do the Browns have any household names anymore?* He worked his way to the film room and got settled.

Epstein checked his notes. He was looking for a play near the end of the third quarter. The home team was winning. The Browns were ahead 15-14 courtesy of five field goals. And they were marching up and down the field against the vaunted defense of the New England Patriots. Their rookie, first-round draft pick, out of USC, Enrique "Riq" Habik was shredding the defense. In less than three quarters he had over a hundred thirty rushing yards and another eighty-two yards receiving.

The plays were indexed on the computer for easy searching. He went down the log and clicked on every running play where Habik was the ball carrier. He studied Habik's behavior before and after every play. He watched to identify any helmet to helmet contact or any time his head may have bounced on the turf. Epstein made little notes on his legal pad as he went. Then he came to the play.

It was second down, thirteen yards to go after a quarterback sack. The quarterback handed the ball off to Habik who stepped forward, dodged left and cut through the defense into New England territory, a twenty-seven-yard gain. It was a shoestring tackle. The defender caught his right ankle and tripped him. His facemask hit the turf but there was no evidence of any head injury. He stood quickly and made his typical gyrations and pointed toward the end-zone, signaling to the world that he made a first down. Then things got interesting.

As he turned. He suddenly gripped his head and collapsed to the ground. Epstein watched him shake his head and then he appeared to shake as if having a seizure. He played the event over and over but he gained nothing else. Then he added the sideline audio. He could isolate the input from the parabolic microphones from the other audio equipment in use. Dr. Epstein listened.

"First down baby! We bad, we bad! We gonna Riq Habik on you! Yeaaaah!" Epstein played the film in slow motion. Nothing unusual. *Typical adolescent behavior.*

Then the audio cut out and he heard a click and buzz sound, pulse-like lasting only ten seconds according to the elapsed time on the film. Almost immediately Habik starting acting strange.

Epstein backed up the film and replayed again in slow motion, watching the position of the parabolic mics. There were two on each sideline. At the beginning of the play they were focused on the offense as expected. At the end of the play, every parabolic mic was aimed directly at Enrique Habik, the running back and he was standing alone on the field.

Epstein picked up the phone in the film room and looked over the directory taped to the wall. *I need the tech guys. Here it is, Jacob Johnson, director of technical operations.* He punched in the four-digit number beside Johnson's name.

"Johnson here."

"Hi, Mr. Johnson, I'm Dr. Larry Epstein head of the concussion project for the NFL. Can I meet with you? I have some questions which you might be able to answer."

177

"Sure. Come up to my office. Room 324...Tough game last night. Terrible thing about Habik."

"That's why I wanted to talk to you, I have some questions about his concussion."

"Concussion? Didn't you hear?"

"Hear what?"

"He had a stroke. He's paralyzed on his right side and he can't talk."

Chapter 25

Be careful about reading health books. You may die of a
misprint. – Mark Twain

Saturday night, University of Minnesota Hospital Cafeteria.

"What do you know about *Catch-22*?" Molly asked.

"The book?"

Molly could see Dag was confused by her question.
"Yes, the book. Is there another?"

Dag seemed deep in thought for a few minutes and
blurted out everything he could remember from the book.
"I read it in college, for an English class but it's been a few
years."

Gladys pulled her dog-eared copy from her handbag
and slid it across the table toward Dag. "It's a first edition
copy, don't lose it."

Dag picked up the book and thumbed through the pages. Most of the story came back to him as he skipped and read at random. "John Yossarian, the name mentioned on the letter from the FBI. It doesn't make sense."

"I agree," Molly said. "I can't think of anything in my life connecting me to *Catch-22*."

"OK, but what's your connection to Robert Smith?" Dag asked.

"He was a college professor during my undergrad, in creative writing."

"He's a communist," Gladys said.

"Why do you say that?" Dag asked.

"I read many of the academic newsletters from area colleges. I don't like the way he writes." Gladys fidgeted in her chair.

"It isn't illegal to be a communist in America," Dag said. "At least not since the McCarthy hearings."

"When I went to the student health clinic, there was a doctor Neil Simon who asked me lots of questions that didn't make sense. Then at the end he said something strange." She paused for a minute. "He said, *too bad about your professor*. I didn't understand. Then he added, *they found his car in the river*."

"And you think this Simon guy was FBI?" Dag asked.

"He didn't say he was FBI, but he gave me the letter." Molly said.

"When was this?"

"Last week."

"And Smith was the one who gave you the package with the cash?"

"Yes."

"Who was the other guy?" Dag asked.

"It only gets more confusing," Molly said. "I remembered some things from the logo on his coat and his Freemason ring. Bobby Smith said they came from Chicago together. So, I did some searching on the internet and found him."

"In Chicago?"

"Yes, his name is Elmore Riley. He goes by Tuck. He is the executive vice president of Mork Engineering, a division of Mork Industries," Molly said.

"So, what was he doing in Minneapolis with an ex-professor from a small midwestern college, who's wanted by the Mob for big gambling debts?" Dag asked.

Gladys spoke up. "What about the money? Why would they give you ten thousand dollars in a wedding shop?"

Dag folded his napkin and took out his pen. He made a list:

-Molly Mae Seymour, student

-Robert Smith, Professor, gambler, English teacher in Russia

-Elmore "Tuck" Riley, executive with Mork Engineering

-FBI with letter

-John Yossarian, Catch 22

-Barry Manilow, old singer/songwriter

-Gladys Keller, widow

At the bottom he drew a line and added his own name to the list, Dag Rasmussen.

"Here's our working list." Dag turned the napkin so each person could see what he had written. "What connects them?"

"My first question is about the FBI. What do they want with me?"

"The answer has to lie with Barry Manilow and *Catch-22*...and Robert Smith." Dag said. "All of them are linked in the letter from the FBI."

"Tell him everything," Gladys said to Molly.

"What else?" Molly asked.

"What you told me."

"Dr. Simon, or whoever he was, talked about a paper I wrote in high school and about my uncle Phineas."

"OK?" Dag tipped his Twins baseball cap back and brushed his hair away from his good eye. "Tell me about the paper."

"It was a physics project about sound waves. Uncle Phineas was in a doctoral program for music and he became interested in how music interacts with biological systems." Molly leaned back in her chair and crossed her arms. "I took his ideas and expanded them. Then in college I wrote a science fiction paper in Professor Smith's class about using sound waves to influence people...and as weapons."

"Maybe that's the link to the FBI. Was your story shared anywhere? Have you heard about the American Embassy in Cuba?" Dag asked.

"I think I know what the Cuban's did." Molly said.

"You do?"

"They used pulsed, high intensity, low frequency subsonic acoustic waves, directed at the Embassy. It's below our hearing threshold but it makes you sick."

"How do you know this?" Dag asked.

"I posted it on my blog." She said. "But it was only my opinion."

"Molly, do you know the full story about your grandparents?"

"Most of it."

"We...the government, does data mining. We can do widespread searches using keywords. If things pop up, we investigate." Dag said. "It was a simple keyword search that led me to your grandparents and eventually to Javier Espinosa and a link to the Sinaloa drug cartel."

"Do you think that's the link from the FBI to me?"

"Probably, but there must be something more to it. I think the key lies with Robert Smith."

The overhead lights in the food section of the cafeteria blinked off. If they wanted to eat or drink anymore, they had to go elsewhere or find a vending machine. Dag checked his watch, 10:03. They had been talking for nearly two hours.

"And Tuck Riley," Molly said.

Gladys stood and gathered her handbag and coat. "If you excuse me. It's past my bedtime."

"Ma'am, please let me walk out with you. It's late." Dag said.

"You're such a nice young man," she said. "Thank you, but I'll be fine. I've lived alone for the past seventeen years, since Otto died. I'll probably make it another day." She turned her back on the two and they heard her shoes tapping on tile floor as she turned the corner and walked out of sight.

When she was out of sight Dag asked, "does she drive?"

Molly smiled, "she has a 1947 Nash Ambassador coupe."

"She drives it?"

"No, she hasn't driven in years. But it's a really cool car. You'd love it."

"OK, what do you want me to do?" Dag asked as he folded his napkin list and pushed it into his pocket.

"Here," Molly said. She took the first prepaid cellphone from her pocket and handed it to Dag.

He picked it up and pushed the power button. It was fully charged. He looked at Molly waiting for the rest.

"About Tuck. I killed him three hours ago. His obituary will be in the Chicago Tribune tomorrow."

Dag raised his eyebrows but said nothing.

"Someone's going to call this number. I need you to track it and find out who it is."

"And if I do?" He asked.

"I'll be in touch."

Chapter 26

Words are easy, like the wind; Faithful friends are hard
to find. - William Shakespeare

Dr. Epstein's face went blank. He stared ahead, focused on
nothing. *Riq Habik had a stroke?* "Are you sure?"

"That's what the media reported this morning. I haven't heard an update from the coaching staff. I just got
into my office about an hour ago."

"Where was he taken?"

"University Hospital."

Dr. Epstein dialed his office number again. The receptionist answered. He asked, "Who was the staff neurologist
on call at University, last night?"

"According to our list, it was Dr. Andrew Boyer."

"Thanks." He checked his contact list and dialed. Dr.
Boyer answered.

"Andy...Larry here. What can you tell me about the Habik case?"

"Hi Larry. It looks like a spontaneous bleed. He was taking aspirin for pain already, probably made it worse." Andy asked, "You looking for cases for your concussion study?"

"I'm at the Brown's facility now. We were just talking about it. Thanks. Sorry to bother you."

"No problem. You know it's an interesting case. He had an angiogram two years ago for headaches, looking for aneurysms. None found."

"Oh? Keep me posted." He ended the call and sat back in his chair. *Spontaneous bleed? No history of aneurysm?*

He looked around the office of Jacob Johnson. Epstein guessed this guy had never been to a Led Zeppelin concert. Everything appeared techie. Game of Thrones posters hung behind his desk. Several gadgets were apart on a small table to the side of the room. He had two large computer monitors on his desk, each displaying a variety of diagrams, graphs and rows of data.

"Is there something I can help you with?" Johnson asked.

"What do you know about the broadcasting teams, you know...the network people?"

"Not sure what you mean. We work closely with them. They're part of Fox or ESPN or whoever has the rights to the programming. Why?"

"If I wanted to inspect a piece of their audio equipment how would I go about doing it?"

"I guess the best way would be to contact the broadcasting teams which own the rights to each game."

"Can you help me with that?" Epstein asked.

"Sure, let me get some phone numbers for you."

"Now I have a tech question for you. Can a parabolic microphone also project sound?"

"They are designed only as a listening device. Why"

"Just curious."

Epstein thanked him and got up to leave. As he was exiting the office, Jacob said, "You know, a parabolic device can project sound very effectively but it needs the right components."

"Could they both be present in the device, allowing a user to switch from one to the other?"

"Electronics are so sophisticated now, you can do almost anything."

"Thanks. Sorry to bother you." Epstein got up to leave.

"What do you think about Riq Habik's chances?" Johnson asked.

"Do you mean his chances for recovery?"

Johnson nodded.

"If he recovers at all, he'll be a spokesperson for a wheelchair company."

"That's sad. You just never know when God's going to punch your timecard." Johnson shook his head.

Epstein turned and walked out the door. *Somebody else punched his timecard. It wasn't God.*

#

She's in grave danger and it's my fault. Bobby felt his stomach rumbling as he took the bus back to his apartment. Cabbage and vodka might be staples in Russia but it wasn't for a midwestern city boy. His ample midsection felt sour as he thought about the fate of Molly.

The brakes of the bus squealed as it came to a rolling stop, two blocks from his apartment. He stepped off into thick fog. It was nearly freezing and the fog was covering everything with a hoarfrost. In the sunlight it was beautiful, at night it was doom and gloom.

His hand trembled as he fit his key into the old lock on his door. It clicked and he pushed his way in. Cold, empty, alone. His life had come to this. The only light was from a single bulb hanging from a wire in the middle of the kitchen. The heat register groaned and creaked, just like in the classroom. He took off his boots and hung his coat on the nail sticking out of the wall behind his kitchen door.

He sat on the cold metal folding chair and rested his elbows on the table. He rubbed his eyes. *How did it go this far? It was the curse, that stupid Billy-goat curse against the Cubs that started everything.*

His hands still had a slight shake but his trustworthy vodka calmed him. He poured himself another glass. *I hate this stuff.* In just a few short weeks it had become a constant companion, as it was for so many of his fellow residents in the stark concrete apartment building they called home.

Not until after he had downed his second glass did he have enough courage to read the list he received from Natasha.

Six stops. Six numbers. Switzerland, Bermuda, Grand Cayman, Miami, New York, Chicago. Lots of big numbers. Six big question marks. *What does it all mean?*

This much he knew. He was dealing with ruthless people and lots of money. And he wasn't teaching English anymore. Switzerland, Bermuda and Grand Cayman probably meant offshore accounts. This time he was given sealed envelopes with names for each stop. He was expected to make deliveries. He would receive instructions from some source when he landed. *Different than last time. Probably money laundering. From where?*

How can I warn her without risking her life? I am leaving in two days. Who can I contact? The US must have CIA operatives here. The US Embassy is in Moscow, can't go there. If I make it to Chicago, I'm not coming back. I need to make contact and disappear. But how?

The image of her photo pinned to the table with a nail file was branded into his memory.

Molly must be warned. There's a way...

#

Dag spent the night in his Airstream camper, parked in a Walmart parking lot. He wasn't sure where he was. After leaving the University Hospital he drove north on 35W until he saw an exit sign and a Walmart sign together. The suburb was Lino Lakes. He had never heard of it before. It didn't matter. Walmart parking lots were as good as home. What did matter was Molly. He wrestled with the information from last night. None of it made any practical sense. He knew there was more to it, much more, but he didn't know where to look.

His 2500W onboard Honda generator hummed during the night so his furnace could run. It was too cold to go without heat, even with a down sleeping bag. He rolled out of the sack at 6 AM, angry at himself for getting lazy. Just a few short months ago he was sitting at his desk by 6 AM. Dag punched the button on his Keurig and picked out a

French roast K-cup. Retirement bored him. Last night's meeting with Molly and Gladys invigorated him. He felt alive again. He had a purpose for living. He had mysteries to solve and evil to fight.

He pulled his ragged hair back into a bunch and tied it out of his face. As he brushed his teeth, he contemplated trimming his beard or shaving. He was reaching for a hair trimmer when the phone rang.

It was Molly's tracfone. The only person he expected was Elmore "Tuck" Riley or someone under his command. Dag checked the number. The area code matched wireless phones from the Chicago area. Dag let it ring four times before he answered.

"Pinkerton Private Eye," Dag said as he picked up the phone.

"Who is this?" Said a voice on the other end. It was clear to Dag the person was confused and concerned.

"Fritz Pinkerton. Who is this?"

"Who I am is none of your business. Tell me about the joke in the paper."

"To which joke are you referring? The White House or your obituary?"

There was a long pause. Dag could hear the person taking a couple deep breaths and some papers were ruffled. He probably had the Sunday Paper in his hands at that moment. Dag glanced at the clock on his microwave. It was only 6:17 AM. *This guy is an early riser. He's either in charge or someone's leaning on him.*

"What do you want?"

"Don't you remember what you learned in kindergarten?" Dag wasn't sure where this was going but the longer he could keep him on the phone, the best chance he had of getting information.

"Kindergarten?"

"Share and share alike."

"How much?" Tuck asked.

"You don't think I would ask for a specific figure, do you?"

"Does Smith have anything to do with this?"

"Smith who?"

"Forget it. You don't have a clue what you're sticking your nose into. Hang up and walk away. If you don't, I'll..."

"You'll what? Send the bad boys from downtown to pay me a visit? Listen Tuck, or is it Tucks, like the hemorrhoid treatment? If you think I'm joking, check the little word scramble in the Tribune tomorrow."

"Word scramble?"

"Do you have a problem with that? Don't know how to read?"

"Then what? Call you for hints?"

"This number doesn't exist anymore. I'll be in touch."
Dag ended the call. He wrote down Tuck's number, then he took the tracfone apart, removing the sim card and battery. If Tuck flew on private jets and had the ability to manage some type of widespread or even global project, he had re-sources to track this phone and location.

He laughed out loud. He felt alive again. Dag looked back in the mirror at his beard. *Leave it. I look great.*

He had to find Molly and put a word scramble in the paper. Just like old times.

Chapter 27

We don't see things as they are. We see them as we are.
– Anais Nin

Monday Morning, Dinkytown

After his Sunday morning conversation with Tuck Riley, Dag drove back down interstate 35W and exited onto University Avenue heading east. Molly agreed to meet him along the street near Dinkytown. He saw a young woman wearing surgical scrubs waving at him from a street corner. Dag circled the block until he found a place to park his pickup truck and camper. They walked three blocks to Al's Diner and sat on the two remaining vacant stools at the counter. It was usually busy with students and locals but on a Sunday morning it was quiet.

Dag ordered a short stack of pancakes, two poached eggs, hot sauce, ham, and a large orange juice. Molly had a bagel with blueberry cream cheese and coffee.

She asked, "Well...did you hear anything?"

Dag smiled. "I pushed his buttons. He squirmed like a worm on a fish hook."

"Did you get his number?"

Dag nodded. "I already called George, he was my second in command. He'll track the number and let me know. I should have names, numbers, addresses, and favorite pizza toppings before lunch."

"Now what should we do?"

"I need you to hack the Tribune again. I promised him a word game tomorrow. Can you do that?"

"I think so. If I have a computer and enough time."

"What should we do with the FBI? You'll have to face them someday?"

"I don't know if I trust the FBI. If they really want something from me why don't they just ask. What's with the secret letter?"

"They're searching for information. If they had something they wouldn't play secret agent with you. I've been there."

While they were talking, a platter of pancakes, eggs, and ham with hot sauce appeared before Dag. He turned his attention to the food. It gave him time to think. Molly did the same with her bagel. She felt comfortable with Dag. He was like another grandfather to her. Sometimes a grandparent is the best friend you can have. Between bagel halves, she leaned to the side and rested her head on his big right arm.

"Thanks," she said.

"For what?" he asked, mumbling through a mound of poached eggs and hot sauce.

"Nothing."

A small tear welled up in the corner of his good eye. He dabbed it with his napkin. "Hot sauce," was all he said.

#

Later Monday Morning, Heading North

After breakfast at Al's Diner in Dinkytown, Molly used her second tracfone and called her college roommate.

"Hey Gretta, I need something. Can you help me?"

"Sure. What?"

How can I say this and not sound crazy? "I have a guy who I think is stalking me. That's why I've been staying away. Can you put some of my clothes in a suitcase? I'll send someone over to get it."

"That sounds creepy. What do you need?"

Molly gave her a basic list of items and added, "any-thing else you can fit into the case." She wanted to pretend everything was normal.

Molly and Dag sat in the cab of his Chevy Silverado with the motor running. Parked on a side street, out of traf-fic, it was a safe place to rest and make a plan.

"Molly, I'm not going to tell you what to do but you need to find a safe place. You can't stay in empty rooms at the University Hospital."

"I realize that. I got kicked out of one of the call rooms last night. I pretended to be a confused med student."

"Then I need to talk to the FBI, face to face. I know how to play their game."

"Should we keep testing this Mork guy, Tuck Riley?" Molly asked.

"Carefully, as long as we don't let him know it's you. Right now, he thinks it's me pushing his buttons. I let him believe I was trying to blackmail him. But we're walking on a dangerous path. These people play for keeps."

Dag put his truck into gear and after making a few turns he got back onto interstate 35W heading north.

"Take this exit," Molly said. She pointed to county road E-2.

Dag follow her directions to Penrose Christian Univer-sity. It was late Monday morning and there was plenty of traffic coming and going and no one in the security shacks at the entrance. They pulled through the narrow streets of campus until they got to an area of public parking.

"Park here. I'm going to find a friend who can go to my room and get my stuff. It shouldn't be more than fifteen minutes."

"No problem."

Dag put his truck in park and turned off the key. He went back to his camper and got out his personal phone. He called the unlisted number for his old office in Virginia.

"Georgie...it's good to hear your voice again." Dag smiled.

"Dag, you old goat. I thought you sailed off into the sunset. Where are you?"

"If I told you, I'd have to kill you."

"I've heard that before. What's up?"

"I need to keep this off the record. I think I'm involved with a big white-collar crime issue but it's involving one of the Ambrose granddaughters."

"Why not turn it over to the FBI?"

"The FBI is involved but they're looking the wrong way, and maybe they're involved. Who knows? The kid is inno-cent. I think she's being framed by someone. But I don't know why."

"What do you want?"

"Get me any information you can on a Professor Robert Smith, Penrose Christian University in St. Paul, Minnesota and Elmore Riley, with Mork Engineering in Chicago. I think Riley's dirty."

"Do you want me to send it by email?"

"No. I'll find a private fax machine somewhere. I'll call you with the number."

"Dag, you sound good. I'm glad retirement is treating you well."

"I've still got it, George. I've still got it."

As he terminated the call, Molly came knocking on the door. She put the suitcase into the camper. They climbed back into the cab and headed north. She had her own laptop. She flipped it open and logged on.

Molly tapped away at the keyboard trying to organize her thoughts. "OK, here's what I want to do. Tell me if this is wrong."

"Before you start talking, I have a question. When are you getting married?"

"The first weekend of February."

"Super bowl weekend?"

"I know. It was the only weekend we could get the conference center."

"Where?"

"Trego Wisconsin, about thirty miles from Namukwa, where Grammy and Papa lived."

"Next week is Thanksgiving. You have two months to get ready for the wedding and get rid of Tuck Riley and Bobby Smith. Do you think you can do it?"

"We can do it."

"You would make a good agent. Have you thought about the CIA or NSA or Secret Service?"

"Ask me again in two months."

Dag headed north out of the metro area. At the North Branch exit, he pulled off and found the public library. They parked right next to the side of the library. The public open wi-fi signal was strong enough for Molly to pick it up on her laptop.

This time it took her less than twenty minutes to hack the Chicago Tribune. Using her own computer and software was much easier. She scrambled six words which Dag suggested and put them into the Word Scramble game in the Life section of the paper. It would be on Tuck Riley's desk Tuesday morning.

edlfrea

suiars

nsgeintviaiot

udlairngen

rubaue

nuygath

She smiled as she logged out of the library. Riley better use plenty of antiperspirant in the morning.

#

Monday Evening, Cleveland

The Epstein home was upscale by most standards and ostentatious by others, but it was home. He loved his work but he did his deep thinking at home. When he wasn't reading the Wall Street Journal, he was reading about head injuries and concussions. He loved it. His favorite nursery rhyme as a child was Jack and Jill, when *Jack fell down and broke his crown...* But it wasn't fun anymore. If he was a child again he would claim there was a monster under the bed. He didn't believe in fairytales anymore, but the monster was still there, he just couldn't see it.

"You seem more quiet than usual. Anything wrong?" His wife asked.

Larry Epstein turned his vacant stare from the corner of the room to his wife. It had been a tumultuous several days and it was only Monday. "Sorry, just thinking."

"Honey, you were gone all morning, you cancelled your afternoon schedule. Your daughter passed her driver's test today and you've hardly said a thing." Ellen Epstein sat back in her chair. She swirled her glass of Rutherford Hills merlot and watched the wine streak down the inside. After

202

a generous sip she asked. "Anything we need to talk about?"

"Ellen...never mind." He leaned forward and rested his elbows on the table.

"Larry, talk to me, maybe I can help."

"Alright...If you think something is seriously wrong, probably illegal, but you don't know where to turn or what to do...What would you do?"

"I think you need to tell me more."

"Ellen, you're a lawyer. If I tell you, then you're involved. It could affect a client of yours."

"Larry, I don't have clients in the true sense. I do corporate law. Big companies and such."

"I know."

They were quiet for a few minutes. The dinner had been excellent. Braised lamb shanks with rosemary, roasted root vegetables and a side of couscous. He poured himself another glass of wine and pushed his half-finished dinner plate away from the edge. He looked at his wife with a hint of a smile on his face.

He had a dream life. A nice house, a great job with security, and a beautiful, respected wife who makes plenty of money. He loved working as a neurologist, heading up the national project on concussions. But something made him uneasy and he couldn't define it. Maybe it was the stroke

Riq Habik suffered; maybe it was unanswered questions about the parabolic mics; maybe it was the lack of cooperation from Tuck Riley. Maybe it was simply unchartered waters beyond the egocentric athletes with rattled brains. Maybe it was the fact that Ellen was corporate counsel for Mork Industries. Obviously, she wasn't their only lawyer but she was high enough on the ladder to have influence. But he worried about influence which could be turned on him if he asked the wrong questions.

"OK, let me ask you a hypothetical question," he said. "If you suspected a company of criminal activity but you can't prove it. Should you tell someone?"

"That depends."

"Depends on what?"

"Many things."

"Oh please...you sound like a lawyer."

"Don't accuse me of talking like a lawyer, I am one. You usually spend the first half of dinner flapping about cerebral cortex brain waves and the problems of medical malpractice."

"Ellen. Listen to me. I didn't mean to offend you. I...I just don't know what to do."

"I can't help you unless you tell me."

They stared at each other for several minutes. He weighed the consequences of what he wanted to say. She looked straight through him. He blinked.

"I think Mork is making acoustic weapons and using them against football players."

"Do you know how crazy that sounds? For what purpose?"

"I'm not sure." He drained the last of the merlot. Larry looked away, to avoid her direct glare. "I'm going to Green Bay on Wednesday. They have a Thursday night football game against Chicago. I'm meeting Jim Frederick. He's an electrical engineer from Milwaukee. I want him to give me his opinion on some audio equipment."

"Did you hear what you just said? You're going to ride into Green Bay Wisconsin in November wearing a yarmulke on your head? You'll look like a Rabbi Lone Ranger and Tonto."

"Thanks for supporting me."

"What if you find something, then what?"

"Then I need you to take some plans from Mork."

"Steal plans?"

"I didn't say *steal them*, you did."

"I wish you hadn't told me that."

Chapter 28

Liberty means responsibility. That is why most men
dread it. – George Bernard Shaw

Bobby Smith slept like a baby. He was up every two hours,
eating and crying. By 5 AM he gave up trying to sleep and
took a cold shower. There was one more class before he left
on the next assignment. He realized his English class was a
joke. By now Bobby considered everyone KGB. He couldn't
get used to calling them anything else. Just like when the
Minnesota North Stars went to Dallas. He couldn't change
his way of thinking. There were the still the North Stars in
his mind. *The good old days.*

Warning Molly without anyone knowing wasn't going
to be easy. *They're using her for leverage to keep me from
talking. If I talk, she's dead and then I'm dead. No one
wins, Catch-22.*

He went through every possible scenario looking for a safe and reasonable way to contact Molly. He couldn't see a way out his predicament. Over the next hour or so, he retraced the path that brought him to this point.

A small college professor didn't drive Mercedes and BMW's. He could have had a comfortable living but he always wanted more. Despite signing a personal statement of faith and moral conduct prior to him taking his position at the college, he deviated widely from the path he professed to follow. Alcohol was a frequent companion and most weekends he spent at one of the tribal casinos just over the border into Wisconsin.

He wasn't a good gambler. Instead of following a logical, objective, statistical approach to playing, he was emotional. When he had a good hand at blackjack he cashed out rather than doubling down. Then when he had a mediocre hand, he bet big as if trying to manipulate the dealer. He did the same in the stock market. Buy high, sell low. It didn't work. He had small winnings and big losses.

One spring while watching the Chicago Cubs during preseason baseball, the announcer was discussing the famed Curse of the Billy Goat by tavern owner William Sianis, in 1945. Smith was struck with the idea of betting against the Cubs, no matter what, because of the curse. *Them Cubs, they ain't gonna win no more,* were the words uttered by Sianis and they held true. He could bet and bet big and always win. It didn't make sense to bet on individual games because the outcome was usually unpredictable but to bet on a season, to win or lose the World Series was no different than an actuary betting on the average lifespan of a given population.

Bobby sought out bookies willing to handle illegal sports bets. Many average-joe baseball fans were willing to drop a $50 or $100 on the cubs at the beginning of the season with high odds against winning the Series. The payout was sixty to one. If they won they made $6000 bucks on a modest bet. But they always lost. Because of the curse.

The years Chicago went to the postseason were stressful and exciting for Bobby. Every time they won a postseason game the bets increased. People were betting rent money, grocery money and their kid's weekly allowance, believing this was the year the curse would be broken. But Bobby had faith in the curse. Thousands pour into bookies and he mortgaged everything he had to counter the bets. He won and he won big.

Bobby got a reputation for his gutsy betting. At Penrose Christian he was Professor Smith, but on the street, he was something else. In his mind he was ranked up there with Teflon Don. He was Ballsy Bob.

Bobby's life changed after that. After a couple years of success, he moved out of his 1969, nine hundred square foot rambler and into a gated community in North Oaks. He sold his home for $79,599 and paid cash for his new house, $849,000. He bought a mint condition, vintage 1945 Studebaker and had custom plates **BB** for Ballsy Bob. He had the upholstery redone in soft creamy goatskin. He only drove it after the Cubs were eliminated from postseason play. When the Cubs lost the last game of the season, he lit a big Cuban and drive to Chicago to collect his winnings, in cash.

He was living large. The Cubs got better, the bets got bigger and he got richer. He spent what he wanted without a thought for tomorrow. He kept his teaching job because he was bored and teaching gave him something to do. And the regents at the college didn't know about his side gig so they didn't have a reason to fire him.

He remembered the first time he met Molly. She was sixteen years old. Bobby sensed something different about her. She was confident and smart, way above the average college student. But she was quirky. She was social but she didn't follow the crowd. He once watched her walking with a small group of friends. When they came to a small footbridge over a trickling brook, on campus, she stopped. It was ten feet above the water, surrounded by handrails and trees. He recalled her abrupt change of behavior. Molly stopped and let her friends continue on. She walked at least three hundred yards out of the way in order to cross the brook on a road rather than a footbridge. He was intrigued but never mentioned it to her.

Her writing skills were exceptional. Her creative writing papers were honed and polished. Opening lines grabbed you, vivid scenes flashed into existence, and when her words cut, they cut deeply and the bleeding wasn't easily staunched. He thought about the paper. The original writing project that saved him and killed her. Or might kill him, too. *Man of War, Weaponizing Barry Manilow.*

He laughed at the title. It sounded so absurd he had to read it. It was a science fiction thriller about using sound and music to fight battles and conquer enemies. Armies were vanquished by blasting the ballads of Barry Manilow into secret enclaves and battlefields.

Then there was the weapon. The Cossack Weapon. Molly had schematics and details, carefully designed and drawn out. Bobby remembered reading the story. He was enthralled, fascinated. Bobby didn't know if it was functional but knowing Molly as well as he did, he believed it to be real and operational. He had asked her to expand the story and the plans, with the idea of submitting it for commercial publication. She did. He made a copy of the

Cossack Weapon schematics, but he never contacted a publisher as he promised. It was safely hidden until he sold it to Vladimir Kalishnov, to save his own skin.

The year the Cubs won the World Series, his world collapsed. When they made the playoffs, he upped his bet. *Like taking candy from a baby.* He loved the Cubs and was thrilled they finally won, but the curse was broken. Reality was a stern taskmaster. Many hundreds of thousands of dollars were immediately gone. When he couldn't pay the balance, they came at night and trashed his house and took his car. The last time he saw his beloved Studebaker was when the tail lights flickered under the waters of the Mississippi River. They gave him three days to pay or he would join the car in an icy grave.

Bobby sat at his kitchen table wondering how it all happened so quick. Kalishnov came to him. Ballsy Bob was a street legend, known for big bets and big winnings. Reputations like that attract rats and flies and other vermin. Kalishnov was no stranger to the gambling world. It was a way to launder money from extortion, drugs and black-market arms dealing.

Kalishnov believed Smith could be an associate in his organization. Smith had guts, connections and baggage. Baggage which Kalishnov could use as leverage. One act of disobedience and Smith would follow the Studebaker into the river.

When they first met after the Cubs won, Smith would have done anything for protection. That's when he sold the Cossack plans.

After Kalishnov reviewed the plans, he shared them with one of his American partners, Mork Industries. They developed and tested the weapon prototypes on street walkers and homeless people. It worked. They sold variations of the plans with the Cubans, who used it against American Embassy workers. It worked. They refined the weapons and applied it against company leaders and politicians. It worked.

And now there was *Catch-22*. Kalishnov never shared the details of *Catch-22*, but Bobby pieced it together. He knew it involved the Cossack Weapon.

It was time to go.

Bobby looked around his grungy dark apartment. He had fallen far and fast. He had nothing left, not even his pride. He sold that along with the plans. If he couldn't save himself, he would try to save Molly.

Oh God...what have I done. I hope it's not too late.

Chapter 29

We are all born ignorant, but one must work hard to
remain stupid. – Benjamin Franklin

Interstate 35 heading north was quiet. Weekdays the traffic went south in the morning and north in the evening.
Weekends the flow reversed. Hoards released from the
drudgery of the time clock, headed out of the city to cottages, cabins and casinos in the north woods. Every mile
north they traveled the clock ticked just a bit slower. Molly
loved northern Wisconsin. She spent much of her childhood there; chasing frogs and fireflies in the summer and
snowflakes on her tongue in the winter. Molly noticed Dag
was fidgeting and guessed he had something to say.

"Molly, I don't want to sound like your father," Dag
said, "But you need to go home."

"I know my mom is worried." Molly reflected on the years after Costa Rica. Thankfully she didn't remember details. Olivia paid a steeper price than she did. It wasn't terrible but it wasn't peaches and cream either.

"When are you going?"

"Not yet."

"Why?"

"Libby's fifteen."

"So?"

"Have you ever lived with a fifteen-year-old girl?"

"Nope." Dag smiled.

"You're lucky. I was much more mature than she is."

"You think so? Maybe we should ask your mom and dad." Dag smiled.

Molly turned away and looked at the highway signs as they passed. "Let's stick to the plan. I'll call her from my aunt's house. I promise."

Dag took the exit at Pine City and headed east toward Wisconsin. According to his GPS, they would arrive at Namukwa in seventy-five minutes. "I haven't been up here since I talked to your grandparents, almost twenty years ago."

"It hasn't changed much. They have a new library and a new clinic where the old school was, along the highway. Other than that, it's the same cars in front of the same bars." She closed her eyes to rest. She was tired. Tired of feeling chased, tired of running, tired of planning her wedding. She just wanted to run away. *I am running away. What am I thinking?*

Molly woke up suddenly as Dag turned his truck into the driveway of the old Ambrose place. Molly realized she had slept the past hour. She stretched and yawned. The old house always looked the same; a green roof, cedar shake siding and a big deck perched on the shore of Namukwa Lake. Petunia's pig pen was gone but Tom and Luella had chickens now. Dag grunted something under his breath when he saw them scatter, in front of the truck. He parked by the big white pine tree and adjusted his eye patch before getting out.

She pushed open the passenger door on the truck and stepped out. A cold November breeze came off the lake. The weak afternoon sun flickered through the bare branches of the trees along the yard. It carried no warmth, only a promise of colder days to follow.

Her uncle Tom met them at the door. "Hi Molly." He gave her a brief hug and held the door open so she could go inside.

"Mr. Rasmussen. Welcome back." They shook hands.

"It's Dag. Glad to be back. It looks the same as I remembered."

They huddled in the kitchen for a few minutes. Tom took their coats and gloves and hung them on hooks in the entry closet. Molly was the first to speak.

"When I called earlier, I wasn't sure you would let me stay. I really appreciate it."

"Molly, we're family. That's what families do for each other." Tom said, "Luella should be home soon. You can stay in the second bedroom. She has it all made up for you."

The warm house helped them relax. Molly loved all of her aunts and uncles, but coming back to the old house on the lake was special. It pushed her worries into the back corners of her mind. She looked out the window toward the lake. It was down on the sandy beach were Chuck proposed to her. Beside a summer campfire with all of her family watching. She said yes and she cried. They all did. It seemed so long ago.

"Can I use your phone. I need to call mom."

"Sure. Help yourself." Tom turned to Dag. "Are you staying? You're certainly welcome."

"If you don't mind I'll park my camper by the garage."

"No problem. I'll help you get settled." They went outside while Molly talked on the phone.

"Mom..."

"Molly, where are you?"

"Tom and Lu's place."

"Why don't you come home? We've been waiting for you. Am I the reason...?"

"No mom, it's not you...It's me. I can't explain right now."

"You know...your dad and I love you very much..." Molly could hear her sniff and blow her nose. She felt guilt pushing up from somewhere in her middle. Her face flushed. She wanted to cry but she bit her lip and closed her eyes.

"Can I change the subject?" Molly asked.

"Of course."

"Is everyone still planning on a family Thanksgiving dinner up here at the lake?"

"Yes, as far as I know. Did Luella say something different?"

"No, she's not home yet. But I'm planning to stay here for a few days and Thanksgiving is next week. I miss you and dad."

"Are you alone?"

"No. Dag is with me."

"Are you still worried about the FBI thing? Is that what happened at the dress shop?"

"I'll give as many details as I can next week."

"So...you aren't taking any medications?"

"Mom. Forget about medications. I'm not sick or crazy or whatever you think. Why do you think I'm making this up? Do you think ten thousand dollars in cash comes from my imagination?"

"Molly, I'm scared. Dad is too. We just want you to be safe and happy. That's all."

"I know..."

"I have your dress. I hung it in your closet. Grandma would be so proud of you."

"I think it's perfect. Sorry I dropped it on the floor and ran out on you."

"Yeah...Dad said Chuck called."

"What did he say?"

"Well...You should talk to dad when he gets home."

\#

Bobby mumbled through the last hour of his English class. It lacked interest and direction. Only seven students attended, Viktor was one of them. Dag tried to avoid eye contact but Viktor seemed to smile and gloat.

"Mr. Smith. My Natasha said you leave tonight. Where going you?"

"Where are you going, Viktor." Bobby corrected.

"Nowhere. Why ask you?"

"Never mind."

Viktor didn't mind. Bobby was sure he had other things on his mind, something other than learning English. And it wasn't Natasha's beautiful smile.

As the class ended Bobby watched everyone file out except Viktor. When they were alone he left an envelope on his desk and smiled.

Why is he smiling? Is he a messenger for the KGB...I mean FSB? Is Natasha directing him or is he directing her? I'm not coming back.

"For you," Viktor said

"What is it?" Bobby asked.

"We're getting married. You, best man."

Bobby opened it. There was a polaroid photo taped to folded construction paper. Viktor and Natasha looked happy. Her toothy grin was centered in the photo. Viktor's vodka enhanced waistline and Natasha's ample chest complimented each other like two used bookends at a thrift sale.

Too bad I'll miss the wedding. It would be a hoot.

Chapter 30

There are two ways you can live: you can live as if nothing is
a miracle; you can live as if everything is a miracle.
– Albert Einstein

Bobby Smith tucked the wedding invitation into his coat pocket
and walked out his classroom for the last time. The Baltic gloom
moved in from the sea and filled up the streets. The sparse street
lamps in Bobby's neighborhood flickered and buzzed, spreading
joy like an Alfred Hitchcock movie.

The bus stop was quiet. Fewer commuters than usual but he
was late. Bobby coughed when his bus belched out clouds of
black diesel exhaust. He climbed aboard and sat in the first
empty seat, three back from the driver. It wasn't cold by Minnesota standards but the dampness gave him a chill. He counted
the blocks and the stops until he reached his corner.

As he stepped off, another followed. Bobby hesitated in the
bus shelter, glancing out of the corner of his eye. The man did
the same. Bobby started off walking his usual pace. He counted

steps, *1,2,3,4*...he counted lamp stands, *1,2*... he counted windows. Bobby could see the entrance to his apartment and started to hurry. The man followed. As Bobby ducked inside the man continued on. *Just nervous, nothing to worry about.*

In his room the single light flickered. His suitcase was basic, with barely enough room for a change of clothing and some personal items. He packed what he had and left the rest. He wasn't coming back.

He looked at the picture Viktor gave him. He smiled. *They believe I'm coming back. Good.* His flight left in three hours. It gave him plenty of time to think. He needed to contact Molly without alerting his superiors or anyone else. *There has to be a way.*

His plane landed in Switzerland on schedule. Zurich was all business, all the time. The streets were well groomed, the taxis were prompt, the people were efficient with conversation. No one talked about the weather or politics. He made his first call and handed off the envelope. His itinerary through Switzerland, Bermuda and Grand Cayman followed the offshore banking business. Every place he logged in, every time he made the contact, every button he pushed, transferring millions from one secret account to another was in his name, his signature, his face. He had no way out.

From Zurich he again had a late-night flight into Bermuda. Kalishnov allowed him no free time between destinations. Bobby barely had time from airport to bank and back again. But Bermuda beckoned. The taxi ride from the airport on the northeast end of the country to Hamilton was enticing. Despite the cool autumn weather, the aqua blue water made the deserted pink sand beaches more beautiful. He repeated his banking routine in Hamilton and then it was back to the airport. *It was only five million this time.*

Grand Cayman was the most beautiful and alluring. The difference from St. Petersburg to the Cayman Islands was a world apart. The air was warm, the breezes soft and the food wonderful. His flight landed mid-morning. He had all day until his night flight into Miami so he decided to make the most of it.

Once his business was transacted he bought shorts, and a tropical patterned shirt from a beach front store and rented a moped.

"Can I leave my bag?" Bobby asked the guy renting scooters. They guy nodded and put his dented and scarred suitcase in the back. Before leaving the shop, Bobby asked again, "Any good places to eat, down the island?"

"What do you want? Seafood? Sushi?"

"I don't know. Recommend something."

He pulled out a tourist map and circled a couple of places. "If you like fresh fish this is the best place, Catch-22. About a mile from here." He pointed up the coast.

Bobby took the map and headed out. Originally, he intended to spend the day touring, but fatigue and jet lag changed his mind. He found a beach bar grilling shrimp. After a couple fruity drinks with paper umbrellas he was done. The hammocks tied between palms, engulfed him and he slept the afternoon away.

Three hours later he was refreshed but he had no better ideas to alert Molly. Bobby contemplated hiring a boat and disappearing into the ocean but Molly was still on the hook. The November sun sets early, even in the Caribbean. As it was getting dark he found a parking spot for his scooter at the Catch-22 seafood restaurant. It was busy.

"Do you have reservations?"

"No."

"We have seating at the bar." The waiter was friendly enough but he wasn't in the mood for idle talk.

"That's fine." Bobby accepted a place at the bar. He was seated between an overweight sunburned tourist from Arkansas on his right and a pierced and tattooed college student from southern California, on his left.

Bobby ordered Conch fritters and raw oysters to start and the grilled sea bass. He checked his watch. *Plenty of time.*

"You come down here much?" The Arkansas guy asked.

"Nope, first time," Bobby said.

"They don't mess around," Mr. Arkansas said. His eyes darted around. He took another gulp of rum.

"What do you mean?" Bobby moved his drink to make room for the fritters. They smelled great.

"The Cayman government. No guns, no drugs, nothing. You get caught down here messing around and they lock you up." He added, "You get seven years for being cross-eyed and life for anything serious."

"That's good isn't it? I mean law and order." Bobby dipped the first fritter into a spicy cream sauce and took a bite. It was so hot he nearly burned his mouth and took a gulp of his rum punch to calm the burn.

"Too much government is never good and no privacy." Mr. Arkansas was on a roll. Bobby cautiously eyed his dinner guest. *Right Winger...maybe worse. Here comes the second amendment and Hillary Clinton thrown in for good measure.*

"I'm American but I live in Russia." Bobby could have hit him with a brick and not caused a greater reaction.

"What? Are you a commie?" His reddened face morphed into a shade of blue around the nose and eyes. "Do you see that?" Arkansas aimed his stubby fingers in the direction of a television mounted above the bar.

"What are you pointing at?" Bobby slurped the last of his oysters down. He burped and wiped his chin on a napkin. He lookup trying to follow the trembling Arkansas finger.

"Hidden cameras. They're everywhere." He pointed out toward the entrance to the restaurant. "You didn't see them when you walked in?"

"I guess I wasn't looking," Bobby said, "Are they bad?"

"Bad?" The big man raised his voice half of an octave. He jerked his arm around and knocked Bobby's drink onto the floor. His face twitched and the fat on his chin jiggled. "They're recording us right now. The CIA, the FBI and the Secret Service can access this camera and find you anywhere in the world."

"Really? You know that for sure?" Bobby let him talk. It gave him time to think. The sea bass was steaming hot. He squeezed a wedge of lemon and let the juice drizzle over the grill marks on the side of the fish. It was the best food he had eaten in months. When the bass was reduced to bones he smiled to himself. *If this is my last supper, it was good.*

Bobby ordered a cup of fruit layered with a sweet cream and topped with a jigger of rum, for dessert. He forced himself to finish it. Mr. Arkansas continued his rant. Bobby smiled and nodded whenever the flow of words slowed to a trickle. Within an hour they were best friends.

Bobby stretched as he got off his chair, Arkansas offered some more advice. "You should wear a cap pulled down over your eyes. It's harder for them to see you, you know."

"I'll remember that." Bobby went to the receptionist to pay his bill. Behind the counter hung t-shirts and caps emblazoned with the name of the restaurant, CATCH-22. The idea hit him.

"I'll take three hats," He said. He paid cash.

Back at the airport Bobby found a black felt tip pen. Taking the first hat he wrote in big letters, ***Molly Hatchet-Flirtin' with Disaster.*** *I hope this works.*

Chapter 31

The question is not what you looked at,
but what you see. – Henry David Thoreau

Tuesday morning. Namukwa

Tom had a fire going in the wood stove and a big pot of coffee ready by the time Molly came out of her room. It had snowed a couple inches overnight and everything looked bright. She blinked as she walked into the sitting room and stood by the warm fire. There was a quietness in the house, the sound you hear when you put your head under a thick down comforter, when you're tired and the whole world loves you. It was a good quiet.

"Good morning," Luella said. She was reading the morning news on her tablet at the old kitchen table.

"Hi." Molly stretched and rubbed her eyes. She realized she hadn't slept well for a couple weeks. Last night was a catch-up night. She felt rested. "Is Dag here?"

"He was in the house for coffee earlier. He left a note for you." Tom pointed toward the note on the table.

Molly inhaled the steam from the cup of coffee and took a slurp. It was good.

> *Molly,*
>
> *Stay here and stay safe. Going to Mpls to see FBI agent Lena Johnson. I have information. Don't leave, and don't call anyone.*
>
> *Dag*

"Aunt Lu, can I ask you a question?"

"Sure."

"When you and Tom were engaged, did you ever have second thoughts...you know...about getting married?"

Luella and Tom exchanged glances. There was a long awkward pause before she answered. "That's a loaded question."

"Forget it. I didn't mean to make you feel uncomfortable."

"No, it's OK. Let me put it this way. Almost everyone has second thoughts at some point in a relationship. Are you feeling that way?" Luella put her tablet down and sipped her own cup of coffee.

"I'm not sure, but I think Chuck is."

"The whole family is coming for Thanksgiving. Why don't you invite Chuck, he's always welcome."

"Thanks, that would be nice. I'll call him."

#

Tuesday morning. Chicago

Tuck Riley left his home before 6 AM and went through the Starbucks drive-up. The cover on his coffee cup wasn't snapped on tight and he spilled a small amount on his leg. He swore loud enough for the workers inside to hear and squealed his tires in the parking lot.

He desperately wanted to get his hands on the morning paper. It was usually delivered to his office by 7 AM. He wanted to be the first to see it.

The parking ramp in his office building seemed empty, but he realized his usual time of arrival was often an hour or two later. He checked his leg. The coffee didn't leave a visible stain on the dark gray wool blend suit. *If the paper shows what I think it will show, the next stain might be blood stains.*

The elevator stopped twice before it reached his floor. He tapped his foot repeatedly at each stop. As soon as others entered or exited the elevator he punched his floor number twice. If it didn't close immediately he hit it again.

The Tuesday morning edition of the Chicago Tribune was folded and sitting on his receptionist's desk. It was still cold when he picked it up. He stuffed it under his left arm and closed his office door behind him.

Riley set his coffee down and flipped open the paper. *No front page, no sports, no market news. Life section...yes.* He opened the front page and scanned down the columns. There in the middle lower section on page two was the word scramble. He took a gulp of his coffee and swallowed hard. *Now what?*

Tuck heard a noise from the front office. He lookout his office and saw his secretary coming in for the morning.

"Marlene, can you come in here?"

"Mr. Riley, you're here early." She hung up her coat, straightened her sweater and walked briskly into his office. "Is something wrong?"

"No problems," He said. "I need you to help with a word puzzle."

"Since when did you start doing word puzzles?"

"Since today."

Marlene glanced over the scrambled words. "This looks different than the usual word scramble. The idea is to..."

"I know what the idea is. I need you to solve it. Now."

"If you want it solved easily, use your computer. There are plenty of websites that can solve word scrambles." She turned her back and walked out of his office.

Tuck could see she was miffed. He didn't care. *Word scramble website? Never heard of it.* He logged onto his computer and found a word scramble solver. Copying the jumbled letters from the first word he typed them in and hit enter. A list of word options popped up. He didn't like what he read.

He repeated the process with each word and picked out the most likely solution based on his situation. When he was done, he printed out the list. He felt weak. Riley realized he had been standing at his desk with his coat on for nearly an hour.

He took off his coat and reviewed the list when it came out of his printer.

edlfrea federal
suiars Russia
nsgeintviaiot investigation
udlairngen laundering
rubaue bureau
nuygath naughty

It has to be Epstein. He picked up the phone. "Marlene, can you get Jeff Mork on the phone."

"The Chairman of the Board, in New York?"

"Yes...Mr. Mork."

#

Tuesday morning, Miami

Bobby stepped off his early morning flight from Grand Cayman to Miami. He had a small carry-on and half of a bag of pretzels in his hand. And his baseball caps.

During the flight he borrowed a black sharpie pen. He had a few hours to think on the flight. By the time he landed he had a plan. *I hope this works.*

He stepped into the shortest line for US citizens. He put on the first cap and got his passport and declaration information. First stop the automated declaration kiosk. He went down the list of questions without thinking. *No, no, no, no, no.* Now the Homeland Security officer.

"Remove your hat please."

"I'm sorry, I didn't hear what you said." Bobby leaned forward as if to hear better and lookup at the camera.

"Remove your hat" the officer said. He rolled his eyes slightly. "Where are you coming from?"

"Grand Cayman." Bobby handed him the passport.

"And where else have you been, on this trip?"

"Switzerland, Bermuda, Grand Cayman."

"Where's your origin?"

"I was born in St. Louis, but my mother was originally from California."

"Not where you were born. Where did your trip start?" The black eyes of the officer bored into Bobby.

Bobby turned his eyes down and looked at the bullet proof vest, the gun and the name tag. *Officer Stromberg got up on the wrong side of the bed.*

"St. Petersburg, Russia."

"What's the nature of your travel?"

"Business."

"What kind of business?"

"Banking."

"Next." Bobby heard the authoritative stamp on his passport. Officer Stromberg, ignored him and motioned for the next in line.

Bobby took one more glance up at the security camera before he walked off into the crowd. He dialed the number on his phone and received a different message. *Leave the envelope in locker #173. Combination 13-3-29.*

8:13 AM EST. My flight leaves in two hours, a two hour-nineteen-minute flight. I'll be in New York at lunch time. 11:32 CST. I hope they get the message.

Bobby ate two egg McMuffins and drank a large orange juice and paced. He walked steady for the first hour and a half, trying to loosen his back and legs. After hours of flying, his butt was numb and his eyes glazed. But he tried to remain focused. *It has to work.*

Bobby took his first baseball cap and stuffed it into a trash can along the concourse. He put on the second one and returned to the departure gate. The sign at the desk frustrated him. *Flight delayed due to weather.* The weather channel displayed travel weather. Freezing rain in New York.

He waited. There was nothing else to do.

#

Tuesday morning. Minneapolis

Dag turned into the Quality Inn guest parking area on James Circle, just off Freeway Blvd, across from the FBI building. He checked himself carefully to eliminate triggering a metal detector and walked across the road and into the front entrance.

"Dag Rasmussen." He said as he stepped up to the reception desk. Dag flashed his government ID. "Here to see field agent Lena Johnson." He pushed his hair back and adjusted his eye patch.

"One moment." He dialed her office number.

"Agent Johnson. I have a gentleman here to see you. Dag Rasmussen."

"What does he want?"

"He didn't say."

"Give me a minute."

Lena typed, *Dag Rasmussen,* into her computer and files started popping up. Her curiosity piqued. Head of DEA counterintelligence, international drug trafficking. Retired. This guy answered only to the State Department and the President. There were files on Columbia, Miami, Sinaloa, China, Nicaragua, Cuba and others. Guys like this don't waste time on social visits.

She pushed the button on her phone. "I'll come to the front and meet him."

"Mr. Rasmussen, it's nice to meet you." She held out her hand. They shook. "Please follow me."

They went through locked security doors and down the hall. Out of habit, Dag counted doors. Fourth from the entrance. *Not a corner office.*

They entered her office and she motioned toward the guest chair. It was a small office but clean, organized. There was a framed photo sitting on her bookshelf. It was a young man, college age. He checked her hand, no ring. *Not married. Boyfriend?* A box of gluten-free crackers sat on the corner of the desk, Trader Joe's. *Health food nut.* Two martial arts trophies sat on the window sill. No dust on them. *Clean freak, don't make her mad.*

"People like you don't make social visits. Why are you here?" She said.

"Do you like coffee?" Dag asked.

"Yes, why are you asking?"

"There's a Caribou Coffee just down the street. I'll buy you a cup. We can talk."

"We can talk here."

"There's an old Bible verse that says *He who has ears, let him hear.* I've worked with the FBI before. I'd prefer if we had our little chat elsewhere."

"No problem." Lena wrapped a scarf around her neck and pulled on her jacket. She paused and looked at the left top drawer of her desk.

"You won't need your gun," Dag said. "I promise to be nice."

She met his eyes and said nothing. As they walked out of her office and toward the lobby the man at the reception desk stopped her.

"Agent Johnson, you have an urgent call on line three."

"Please excuse me." She said to Dag. Lena returned to her office and picked up the phone. "Agent Johnson."

"Lena, Dutch here. Robert Smith cleared customs in Miami a little over an hour ago, coming from Grand Cayman. We had a tag on his passport to notify us of any activity."

"What was he doing?"

"Nothing...but he was wearing a cap that said **Catch-22** from a seafood place in Cayman Islands."

"Coincidence?"

"Doubt it. He wrote on the front of the hat; *Molly Hatchet-Flirtin' with Disaster.*"

"That's an old song from the 70's, isn't it? Is he a music fan?"

"Couldn't tell you. I'm a Lawrence Welk fan."

"Dutch, I have Dag Rasmussen waiting to talk to me. What can I tell him?"

"Don't tell him anything. I don't trust old spooks."

Chapter 32

Twenty years from now you will be more disappointed
by the things you did not do than by the ones you did.
– Mark Twain

Tuesday, late morning, Miami.

Bobby read old newspapers and discarded magazines.
When he ran out those he read signs and labels on discarded Gatorade bottles. Every fifteen minutes he checked
the arrival and departure boards. Flight 348 to New York:
delayed. Other flights in and out of New York and New Jer-
sey were also delayed. Nothing he could do about it. After
his seventh check on the flight he noticed other flights into
and out of New York were no longer delayed. Then the departure time next to his flight flickered to life. *Scheduled
departure 1:12 EST.* He checked the time. Another hour.

He wouldn't make his connecting flight to Chicago. *Stick to the plan.* He pulled out his second cap and checked his notes. *Get it right. No room for error.* When he was done he was satisfied. He would figure out the next step in New York.

#

Tuesday early afternoon, Minneapolis

"Mr. Rasmussen, sorry for the delay." She shifted her eyes away when he looked at her.

"No problem."

"So, you were talking about coffee. It's afternoon, how about lunch?"

"You choose."

"How about the Hummus Grotto?"

"Never heard of it."

"My favorite place. They have a great, lactose-free, soy latté and vegan burgers with gluten free bread."

"Sounds yummy."

It took twenty-seven minutes during midday traffic but the parking lot was nearly empty. *I wonder why? Glad I had a double cheeseburger with extra bacon and a beer for breakfast.*

When they walked in the receptionist greeted them.

"Lena, welcome back. Your usual table?"

"Yes please."

"Is this your dad?"

"No, I'm her fiancé," Dag said. Lena gave him piercing look. He remembered the martial arts trophies.

"Oh, I'm sorry." The receptionist said.

Dag smiled.

The table was in the back corner. From their position Dag could see the front and the rear entrance. His back was guarded. *At least she can do something right.*

Lena ordered the spinach frittata made from free range egg whites and gluten free sourdough toast with sugar-free pomegranate preserves. Dag ordered the organic kale, yogurt and tofu smoothie.

"Do you like music?" Lena asked.

"I only listen to Willie Nelson, why?"

"Have you ever heard of Molly Hatchet?"

Dag perked up at the sound of Molly's name. "Old rock band from the 70's, isn't it?"

"Yes." She was quiet, playing with her fingernails.

Dag could play her game too. *What does she know about Molly?*

"Mr. Rasmussen, you have quite a resumé. Why did you come to me?"

"You shop at Nordstroms and you're interested in photography."

"That's an interesting observation."

239

"Listen. We both know why I'm here. You're following Molly because someone told you to do it. And it's obvious you've been told to withhold information. The only reason you went back to answer your phone was because the Dutchman was calling. You would have ignored anyone else."

"How do you know that?"

"Because I answered to the State Department and the President, no one else."

"You're retired. You don't outrank anyone."

"Old alliances don't die, they just go dark."

"I could be fired for leaking information against orders."

They were interrupted by the all-natural server delivering their food. Dag couldn't wait to try his tofu-smoothie.

"You tell me what you know and I'll help. I don't need publicity and I don't want it. You might come out of this smelling pretty." Dag took a big suck on his straw and started to gag.

"Where's Molly?" Lena asked.

"You couldn't find her with a satellite and a room full of lawyers."

"Are you challenging me?"

"I've spent a lifetime making people disappear, sometimes permanently."

Lena was quiet for several minutes. Dag let her squirm. She pushed her plate away from the edge of the table. He watched her free-range frittata sag.

"What do you know about *Catch-22*?" She asked.

"Not much. If it involves the girl, you should tell me."

"Professor Robert Smith has been flying around the world on someone else's dime. We think he's linked to *Catch-22,* but we don't know what it is...yet."

"What does this have to do with Molly Seymour?"

"They are connected...somehow." She dug into a backpack and pulled out a laptop. "I could lose my job for this."

Dag watched her face as she opened it up and logged on. *She wouldn't make a very good poker player.*

"Here." She turned the computer to see the image. "He came through customs in Miami, this morning. Tell me what you see."

Dag studied the photo carefully. Bobby Smith was looking at the camera. The printed front of the cap said Catch-22 Seafood. Handwritten letters were under the logo. *Molly Hatchet, Flirtin' with Disaster.*

"It's obvious."

"What do you see that I don't?" Lena asked.

"He's defecting and he's sending her a message." Dag checked his watch, 1:13. "Where is he now?"

"On a plane into New York. Should be landing around 3:44 EST."

"Let it play."

"You don't think we should pick him up?"

"Smith is a messenger, a nobody. If you pick him up now, you'll never find the people behind him."

"Dutch already called New York."

"How well do you know history?"

"Fair, why?"

"Then you know the Vikings made it to the New World long before Columbus. The Flying Dutchman never made it to shore."

"What do you have against Dutch?"

"In my opinion, Dutch is a rodeo clown trying to get his picture on the front page."

"I think this meeting is over." Lena put her laptop back into her bag and stood up.

"Leave the girl alone. If you want to talk to her, you go through me."

Dag dropped $20 on the table. Lena avoided eye contact and headed toward the door. Her phone rang. Dag stood close enough to hear.

"Johnson...Dutch. Mechanical problems. Smith's plane was rerouted to Charlotte...emergency landing. He wrote letters on his cap."

"What does it say this time?"

"It's code."

#

Bobby Smith had just dozed off when the plane began to shake. He was used to turbulence but this seemed different. The flight attendants announced their usual 'return to your seats, buckle your seat belts' stuff. First time travelers were wide eyed; seasoned travelers yawned and resumed their sudoku puzzles.

Then the captain spoke. "We are experiencing some mechanical problems and have received clearance to divert our flight. We will be landing in Charlotte, NC. We're sorry for any inconvenience this may cause." The intercom clicked off and the plane made another jerk.

"Please return your seats to their locked and upright position and stow all personal items overhead or under your seat. Thank you." Bobby pushed the window shade up and looked out. *It's a long way to the ground. I've never been in a plane crash before.* He was surprised by his own serenity. He didn't care about New York or Chicago or his instructions. *I need to warn Molly.*

The oxygen masks dropped suddenly from the ceiling. Someone in the back screamed. Bobby slipped the mask over his face and took a deep breath. *It smells like plastic.* He felt the plane dip and start to descend faster than any he ever experienced. His stomach lurched up into his chest. He was floating, then sinking and then rattled side to side. He felt the splash of someone's drink on the back of his head. The plane shuddered and groaned and then as sudden as it started it stabilized.

"Passengers prepare for landing."

The wings fanned and the engines roared. The plane hit hard and bounced. The landing gear screeched in protest. Bobby saw smoke and then flames from the starboard engine. A girl in the seat behind him screamed again and cried. They were on the ground.

The plane stopped just off the runway and emergency vehicles with flashing lights descended on them like flies on dead meat. Levers turned and emergency exits opened. One by one the passengers jumped out the doors onto inflated slides. Bobby left his luggage, his phone and his instructions. But he had his baseball cap.

#

"Lucky for him," Dag said.

"I don't understand." Lena hung up her phone. "They had an emergency landing. Someone could have been hurt or killed."

"Yes, but Smith avoids a free ride in a black suburban, courtesy of your goons in New York."

"Spare me your sarcasm."

"I need to know what his hat said." They walked out of the Hummus Grotto. Dag breathed a sigh of relief and spit on the sidewalk. *Tofu slurpee.*

"This is FBI business. You'll know what we let you know."

"That message is for Molly, not you."

"How do you know that?" She clicked open the locks on her car door.

"You won't be able to crack the code in time."

"In time for what?" She turned and looked Dag in his good eye before driving into the street. "We're the Federal Bureau of Investigation for the United States of America."

"Precisely."

Chapter 33

After a good dinner one can forgive anybody, even
one's own relations. – Oscar Wilde

Wednesday 2AM, Moscow.

Kalishnov listened to the voice on the phone. He nodded. He paced. He scratched. "Nyet, nyet," he paused, "Da."
He slammed the phone down so hard it rang again. Once.

He scribbled a note and handed it to his assistant, Bo-
ris. He grumbled something in Russian, too low for anyone
else to hear and sent him out. Vladimir Kalishnov walked
to his window and raised the blinds. He stared out of his
window to the street lights below. It was clear and the frost
sparkled on the windows, wires and rooftops.

It was the second phone call tonight. The first caused
him little concern. Bobby Smith's plane made an

emergency landing. No problem. He was a stooge, a pawn in the big game. He doubted Smith knew enough to warrant a change in plans. It was working perfectly. Everything was on schedule. Millions in American dollars. And even better, he was undermining the core of American culture. It was time to terminate Smith.

The second phone call was more concerning. Tuck Riley was agitated. *Weak Americans.* Someone knew something and they were trying to draw him out. Quiet them with money but only until the instigator was eliminated. If Riley cracks, he was expendable as well. Kalishnov didn't come this far to roll over and play dead.

The girl is brilliant. She needs to be watched. Kalishnov laughed and pulled the shade.

#

Tuesday afternoon, Charlotte, NC

It isn't going to work. I need to go through security. He stood at the bottom of the emergency slide near the right wing of the Boeing 727, assisting others as they exited the plane and slid to safety. From the terminal a series of vans approached the tarmac to transport the passengers to safety. He expected they would take them into the terminal but he didn't expect to go through the normal concourse.

The loaded vans returned to the terminal. Passengers were ushered into a secure side room and a representative of the airport spoke to them.

"Passengers of flight 1273 from Miami to New York, please listen up." The murmuring of the crowd lessened to the point where Bobby could hear. "If anyone has injuries, we have paramedics standing by. Please let us know immediately. Your luggage will be taken off the plane when it is determined to be safe. We have ticketing agents standing by to assist you in your travel plans. We are sorry for the inconvenience."

Bobby tried to listen but there was a push of people trying to get to the counter for alternate travel plans. He stood back trying to figure out his next step. *I'm not going to New York or Chicago. One chance. Think...no phone, fifty bucks...no luggage.*

He found a vacant chair and parked himself. He still had a sharpie in his pocket. One baseball cap on his head and one in his hands. *Make changes...one chance.* When he was finished he walked out of the holding room and headed toward security. *Don't deviate...walk straight...keep your head down.*

"Stop! You are entering a secured area. Stop!" Bobby heard the warning but kept walking. He heard running footsteps behind him. *Steady...they aren't going to shoot...I hope.*

"Sir! Stop! This is a secured area!" An alarm sounded and two officers stepped into his path. He stopped. He looked up at the security camera.

"Put your hands above your head and turn around." He raised his arms as high as he could reach. Bobby slowly turned. Two more officers held his arms and escorted him back into the holding room. "Sir, did you know you were going into a secured area?"

"I'm sorry. I just got off the plane that had an emergency landing. I wasn't thinking clear." He looked up toward the lights. A sudden spinning sensation hit him. His eyes jerked side to side. He grabbed his cap and fell into the arms of the officers holding him.

"We need a paramedic here." The first officer spoke into the radio. It squawked in response. They lowered Bobby to the floor. *I made it.* He laid on the cold floor and his eyes rolled back in his head. It was the last he remembered until they loaded him onto a waiting ambulance.

#

Dutch watched the security video download from Charlotte-Douglas International Airport. Bobby Smith appeared dazed. Dutch watched the security team warn him and detain him, all without incident or violence. Smith appeared

249

to collapse into their arms and he was lowered to the floor. But just before he collapsed, Smith looked up at the security camera. He reached up and touched the bill of his hat with his right hand and held onto his hat as he swooned.

Dutch zoomed in until he could read the letters. He printed the screenshot and moved forward frame by frame until he was certain he didn't miss any of the letters. He replayed the scene six or seven times until he was convinced there was nothing else to gain.

HZ FB YQ MH DP FV

The letters were all written upside down.

#

Lena broke all the speed limits getting back to her office. She weaved in and out of traffic on Interstate 694 and hit the exit ramp at 70 mph.

Dag sat in the passenger seat and didn't speak a word. He had a knot in his stomach thinking about Dutch Van Tassel. Seven years ago, they were involved with an opioid drug bust in West Virginia. One of Dag's agents was shot and killed. Dag had called the FBI field office for assistance. Dutch was the agent in charge of the FBI side of the operation. First, he tried to muscle in and control the entire operation. When that didn't work he used his leadership position to talk to the press. He was in all the headlines. Dag didn't care about the press. He hated the press. But when it mattered most, Dutch pulled out and left the DEA team vulnerable. Dutch claimed some cockamamie procedural violation. When Dag's man went down, he blamed Dutch.

Dag followed Lena into her office. If she didn't want him there, she didn't protest. She logged into her computer and checked the files sent by Dutch. E-mail recipients included a dozen other agents and cryptology.

"You're going to give me a copy, aren't you?" Dag asked.

She closed her laptop and stood as tall as five feet two inches could stand. "Have a nice day, Mr. Rasmussen."

Dag smiled. "Remember the Flying Dutchman."

He was punching numbers on his phone before he left the lobby.

Chapter 34

Seize the moment. Remember all the women on the Ti-
tanic who waved off the dessert cart. – Erma Bombeck

Wednesday afternoon, Lambeau Field, Green Bay, Wisconsin.

Dr. Epstein walked off the DC-9 at Green Bay regional
airport. He flew from Cleveland to Chicago and then to
Green Bay. He could have rented a car out of Chicago and
drove but he needed time to think. Sitting in airports gave
him plenty of time to think. He walked off the plane and
into the baggage claim area. He had no baggage but that's
where he was scheduled to meet his electrical engineer, Jim
Frederick.

Getting around in the Green Bay airport was a stark
comparison to O'Hare, but he didn't complain. He wasn't

there for sightseeing. The gift shops were flush with plenty of Packer's shirts and cups but he wasn't interested. He was a Steelers fan, always was and always would be.

"Dr. Epstein?"

"Oh, Mr. Frederick. You caught me daydreaming. Sorry."

"No problem. My car is just out front."

The trip from the airport to the stadium was easy. No traffic, no toll roads, no emergency vehicles flashing their lights, and no road rage or drive by shootings. They parked by the pro-shop near the atrium entrance of Lambeau field and went in. There was a buzz of activity, preparing for the Thursday night game against Chicago.

"I know you are working on the concussion project, but what does that have to do with network broadcasting?" Jim asked.

"Probably nothing, but intense noise can create or aggravate concussion symptoms. Inspecting some of the equipment might help us understand the sound experienced by the players."

"Sounds interesting. I look forward to seeing your report."

The receptionist led them to the sidelines where FOX Sports was setting up.

"Hi, I'm Chip. What are you looking for?"

"We want to inspect your parabolic microphones." Epstein said.

"The parabolics? That's strange." They followed Chip out of the stadium and back to the equipment trucks. "It's one of the last things we set up because it's simple and only used on the sideline."

"Who's the manufacturer?"

"I think these are made by Seoul-Chang Acoustics, out of South Korea. Why?"

"I was told all of the mics were made by Mork Industries."

"Seoul-Chang Acoustics is a division of Mork."

"Do you have the schematics for the mic?"

"I think so. We always have back up equipment in case of failure." Chip dug into the back of the equipment trailer and found a large unopened box with a picture of the parabolic mic on the label. He sliced the tape and opened the lid. "Here you go."

"Can we look at the equipment as well?"

"Have at it."

Chip left them and returned to his broadcast setup tasks.

"Jim, take a look at the schematics and the device and tell me if there is anything unusual."

"Like what?"

"Something you wouldn't expect."

#

Wednesday afternoon. Namukwa Lake

Molly spent the morning digging through the old library. Fifteen years passed since her grandparents lived in the house. Tom and Luella were the official owners now. They updated the old house but preserved the library. It was one of Molly's favorite rooms. She loved the old books with tattered covers and yellowed dog-eared pages. She felt a sense of mystery when she parted the old pages and read words printed over a hundred years past.

Grandpa Roy was an amateur cryptographer. He loved codes and ciphers and collected historical books about spies and secret codes. Molly remembered the treasure hunts he designed for her and the cousins. During summer vacation, he made treasure maps and secret codes for the kids to follow. Sometimes the hunt went on for days, from the beach to the old hollow pine tree back in the woods and then to the attic. Grandpa Roy had a big can of coins he had collected from around the world. Melted down they wouldn't be worth ten dollars but to her they were lost pirate treasure. That can of coins had been buried and dug up a dozen times over the years.

She found the book she was looking for. *Secret Codes and Ciphers.* Compared to computerized code breaking today, this was child's play, but to her it was a well of memories.

"Here it is." She stepped from the library, into the sitting room. Tom, Luella and Dag sat together looking over some paperwork.

"This is what was written on the hat?" Tom asked.

"She wouldn't let me get a copy so I memorized it." Dag said. "But I don't trust my memory any more. I called my old office and had them get the security image from the airport." He used Luella's laptop and logged into his gmail account. He opened the photo and enlarged it.

HZ FB QY MH DP OV

"He wrote it upside down." Luella said. "Do you think that means anything?"

"Why do you think this is a message for Molly and not someone else?" Tom wondered.

"Because of the first image in Miami." Dag opened another image on the computer. Bobby Smith was standing in front of the Customs official. His hat said

Catch-22 Grand Cayman
Molly Hatchet, Flirtin' with Disaster.

"Just because it says *Molly Hatchet?* That could mean anything." Luella said. She brought a fresh pot of coffee to the table and sat down. "Forgive me for being ignorant, but what is going on and why does it involve Molly?"

"I don't really know," Dag said. "Molly why don't you bring your aunt and uncle up to date."

"The FBI gave me a coded letter about *Catch-22*. We don't know what it is, but it involves my former professor, Robert Smith. That's him in the photo." Molly picked up the security photo and looked closer. "He was supposed to be teaching English in Russia, but none of this makes sense to me."

"Are you in danger?" Tom asked

"We can't confirm anything at this point," Dag added. "We are working under the assumption she may be in danger."

"So why not work with the FBI?" Luella wanted to know.

"The FBI doesn't know either. They think *Catch-22* is a big operation, possibly terrorist or organized crime. They have some pieces of the puzzle but not enough."

"So why the charade and the letter?"

"They're fishing," Dag said.

Molly placed a sheet of paper on the table. "Here's the lyrics to Flirtin' with Disaster."

I'm travelin' down the road
I'm flirtin' with disaster
I've got the pedal to the floor,
My life is running faster
I'm out of money, I'm out of hope,
It looks like self destruction
Well how much more can we take,
With all this corruption
We're flirtin' with disaster,
Y'all know what I mean
And the way we run our lives,
It makes no sense to me
I don't know about yourself or what you want to be,
yeah
When we gamble with our time

"What do you think? Is this about him? Or me? Or something else?" Molly asked.

"Let's assume you are in danger," Dag added. "The first step is to solve the code."

"Here." Molly opened her grandfather's book and set it on the table. "This is a *Wheatstone-Playfair* cipher." Everyone turned their attention from the security photo to the book. A grid of letters appeared under an old black and white photo of the inventor.

"So how do you solve it?" Tom asked.

"We need the key word. Once we have that, it is easily solved." Molly said. "The problem is finding the key word."

Dag spoke up. "If we assume it is meant specifically for you, then we must also assume it's a word you would know."

"OK, let's think." Molly took a sheet of paper and a pencil. For the next hour they listed every possible word or word combination linking Molly and Bobby Smith.

Penrose, Christian, University, college, education, Molly, Seymour, Minneapolis, Minnesota, Wisconsin, writing, graduation, fiction, creative, school... After reviewing an extensive list, they were no closer than when they began.

"So, what makes a good keyword?" Luella asked.

"The best keywords are longer and don't repeat letters." Molly said.

"Then we can delete most of these words without testing them." Tom said.

After three hours of trying different words, phrases and ideas, they found themselves back at the beginning, wondering what it meant. November evenings come early and the setting sun cast long shadows before the afternoon was gone.

Luella made a pot of chili in the slow cooker. "Hey, do you guys mind if I turn on some music? What do you like?"

"As long as it isn't rap, I don't care." Dag said.

Tom went to the wine cellar and pulled a couple of different California cabs to go with the stew. They set aside the spy business and relaxed by the fireplace. The music genre changed from the *Bee Gees* to the Blues. After many days of playing hide and seek, Molly felt at home.

"How are the wedding plans coming?" Luella asked Molly.

"Mostly good. We had an argument about the reception. Chuck's family doesn't drink so he was embarrassed to serve wine at the dinner. But I wanted to."

"What did you decide?"

"Jesus turned water into wine at the wedding. I didn't think there was any problem with it." Molly said, "Then he argued the New Testament wine was really grape juice...I lost it."

"How did that go over?" Tom asked.

"We're serving wine. I told him, no one was forcing them to drink it." Molly dipped her finger into the cabernet and rubbed it around the rim of her glass. A clear tone rang out and no one spoke. In the background she heard the music, *she'll be riding wildfire...* The fire crackled in the fireplace. The western sky was pink through the bare forest.

Molly swirled her wine and took a drink. "I know the keyword."

Chapter 35

He that is good for making excuses is seldom good for anything else. – Ben Franklin

Thursday morning, Green Bay Wisconsin

Jim Frederick went over the schematics quickly. There was nothing complicated about a parabolic microphone. It was basically a big bowl used to collect and reflect sound toward a microphone.

"Do you see anything?" Epstein wanted to know.

"Nothing unusual. This is an electromagnetic transducer." He pointed to part of the central apparatus.

"What does that mean?"

"It changes sound to an electrical signal for transmission. This one is more sophisticated than a simple microphone."

"So...?"

"It looks like this can transmit as well as receive."

"If you produced sound, could the parabolic dish concentrate it and direct it at specific point?"

"I don't see why not."

Dr. Epstein looked over the parabolic device. "Find a screwdriver."

Jim stepped out of the semi-trailer and found one of the technicians setting up the broadcasting equipment. "I'll bring it right back." He promised.

Epstein unscrewed the base holding the microphone in place. It slipped out the back leaving him with a huge punch bowl with a hole in the bottom. He coiled the wires together and stepped out of the trailer. "Let's go."

Frederick returned the screwdriver and they walked around the north end of the stadium to Frederick's car.

"Let's go to your office in Milwaukee. I need you to test this device and tell me what it can do."

\#

Wednesday afternoon, Chicago

His phone buzzed on his desk. Tuck Riley looked at the screen. *Blocked.* He had to answer it.

263

"Riley," He said.

"Meet me for coffee." Tuck recognized the voice. He didn't know his name.

"Is something wrong?" Riley asked.

"Smith disappeared." The voice said.

"What do you mean *disappeared?*"

"Does *disappeared* mean something different to you? Twenty minutes." The phone went dead.

#

The bright lights bothered Bobby Smith's eyes. Looking up trying to find the security cameras made him dizzy. He was prone to vertigo and he felt his head starting to spin. *I'm falling.* He felt himself being lowered to the ground. *Don't fight, stay down...I'm dead.*

"You violated a secured area." Someone said.

Bobby heard the voice again. He didn't open his eyes. He shook his head slowly. Paramedics arrived and eased him onto his back. They propped his head with a jacket and he felt a blood pressure cuff tightening around his right arm.

"What happened? Are you alright? Do you have chest pain? Are you hurt?" A stream of questions bombarded him. He nodded and mumbled but mostly remained quiet. Within twenty minutes they loaded him onto a gurney and he could hear his heart on the monitor, *beep...beep...beep...*

"Do we have his ID?" Someone asked.

"I have his information. He just came off the flight making the emergency landing," someone else answered.

"I think he was stressed and confused. Nothing to suggest wrong doing."

"File the report as if he's just a confused passenger but check him out anyway." Bobby heard, as he was being wheeled away to the waiting ambulance. He opened his eyes just a crack to glimpse his surroundings. A crowd of onlookers parted to let them through.

At the emergency room he was wheeled onto bay number three and the curtain was pulled. Six people gathered and shifted him from the ambulance gurney onto a hard table. Noise, questions, EKG's, blood tests, x-rays, more questions. He felt a sharp jab in the back of his right hand and watched a bag of fluid start to drip into his veins. They pushed some medications through a needle into the tubing and he felt his head swim and his vision blurred. He tried to block it out. Two hours later, more questions, more lab tests, another EKG, a CT scan of his head. More waiting.

"Mr. Smith, I'm Dr. Jeff Gall, one of the ER physicians." He placed the ice-cold stethoscope onto Bobby's chest and moved it to three or four different spots. "Deep breaths." He said. Bobby complied.

"Good news. All of your tests are normal so far. Probably all in your head."

Bobby nodded. *More than you realize.* "Now what?"

"You have good insurance and we have some empty beds upstairs. I think we should admit you for observation." Dr. Gall didn't wait for an answer. He barked out some orders to the nurse at his side and disappeared behind curtain number three.

Still under the influence of the medication he had been given he didn't protest. His room was nice. He had a view of the parking lot and another big building across the street. Bobby dozed into the evening. It had been years since he slept as well. Evening slipped into night. Someone placed a tray of heart-healthy food on the bedside stand. Dry toast, spinach salad without dressing and bottled water. He didn't eat. Bobby wanted a bacon, double cheeseburger and fries. He pushed the call button.

Forty minutes later two orderlies appeared in his room.

"Can I get something else to eat?"

They said nothing but helped him into a wheelchair and started down the hall. When the elevator doors opened they punched floor number five. Bobby could hear messages paging overhead for Dr. This and Dr. That. The doors closed and reopened on the fifth floor.

It was a long hallway. They passed the first nursing station and then the second. At the end of the hall was a second elevator. When the doors opened the orderlies pushed the ground floor button. Bobby said nothing. He knew nothing. When the doors opened he was in the loading dock area for deliveries.

"Hold this." One of the guys wadded a bunch of gauze over his IV and yanked it out of his arm. "Can you walk?"

"Yes."

"Follow us."

They walked out of the loading dock area to a waiting van with the words, *Hospital Linen Supply* on the side. Bobby was helped into the back and they turned right onto the busy four-lane street behind the hospital and merged into traffic.

#

"I know the keyword." Molly said. She took another sip of wine and set her glass down. Everyone watched as she took the paper and wrote out the grid with the keyword.

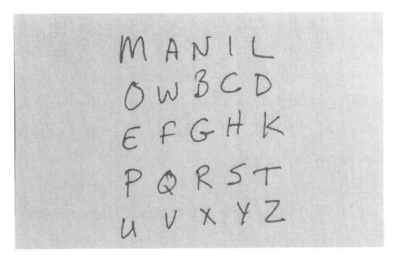

HZ FB YQ MH DP FV

Using the code letters from Bobby's hat she wrote the corresponding translation.

YK WG VS EI TO US

"It doesn't make sense." Molly looked at each face. "Do any of you see anything in this?"

"The last part might mean something. *To US or to us*, and the *vs* could represent *versus or against or between.*" Tom said. "But the other initials don't jump out at me."

"Are you certain about the key word?" Dag asked.

"I thought I was. It was from my paper, *Man of War, Weaponizing Barry Manilow*. He made such a big deal of it. I was certain I had the right word." Molly said.

"Molly...instead of *MANILOWB,* why don't you try *BMANILOW.*" Luella said. "See what comes out."

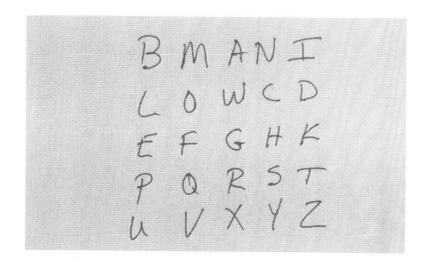

She reapplied the coded pairs and wrote the results.

YK ME VS NF TL VF

"It's worse than the last one." Dag said. "If we don't figure it out, FBI cryptology will. I don't know if that's good or
bad but it's better to be ahead of them if we can."

"Let me see the picture again." Molly said. She magni-
fied the image looking for anything else they may have
missed. "I give up. Let's eat."

They cleared the table of papers and Luella ladled generous portions into rustic ceramic bowls. A loaf of hot
crusty bread from the oven, dripping with melted butter
was the perfect side. They ate in peace.

At the end of the meal, Tom opened another bottle, a
dry French rosé, lightly chilled. "To the future," Tom said

as he lifted his glass. "May we accept it with dignity and survive it with grace."

"Amen," someone added. And they clinked glasses.

When the bottle was empty, Molly caught herself staring into the fireplace and then into the empty bottle. She tried to read the label from the backside. Everything was backwards.

"It's backwards," she said.

"The wine bottle?" Tom asked.

"No, the code. Professor Smith wrote it upside down because it's backwards."

"Show me." Dag said.

Molly got her pencil and paper and rewrote the translated letters.

KY EM SV FN LT FV

"Does that mean something to you?" Dag asked.

"It makes perfect sense. Don't you see?" Molly said. "It's music. The key isn't a real key, it's a key in music." She took the paper and wrote it out for everyone to see.

KY EM SVN FLT FV -Key E minor seventh, flat five. "I think he made a mistake and transposed the **FN**." Molly smiled. "We solved it."

"So what? He likes the blues, but what does it mean?" Dag asked.

"I have no idea," Molly said. "I'm calling Uncle Phineas."

Chapter 36

Part of the secret of success in life is to eat what you like and let the food fight it out inside. – Mark Twain

Thursday, Chicago.

"Mr. Riley, there's an urgent call from shipping."

"Tell them I'm not here."

"Line 3."

"Riley here." Tuck sat back in his chair and gazed out the office window toward Lake Michigan as he listened to the caller's voice. The blustery wind whipped around the corner of the building scattering early winter snowflakes. "Are you sure it's Epstein?"

He scribbled some notes on his desk as he listened. "No, don't call the police or file a report. I'll Fedex a replacement up there. You'll have it before the game tomorrow night."

It'll be an interesting conversation over coffee.

#

"This is an electromagnetic acoustic transducer. It can send and receive sound but not at the same time." Jim Frederick stood at the equipment table in the back of his office building.

"You're sure this can transmit sound?"

"Isn't that what I said?"

"Show me."

Jim Frederick plugged the wires into an audio jack on his computer and opened a music file. Jimmy Buffet came out of the sound apparatus.

"If this were back in the dish, could you direct the sound at a specific point?"

"Sure. The dish can direct sound if the wavelengths are shorter than the radius of the dish. Longer wavelengths can be produced but not focused."

"And what if you had two or three of these focused on one point?"

"That depends on the wavelength and the frequency. They could cancel each other, or they could amplify the intensity."

"Help me..."

OK...have you ever been in a boat that turns around in circles? It produces waves. When the peaks of those waves come together, the resulting wave is twice as high. If the trough and the peak meet at the same point, they cancel...no wave."

"If I aimed two or three of these at someone what would happen?"

"Led Zeppelin and Pink Floyd in the same room."

"I see."

"And the other crazy thing...someone ten feet away might not even notice anything unusual."

#

Wednesday evening, Namukwa.

"What's the point of sending an encoded guitar chord?" Tom asked. "It doesn't make sense unless it's a code or clue for something else."

Dag spoke up. "Do you know if Smith is married, or divorced? Could this be a clue for someone else as well?"

"I never thought of that," Molly said. "Maybe he has a sister or someone else in the family named Molly."

Dag's phone rang.

"Yep" he said as he lifted the phone to his ear. Molly watched his face. If there was anything interesting, he wasn't giving it away by his expression.

"Are you sure?" He asked. Another long pause.

"I'll think about it." He nodded and ended the call. Dag stood and went to the window overlooking the lake. The moon was coming up and it glinted on the thin ice along the shore. It was peaceful and cold.

"Who was that?"

"An old friend, the Flying Dutchman." Dag turned back to the fire. "It's obvious, the agent I had lunch with, Lena Johnson, gave Dutch an earful."

"What do you mean?" Molly asked.

"I'll spare you the finer points. He's giving me ten days to bring you in for voluntary questioning or he's going to get a federal warrant."

"A warrant for what?" Molly asked.

"He'll find a reason."

"What precipitated this?" Luella asked.

"Bobby Smith disappeared from the hospital during the night. FBI checked his hospital records. He was on medication so it wasn't likely he left on his own."

"What does that have to do with me?"

"Your name was on his hat. But that's not all," Dag said. "Smith had a house in North Oaks, a suburb of Minneapolis."

"So?"

"It's on fire."

#

Wednesday evening, Chicago

"Decaf Columbian, cream and sugar." Tuck left a five-dollar bill on the counter and walked to the table in the back corner of Starbucks. Mr. Big was already waiting. Their eyes barely met, they didn't shake hands. Tuck didn't know his name and he didn't want to ask.

"Our friend didn't show up." Mr. Big said. His voice was low and steady. His eyes darted back and forth as if watching a ping-pong match.

"Smith?"

"On the street they still talk about Ballsy Bob. I respect Ballsy. He took us for plenty before the curse was broken. I bet somebody punched his ticket."

"What do you want me to do?"

"You need to guarantee a win."

"Name it."

"Chicago-Green Bay. Thursday night. Packers are 10-point favorites. Bears...by 7."

"I'll give the word."

"Three million on the spread. Pay-off is five to one."

"What if it doesn't work?"

"The girl."

"What about the girl."

"I heard her play Tchaikovsky. She's good, but it's hard to play with broken fingers."

"Why her? Why not me?"

"You're a commodity. I can find a thousand people to do what you do. But she's Ming Dynasty porcelain, one of a kind. You won't let it happen."

"We have a problem."

"No, you have a problem."

"Epstein was at Lambeau." Tuck hung his head as he spoke.

"The concussion guy?"

"He knows."

"Where is he now?"

"Flying back to Cleveland, tonight."

"My cousin, Vigo, has a great restaurant in Little Italy not too far from Dr. Epstein's office in Cleveland. I'll have Vigo invite him to dinner."

"He's Jewish."

"So? Vigo will stick a matzo ball in his cannoli."

Chapter 37

I'm not going to buy my kids an encyclopedia. Let them
walk to school like I did. – Yogi Berra

Thursday afternoon, Namukwa.

"Molly, your mom called this morning. They're coming
up this weekend," Luella said.

"I'm sure she has wedding things she wants to talk
about." Molly sighed and rubbed her eyes.

"You don't sound like a typical bride-to-be. Is something wrong?" Luella stopped putting dishes into the dish-
washer and turned toward Molly.

"I don't know. It's hard for me to talk to my mom.
Sometimes she seems pushy, I can't explain it."

"Listen...when Maddie got married last year it was the
same with us. We argued about everything...invitations,

venue, expenses. I think I know what you're going through." Luella put some lotion on her hands and rubbed them together. "Give her the benefit of the doubt. I know she cares."

"It isn't her. It's me. Don't you ever have doubts?"

"Of course. We all do. But I have faith that all things will work together...for good."

"Sounds too simple."

"It isn't simple. It's much harder than you think."

Molly studied Dag's Airstream through the window. *He's scary looking but he's a good man.* "Hey Aunt Lu, have you seen Dag?"

"Tom took him to his office, in town. He wanted to use the fax."

"Are Phineas and Emma coming too?"

"They're coming for Thanksgiving but I wasn't planning for them, this weekend. You can invite them if you want."

"I wanted to talk to Phineas about the code. He might have a different perspective."

"Give 'em a call."

#

Thursday afternoon, North Oaks, Minneapolis

Lena Johnson parked on the street, a half block from the smoldering remains of Bobby Smith's house. She zipped her jacket up tight to her chin and made sure her FBI credentials were visible.

"Lena Johnson, FBI." She flashed her ID at the fire inspector.

"This is a house fire, not a federal crime scene. What are you doing here?"

"Have you determined that already?"

"Not yet. What can I do for you?" The fire inspector put down his clipboard and wiped some black soot from his arm. "Drew Sketcher." He extended his hand.

"What can you tell me?"

"Started in the garage. Looks like gas or lighter fluid was used."

"Was there anyone here?"

"Nope. According to the neighbors, he hadn't been home in over a month. A tight community. They spy on each other."

"Find anything suspicious?"

"The back end of the house was spared, except for smoke and water damage. What are you looking for?"

"I don't know yet. Maybe I'll know, if I see it."

Lena slipped on some latex exam gloves and stepped carefully through a hole in the wall, into the back half of the house. Windows were broken. Furniture was tipped over, upholstery was cut and ripped. Drawers were pulled out and dumped. In one room she found a collection of bowling trophies and several autographed baseballs. One was signed by Sammy Sosa. Paintings, blackened and curled from the heat, still hung in the hall. There was a framed photo of Bobby Smith standing beside his polished blue Studebaker with license plates, **BB**. The glass was cracked. *Someone was looking for something.*

She snapped some photos with her phone and called Dutch. "Someone was here."

"I didn't send you out there to tell me what I already know."

"Everything's torn apart. It looks professional. What am I looking for?"

"He's linked to the mob from gambling. He's in bed with the Russians. He's traveling on private jets with business executives. And he's sending clues to Molly Hatchet through security camera photos. He was drugged and disappeared from a hospital in Charlotte and his house burned down in Minneapolis. *And...*he's flashing *Catch-22* on his baseball cap. If I knew what to look for, I wouldn't have sent you." Lena heard her phone go silent. Then it rang again.

"Our only link is the girl." He said, as soon as Lena accepted the call. "I told Rasmussen ten days, but we can't wait that long. He's protecting her and I want to know why."

"Do you want me to get a warrant?"

"For what? No judge in his right mind would issue a warrant for her unless there's probable cause."

"We don't know who started the fire."

"I like how you think."

#

Thursday evening, Namukwa.

"The sausages are ready. I need a pan or something." Tom yelled in the back door of the kitchen. Smoke from the Weber grill curled around his head and mingled with his breath in the cold night air.

"Phineas, can you take this out to Tom?" Luella handed him a scratched and dented aluminum cake pan.

"No problem." He pushed open the door with his left elbow, being careful not to spill the glass of Spotted Cow in his right hand.

"Here you go, Tom. Hey...thanks for the invite...this is fun." Phineas sipped his beer and handed Tom the pan.

"It was Molly's idea."

"I know Harry and Olivia are worried. What do you think is going on?"

"Not sure. Mr. Rasmussen is convinced there's something or he wouldn't be here."

"Is there anything we can do?"

"Molly has this secret code thing. She thinks you can help figure it out."

Tom picked every sizzling sausage from the grill and put them into the cake pan. "We can talk about it after dinner. Let's eat."

Dinner was a glorified tailgate party before Thursday Night Football. Olivia, Luella and Emma were wearing Aaron Rodgers #12; Harry wore #15; Bart Starr; Tom and Phineas had Favre, #4 and Dag wore retired #66, Ray Nitschke. Libby wore #52, Matthews, and Molly wore #2, Mason Crosby. The home team was well represented around the table.

When there was a break in the football banter, Phineas said, "I heard you had a music question."

"E minor 7th, flat 5. What does it mean to you?"

"A common blues chord, especially with guitars and piano. Why?"

"If someone went to the trouble of encoding this, what would you think?

"It has to lead somewhere else. Taken by itself, there's nothing mysterious here." Phineas walked over to the upright piano in the corner and played a blues lick. "The chord you mentioned is only four notes, E, G, B♭, D, but you can play them many ways."

When he returned to the table he asked, "What do you think it means?"

Molly shrugged her shoulders, "We don't know."

"It's almost time for the game," Harry said. "Molly, let it go. Let's relax and watch the game."

"OK dad." She gave her dad a hug, "Thanks for coming. I really miss you guys."

"We've been praying for you every day." Harry whispered into her ear.

"Thanks, I needed that."

The television pregame commentary was all about the oldest NFL rivalry between the Packers and the Bears. Molly ignored the hype. She filled her plate with cheese dip and pita chips and found a place at the end of the couch next to her mom.

The commentators bragged up Aaron Rodgers as being unstoppable at home in temperatures below 32 degrees. The Bears were struggling to rebuild but it was a division game and anything could happen. Then the announcers turned serious.

"As we all know, head injuries are a serious matter. The NFL as well as the player's union and team owners are making concerted efforts to prevent serious concussion. Dr. Lawrence Epstein, noted neurologist from Cleveland Clinic, in association with the NFL and a large grant from Mork

Industries, was leading a large-scale study on concussion prevention and treatment. We were saddened to hear, Dr. Epstein was involved in a fatal traffic accident near his home early this morning. Our thoughts and prayers go out to his family at this time. And now a break for a message from your local station."

The television cut away from Thursday Night Football to the local news station out of Duluth, Minnesota. "Authorities are asking for help in solving a recent house fire in the North Oaks area of Minneapolis. The home of Professor Robert Smith was destroyed by fire. Arson is suspected. Molly Mae Seymour, a graduate student at Penrose Christian University is wanted for questioning but is not yet considered a suspect in the arson. Anyone with information regarding the whereabouts of Molly Seymour is encouraged to call 612-955-3099 or their local police." Her Penrose photo ID was displayed on the screen along with a more recent photo.

The room was silent. Molly's cheese dip ran off her plate and onto the couch.

Chapter 38

I used to play sports. Then I realized you can buy trophies. Now I am good at everything. – Demetri Martin

Thursday night, Namukwa.

Mason Crosby sent the opening kickoff deep into the end zone. The first play of the game, Green Bay tackled the Bears starting running back for a loss. The second and third plays were little better. The Bears punted. Tuck Riley's hand shook as he picked up his phone. *Tough night.*

The phone picked up after three rings. "Yes?"

"If the Bears don't score before the end of the first quarter, start working on the Packer's defense."

"Anyone in particular?"

"Start with the line." Riley hung up. He chewed two antacid tablets and poured another drink. Three minutes into the game Packers were up 7-0. By ten minutes it was 14-0.

Riley called again. "We can't wait. Start with their offense."

"Rodgers too?"

"Spare him until the 4th."

"Got it."

Tuck set his phone aside and leaned forward to watch. He had seen it before and was amazed at its simplicity. Riley recalled the first time he witnessed the power of the Cossack. It was preseason football. An undrafted running back for Indianapolis broke several tackles against Jacksonville and waltzed into the end zone. His end zone dance and arrogant rants weren't well received by the crowd. Tuck made the call. The next time that running back carried the ball he jumped up from the turf and announced how good he was.

On cue, the player clutched his helmet, spun like a top and collapsed to the ground. No one else on the field acted differently or reported anything out of the ordinary. The running back was taken off the field on a stretcher.

After Green Bay's second score, the Bears had the ball on their own 25-yard line. The call was a play action pass option. The quarterback fumbled the ball on their own 20-yard line and the Packers recovered. As the nose tackle was getting up from the turf he clutched his helmet and staggered to his left and fell.

"Injury, time out," the official called. The announcers renewed their discussion about the violence of football and the sudden tragic loss of lead investigator, Dr. Lawrence Epstein.

Green Bay took over on the 20-yard line. They were certain to score at least a field goal. Tuck sent a text this time. As the play was unfolding, one of the wide receivers appeared to stumble as he ran an out pattern. He fell to the ground and Aaron Rodgers threw one of his rare interceptions. The corner caught the ball with no one in front of him and ran 80 yards untouched down the left sideline. The score was 14-7. Tuck ate only one antacid tablet this time.

As the clock ran out at half time, one of the television announcers stopped the Packers coach as he made his way to the locker room. "Coach, what can you say about all of the Packer's injuries in the first half?"

"Next man up."

"But four concussions and none for Chicago. Can you explain that?"

"It's a violent game."

"Do you anticipate any changes in the second half?"

"Our players never give up." And he trotted off toward the tunnel.

"There you have it." The sideline announcer added. "The Packers were heavily favored coming into this divisional game, but the half-time score shows a different story. 14-24 in favor of Chicago. Al, back to you."

#

"Molly?" Olivia knocked lightly on the bedroom door. When the local news mentioned Molly's name in conjunction with the North Oaks house fire, she had no interest watching football. "Molly?"

"Mom, I don't want to talk right now."

"Honey, it's Chuck. He called on my phone."

Molly pulled open the door and retreated back to her bed. "Tell him I'm sick."

"Just say something. He's worried."

Molly took her mother's phone and pushed the door shut. "Chuck?"

"Molly, my father called me. He heard the news."

"I can't imagine what he had to say."

"He's worried about his image."

"His image? What about my image?" Molly coughed and rubbed her eyes. "I didn't hear his name on television."

"You know... he's the director of one of the biggest political action committees in the country."

289

"So?"

"He said, he didn't want me to marry a fugitive. Bad publicity could hurt fundraising."

"And you didn't defend me?"

"It's hard to stand up to my father."

"You can print his image on a roll of toilet paper and hand it out at the next event. Maybe that'll help. And you can have your ring back. It's over."

"Over? Wait...Molly."

"I'll call you when I start medications." She threw the phone against wall.

#

Friday morning. Chicago

Tuck turned to the Tribune sports page and smiled. Green Bay had come back within a touchdown and Aaron Rodgers was leading them down the field with 3:19 left in the 4th quarter. He was working his magic and the hometown crowd was getting excited. The noise was intense. Riley made another call, but the guys on the sidelines weren't coordinated. The running back and the quarterback were the targets. But the effect it caused was even better. Suddenly they both acted confused. Rodgers was tackled and the ball came loose. Bears recovered. Game over. *I love football.*

He flipped through the paper and found the article about Dr. Epstein and his work with concussions. It was so tragic to lose a brilliant physician helping to change the lives of many athletes. The family was planning a private burial. It was an interesting read, but Tuck knew that many of the concussions reported over the past few years, weren't concussions. They were acoustic injuries. *Epstein knew. Smith knew. What if the girl talks? What does she know?*

There was another article on head injuries and the work being donated by Mork Industries. Mork Industries gave a $500,000 grant to college programs and NFL football to refit helmets with a shock absorbing gel liner. It was pliable and formed to the shape of the athlete's head, making it more comfortable. The gel was better at absorbing and dissipating blunt force. But Tuck knew it was part of the plan. Gel transmits sound waves ten times better than air. Gel helmet liners combined with short bursts of concentrated acoustic waves disoriented or disabled an individual in seconds. Anything more than a few seconds caused loss of consciousness. The first week the helmet liners were used, Mork recouped their $500,000 investment several times over.

The plan was working perfectly. Smith had gambling connections and debt the Russians could exploit for gain. He also had the plan, the original simple plan designed by the girl. It was so simple it was genius. A weapon disguised as a simple listening device, controlled and operated from a remote computer. People were willing to pay huge sums to influence the outcome of NFL football. And if people paid for their services, you could blackmail them until the end of days. If the fans knew what he knew, there would be riots.

Kalishnov expanded the concept into other sporting venues and there was talk about the Olympics. Tuck protested, concerned that wider use would risk exposing them. He didn't want to kill the goose that laid the golden egg.

Riley folded the morning paper and set it aside. He stood and stretched. It was a rare sunny November day in Chicago. The morning sun poured into his east facing townhouse and it felt warm on his face. He wanted to sit and soak it all in but something still wasn't right.

He picked up the life section of the Tribune and checked the obituaries. Nothing unusual. He checked the scrambled word puzzle. It looked normal. He reviewed the crossword puzzle. No problems. *It wasn't Epstein. Too creative. I'll send my own message and see what I catch.*

Chapter 39

Siblings: your only enemy you can't live without. - anonymous

Friday morning, Namukwa.

"I'm ready to talk."

"It's about time," Olivia said, "You broke my phone. And what about the wedding?"

"I don't want to talk about the wedding. It's over." Molly poured herself a mug of black coffee. "I've been having second thoughts anyway and last night confirmed it."

"Poor Chuck," Libby was curled into the corner of the couch with her flannel pajamas tucked under her feet. "I bet he cried all night."

"Shut up Libby."

Molly pulled out a chair and sat next to Olivia. "Mom, I want you to know, I'm really sorry about the wedding. But I don't think I can marry Chuck. Not anymore."

"Maybe you should see a counselor," Olivia said.

"There you go again with your counselor thing. Pretty soon you'll be talking about medications and before Thanksgiving I'll be locked up in a rubber room." Molly got up from the table and walked to the window. *This was always such a happy place. I miss Papa and Grammy.* It was cloudy again. The morning sun fought to make itself known. Chickadees flitted from limb to limb eating sunflower seeds from the birdfeeder. A big woodpecker tapped out another Morse-code message to the forest dwellers. A pair of squirrels snuffed about on the ground, dining on seeds dropped by the birds. A goshawk with fierce eyes slashed through the trees. The little birds froze. The woodpecker ducked for cover. Molly blinked. There was only one squirrel remaining.

"Mom, I'm leaving."

"Oh Molly, every time something difficult happens, you run away." Olivia sighed, "I don't know what to do with you anymore."

"She's going to Italy." Libby's eyes darted from Molly to Olivia. "I found her tickets."

"Molly, is that true?" Olivia asked.

Molly gave a sharp sideways glance at Libby. "I'll be twenty-two in March."

"So, you're old enough to turn your back on your family? Is that what you're saying?"

"I'm not turning my back on you or anybody. I don't know what I'm saying." Molly pulled on a coat, hat and gloves and stepped outside. *I don't know.*

#

Dag Rasmussen parked his pickup truck and shiny Airstream trailer in the parking lot at Canal Park in Duluth. He pulled his bomber hat down tight over his wild hair and slid his arms into a black and red plaid Mackinaw coat. He glanced into the mirror in his camper and one word came to his mind: *Fargo.* He felt out of place but he looked like most of the other guys out for a walk in the blustery wind along Lake Superior. *Look for the man with the tartan cap.*

Dag zipped his coat tight to his chin and blinked back a tear. The wind was brisk across the lake and waves rolled across the channel, under the bridge and into the harbor. Windsurfers in black neoprene suits clung to miniature sails, on the water, bobbing and scooting where the wind took them. The only other people on the boardwalk were joggers, walkers, lovers and singles with dogs on leashes. Just another day in Duluth. *These people are crazy.*

Dag walked from the parking area toward a concrete house, tilted and empty in the water; the shell of a prehistoric hermit crab, vacated and forgotten. One fellow with a hairy mutt on a blue nylon leash sat on the bench reading the morning newspaper. He had a tartan cap in place and a curved pipe like Sherlock Holmes.

"Are you from the MacDonald clan?" Dag asked.

"Nay, but I've been to Glasgow, and I had a nip of Dalrymple last night," He replied.

"Dalrymple's good but I prefer Glenmorangie." Dag nodded and sat beside him staring over the icy inland sea.

He tried to remember the last time he was in Duluth. It was years ago when old man Ambrose went bonkers and was in the hospital on the hill. Dag shifted his gaze from the wind surfers to the hospital on the hill, overlooking the port. It was summer then and it was still cold.

The man with the tartan cap reached down to his dog and unclipped a small plastic container from her collar. He handed it to Dag. "It's all we've got." He pulled the collar of his coat up around his ears. "The weather man said you'd best get out your woolies." He stood and walked down the boardwalk with his dog. The waves crashed against the riprap, the surfers frolicked in the frigid water and Dag sat alone, wondering, *what next.*

#

Tuesday morning, Oak Grove, Wisconsin.

It had been a testy weekend with parents, first at Namukwa and later at home in Oak Grove. Molly felt pressure on many fronts. They were paying for school and she quit attending. They were paying for the wedding and she called it off. She had beautiful long dark hair and she cut it short and got a tattoo. They thought she was depressed and she was giddy as a child at Christmas. Well maybe not that giddy, but she wasn't as melancholy as everyone thought and that frustrated her. She wanted everyone to leave her alone until she could figure out what was happening in her life. She checked the clock on the microwave. Time to leave.

It was all arranged. She was going to meet Lena Johnson, the FBI agent. Dag was still AWOL, apparently camping in Duluth. She wanted him along, but it didn't matter. She needed to get it over and done. Molly was tired of playing cat and mouse.

"Mom thanks for letting me borrow your car. I'll drop Libby off at school on the way and I expect to be back for supper." Molly pulled on a ski jacket and stocking cap and gave her mom a hug.

"Molly, I'll be praying for you."

"Everything's going to be OK. I promise." Molly hurried out the door. As they drove out the driveway, Molly looked back at the front window. Olivia was framed in the glass, pressing a tissue to her nose.

"Do you want to know what Dad said about you, last night?" Libby asked as they turned onto the main road.

"Does it matter?"

"He said you were strong and brave and we needed to trust you."

"Dad said that?"

"Yep, and then he said you were too smart for your own good, and you were probably going to learn a hard lesson along the way."

"That sounds more like him." Molly turned the Toyota Rav4 into the school parking lot and dropped Libby at the curb. She had an hour's drive before the meeting. It gave her time to think.

If Dag didn't trust the FBI, then she didn't. Molly called the shots. The meeting was arranged at Tavern-on-Grand in St. Paul. Gladys Keller's house was easy walking distance from there and it gave her a chance to see the old woman again. Her house also had a secret entrance and exit though the cellar. It gave Molly a better chance to disappear if necessary.

At 1710 Summit Avenue, Molly drove into the driveway and opened the garage door. She pulled the Toyota into the empty space next to the 1947 Nash and closed the door behind her. Gladys was waiting in the kitchen.

"Molly, it's nice to see you again." Gladys gave her a warm hug. "You've got some schumtz on your cheek." She licked her fingers and rubbed the mark away.

"Thanks Gladys."

"Are you all set?"

"As well as I can be," Molly said. "Is it OK with the Henkel's?"

"I call them yesterday. They're glad to help."

Gladys lead Molly down the stairway into the cellar. In the corner was another door leading into a small dark room. On the back wall of the second room was another door made to look like a narrow cabinet. Gladys pulled the latch and the cabinet swung open, revealing a dark tunnel. Stone steps went down and turned out of sight. "Don't forget your flashlight." Gladys gave her another hug and clicked the false door shut behind Molly.

The tunnel dated back to Prohibition days. It smelled old and musty and the damp chill did little to comfort her. She waved the flashlight around, trying to illuminate her path. Several old crates and bottles were stacked against the wall, remnants of a different era. The passage made two more turns and went down several more flights of stairs. There were forks in the tunnel and she remembered to keep left. Finally, at the end she saw a crack of light coming from the root cellar connected to Henkel's garage. Coming out of the tunnel she found herself on Grand Avenue, a block east of the Tavern-on-Grand. Molly waited until there was a small group of people walking by and she joined them. She walked two blocks past the Tavern before crossing the street. Molly entered the Tavern through the service entrance, acting as if she owned the place. No one said anything.

The dining area was rather dark, but Molly could see Lena Johnson sitting alone in the booth in the back, left corner. There was a man, alone in a booth near the front entrance. Agent Johnson and the man looked at each other. Molly knew they were together.

Molly took out her phone and sent a text to agent Johnson. *Tell the man to leave.* Molly watched to see what would happen. Johnson coughed and the man turned in her direction. She gave him a signal and he got up from his place and walked out the front door. Molly figured he would be sitting in a car, watching the front entrance. When he was out of sight, Molly went back into the kitchen area and slipped on a uniform top which was hanging on a hook near the walk-in cooler. She grabbed a glass of water and a menu and walked to the table.

"Are you expecting anyone else?" She asked as she approached the table.

"Yes, I'm waiting..." Lena lookup at Molly and realized she had been duped.

"I said I would only talk if you came alone." Molly said.

"I am alone."

"If you lie to me about simple things, how can I trust you with important things." Molly turned to leave.

"Wait...Professor Smith disappeared. We need to talk."

"I know about his hat trick," Molly said.

"There's more."

Chapter 40

Double, double, toil and trouble; Fire burn and caul-
dron bubble. – William Shakespeare

Tuesday, Noon. Grand Avenue, St. Paul.

Molly hesitated at the kitchen entrance. She felt like running, but she wanted to hear what agent Johnson had to say. She stepped behind the door and stripped off the uniform top and hung it back on the hook. Molly picked up her coat and hat and returned to the booth with Lena Johnson.

"Where's Mr. Rasmussen?" Johnson asked.

"AWOL."

"When?"

"Three or four days ago. What does it matter? He doesn't trust you and you don't like him."

"Ms. Seymour, I'm going to be straight with you."

"Meaning...you weren't before?"

"Listen...something's going down. It's called *Catch-22*. We still don't know what it is but you're involved. We think you have answers and until we get some answers we're going to ride you until we learn something."

"Start talking, I need to pick up my sister from school at 3:30 and I have an hour drive."

"How well do you know Professor Smith?"

"He was my college professor a couple years ago. Nothing else."

"Why would he send you a coded message on his cap?"

"Why don't you ask him? You're probably waterboarding him right now."

"Don't be stupid. That's against the law."

"What does the law have to do with it?" Before Lena could respond, a waiter came to their table. Molly figured Agent Johnson was buying so she ordered the house salad with gorgonzola, a bowl of lobster bisque, the deep-fried walleye sandwich and a sixteen-ounce glass of Summit beer, on tap. Lena ordered the gluten-free, lactose-free, non-GMO, vegan burger and a sugar free lemonade.

"Who's this?" Agent Johnson asked after the waiter left.

Molly studied the photo of Professor Smith standing beside a woman. She appeared slightly older than he did. The photo was blackened on the edge and curled.

"Never saw her before."

"Her name is Margaret Axtel. She's an artsy recluse. She does pottery and lives alone in Cornucopia, Wisconsin."

"So? Maybe he had a girlfriend. Why don't you talk to her?"

"We tried. Court records show her to be an older stepsister to Bobby Smith. Smith was adopted. She has no phone. Neighbors claim she's psychotic and deaf. There was an incident with the Bayfield sheriff a couple years ago. She threatened him with a shotgun."

"Maybe you should try acting nice."

Agent Johnson reached into an envelope and pulled out more papers.

"Here's the Star-Tribune, today's issue. Have you seen the obituary section?"

Molly swallowed a gulp of hot soup and turned the page.

Molly Hatchet age 22. Died suddenly in her sleep. She was preceded in death by her sister from a tragic accident. Both deaths are under investigation. Anyone with information is encouraged to call the Minneapolis Police Department.

"What does this mean to you?" Johnson asked.

"Someone is playing games."

"Aren't you worried. I'd consider this a threat, if I were you." Johnson asked. "Who is it?"

"Why should I know. Call the paper."

"We did. We traced the call back to Chicago. The office of Elmore Riley. Do you remember him?"

Molly cleared her throat and swallowed. She said nothing. After a moment she pushed her lunch back from the edge of the table. "I need to go."

"Riley and Smith visited you at the dress shop. I was there taking photos." Lena put a few more photos on the table. "Remember?"

"I didn't do anything wrong."

"I think you're hiding something. If you tell me what you're hiding, you're guilty. If you don't tell me and we find out, you're still guilty. It seems you have your own *Catch-22.*" Johnson smiled.

Agent Johnson's phone alarm went off. *Amber-Alert.* She turned off the audio and checked the message. "This is interesting." Lena put her phone down and looked into Molly's eyes. "A fifteen-year-old girl was abducted from your old high school. I think you know her."

"I need to go." Molly ran out the back.

Johnson called her partner. "She ran out the back." She got up to follow and the manager of the restaurant stepped in front of her with the bill.

"FBI." She flashed her credentials.

"Owner." He flashed a smile. "We take cash or credit cards."

#

Tuesday morning, Duluth, Minnesota

Dag returned to the *Silver Bullet* with the chip. He was back in the game. He didn't need his name on the door or a title to feel good again. Years of clandestine work left him with many dark-alley contacts who owed him favors. He hoped this would shed some light on the problem.

Dag pushed the SD chip into his laptop and clicked on the icon. A dozen files were displayed in the menu. Dag started at the top and worked his way through. There were files on Robert Smith, Kalishnov, Elmore Riley, Molly Seymour, Lena Johnson, Dutch Van Tassel and Margaret Axtel.

He sat in the parking lot for three hours pouring over details until his computer battery flashed *7% battery life remaining*. Then he found it. There was no mistake.

Molly was in trouble. He needed to find her fast.

#

Tuesday afternoon, Oak Grove, High School

Tuck swore under his breath. Libby was tougher than he suspected. She bit him on the hand and she scratched his face, but he finally pushed her into the back seat and drove off. He thought he could just drive up to the school and scare her into coming with him. It wasn't so easy.

The black suburban was equipped for transporting detainees. There were no latches on the inside of the back seat, the windows didn't open and there was a bullet-proof glass between the front and back seats, so he couldn't be attacked. It wasn't his, he borrowed it.

He turned up the radio to help drown out her screaming and yelling. She took off her shoe and pounded on the side window, then on the glass between them. He glanced into the rear-view mirror. Libby's mascara streaked and ran down her face. Her eyes were red from screaming and crying. She looked like a wild animal.

Tuck found himself in unfamiliar territory. He had goons at his bid and call. He didn't like the dirty work and he was trying to remember why he insisted on doing this alone.

"My sister's gonna kill you!" He heard her yell through the glass. He pushed the intercom button.

"I'm not going to hurt you," He said. He didn't sound very convincing. *Her sister? What about her dad or the police?*

Libby went quiet. Her changed behavior unnerved him. *What's she doing?* He drove slower so he could think. The drop was ten minutes away.

Libby slipped down on the seat, low enough, making it hard for him to see her. She started to shake and jerk. Tuck could see her eyes roll back in her head and spit ran out of her mouth and onto the seat. *Oh God...she's having a seizure.*

Tuck didn't know what to do. He pulled to the side of the road and opened the back door. Libby continued to shake. Her breath was gurgling and labored. He pulled her toward the door trying to turn her so she wouldn't choke.

Libby kicked him in the crotch as hard as she could. Tuck groaned and doubled up, grabbing himself. She stuck her thumbs into both of his eyes and gouged as deep as possible. He screamed. Then she kicked him again in the stomach.

The air rushed out of his mouth and he collapsed on the ground. Libby kicked him one more time in the face. Blood spurted from both nostrils. Libby ran into the street.

Tires screeched. Tuck turned in time to see a young girl flying over the hood of a rusty Ford Escort. *Her sister's gonna kill me.*

Chapter 41

Never interrupt your enemy when he
is making a mistake. – Napoleon Bonaparte

Tuesday afternoon, Grand Avenue, St. Paul, Minnesota.

Molly ran out the back of the restaurant. There was a garbage truck picking up the dumpster. She didn't hesitate. She ran to the cab and opened the passenger side.

"Some guy is chasing me," She said.

The driver jerked his head around and looked at both mirrors. "Get down," he said. She crouched low in the seat and he flipped a jacket over the top of her. As soon as she was out of sight he maneuvered the lift arms into the sleeves on the dumpster.

The hydraulic lift hummed as the dumpster raised off the ground. A man ran around the side of the building. "I see your friend." The driver said.

"What's he doing?"

"He isn't looking for Easter eggs." He opened his window and yelled at the guy. "Hey Buddy, get out of the way. You could get killed."

The agent ignored the driver and did a quick search around the back of the restaurant and back parking lot. Seeing nothing, he ran back toward the street.

"Hey little girl, your friend is gone."

"Are you going up the block?"

"Yep. Wanna ride along?"

"Thanks."

Three dumpsters later, Molly raised her head up and peered over the bottom edge of the windshield. "Thanks again." She said and opened the door.

"No problem. If I see the creep, I'll put a dent in his car."

Molly smiled and slipped out of sight. She blended with a group of pedestrians and crossed Grand Avenue to the north side. Once on the other side of the street most of the people turned west. One or two went with her to the east. A block short of the Henkel house a car suddenly turned mid-block and came toward her.

"Stop her!" Someone yelled out the car window.

Molly didn't wait around. She ran east as fast as she could. The car was closing the distance but there was a city bus and delivery truck in the lane between them. Just as she reached Henkel's place the bus obscured her from the driver's vision. She darted through the garage and into the root cellar attached to the back of the garage. She grabbed the flashlight, left on the work table, and slipped into the tunnel. Molly pulled the door tight and latched it from the inside. She took a deep breath to steady herself and walked into the dark labyrinth.

#

Tuesday afternoon.

Libby took her shoe off and pounded the window. She screamed. She kicked. She yelled. She was trapped. *What's happening?* Suddenly Molly's travails started to make sense. *This must be related.* She stopped her frantic flailing. *What would Molly do?*

Libby put her shoe back on and lookout the window. They were heading west. *But where? Why?* Libby became very still and lowered herself down on the seat. *Make him stop. Make him open the door.* She made herself start to shake, first her arm then her whole body. *He's slowing down.* She closed her eyes, then opened them. She rolled her eyes back as far as she could and let the spit run out of her mouth, down her cheek and onto the car seat. *He's stopping, keep shaking.*

The suburban came to a stop on the shoulder of the road. She heard the driver's door open and slam shut, then the rear door.

"Hey. Are you OK?" She heard him ask. He grabbed her jerking legs and pulled her closer to the open door. She felt herself moving. *Keep twitching.* When her feet came close to the man she pulled them back and tensed. She made a sudden violent move, with as much strength as she could muster, Libby jammed her foot directly into the man's groin.

"Ugh!" Was all she heard. He bent forward involuntarily. She reached up and jammed her thumbs into his eyes. "Aaaah." He yelled and blinked. He reached up with both hands to protect his face and she launched both feet directly into his stomach. Libby heard the air rush out of his mouth and he fell back onto the pavement.

Libby jumped out of the car and gave one final kick into his face. She felt his nose snap and she tried to drive her heel through his face. Blood flowed freely down his cheeks and onto the road.

Run. Libby turned to run and heard a car horn and screeching of tires on pavement. The last thing she remembered was crushing pain and blackness. Everything went quiet.

Cars were stopping. "She just ran in front of me," the driver said.

"Did anyone call 911?" someone else yelled. A third driver ran to Libby. He took off his coat and gently placed it under her head. She was breathing. Her leg was crooked. Her skin was scraped and bleeding. She was still alive.

In the chaos, Tuck pulled himself back into the black suburban and drove away.

#

Molly hurried up the tunnel. The flashlight was barely bright enough to illuminate her path. The tunnel forked, and she went right, up the stairs, turned again, down the short hallway. She came to the secret entrance of 1710 Summit Avenue East. Gladys was waiting.

"They took Libby." It was the first thing out of Molly's mouth. "I need to call my parents."

"Mom. They took Libby."

"Molly...who..." Olivia asked. "The police are here now. They want to talk to you."

"I'm not talking to the police. Tell them to call Lena Johnson, FBI. She can answer their questions."

"Stop it! Stop talking about the FBI. Libby is missing. Someone took her from school."

"Mom, don't you believe me? This is all related. Wake up!" Molly thought for a minute. "Alright I'll talk to the police. Maybe they'll believe me."

Molly gave the officer all the pertinent information he wanted. When she mentioned FBI the tone of the officer's voice changed. She could tell he was skeptical. As she spoke on the phone she could hear the police scanner in the background. A possible assault or hit and run accident on state highway 35, south east of Hudson, Wisconsin. An adolescent girl was injured. Ambulance was paged. *It has to be her.*

Molly hung up the phone. *Hudson hospital.*

Gladys sat impassively listening to one side of the conversation. When Molly hung up the phone she asked, "What can I do?"

"Just pray."

Molly gathered her things and gave Gladys a quick goodbye hug.

"Where are you going?" Gladys asked.

"To the hospital in Hudson to check on my sister and then Cornucopia."

"Where's Cornucopia? Why there?"

"To find the real Molly Hatchet."

Chapter 42

The human voice can never reach the distance of the still, small voice of conscience. – Mahatma Gandhi

Wednesday afternoon.

"You're an idiot." Tuck listened to the voice on the phone. "And I'm an idiot for letting you go alone. This won't be easy to clean up."

"I don't think anyone recognized me," Tuck said.

"There are security cameras everywhere. Your face will be on every police bulletin within the hour."

"What should I do?" Tuck asked. He looked at himself in the rearview mirror. His nose was crooked, and blood still oozed out the right nostril.

There was a long pause. Tuck waited for instructions.

"Go to the safe house. I'll have someone meet you there."

Tuck heard a click as the call ended. He entered the address into Google maps on his phone and drove north on Wisconsin highway 35 to interstate 94 and then west into Minnesota. He turned onto 494 and then turned south into Apple Valley. Tuck followed the GPS prompts and drove slowly into an upscale residential area. By the time Tuck arrived someone was waiting for him.

The garage was open. He pulled the suburban inside and closed the door behind him. Tuck felt nauseous from swallowing so much blood. He gagged up a big blood clot and spit onto the garage floor.

The man helped him into the house and handed him a glass of water. "Here's some pain pills. Your nose is crooked."

Tuck grunted out, "thanks", and swallowed the pills with a gulp of water. After a few minutes he started to feel relaxed. He wanted to take a nap.

The man came to him with a piece of paper and a pen. "Write 'I'm Sorry'. And sign your name."

Tuck was confused but he was feeling too tired to protest. He scribbled out the note and signed his name. There was a smear of his blood on the paper. He tried to wipe it but only made it worse. Tuck stood up and staggered. He nearly fell. The man caught him.

"Do you need to lie down?" He held Tuck's arm and escorted him back to the garage and into the suburban. Once he was back in the driver's seat, the man pushed the seat button and Tuck reclined. Tuck took a deep breath and relaxed. He fell asleep.

The man took a hose and shoved it through a crack in the side window and ran it back to the exhaust pipe. He stuffed some rags into the pipe to keep the hose in place and started the engine.

"Nighty-night."

He wiped down everything he had touched and went out of the house through the back door.

He sent a text.

Done.

#

Molly drove as fast as she dared and got to Hudson Hospital in forty-five minutes. She entered the emergency room and offered her ID to the desk.

"Hit and run victim, I'm her sister." The receptionist took Molly back immediately. Libby was lying on a gurney. Her clothes were cut away and she was covered loosely with a thin cotton gown and a blanket. Her left leg was wrapped in a big splint from above her knee to her toes. An IV bag dripped into each arm. Her right eye was swollen shut and her hair was matted with blood on the side. The heart monitor beeped a steady 84. Molly watched her chest move up and down. She was asleep.

"Lib?" Molly reached her hand and touched Libby's shoulder. Molly tried to sniff back her tears but they ran freely.

Her good eye fluttered open and she tried to smile. "Molly."

"Libby, what happened?"

"I don't remember exactly. This guy grabbed me at school and shoved me into the car. There weren't any door handles. When he opened the door, the last thing I remember was kicking him and running."

"Are you her sister?" A police officer came into the emergency room bay with a clipboard. "I'm state trooper Marshall."

"Molly Seymour. I'm her sister." Molly turned from the bedside to face officer Marshall.

"Witnesses at the scene reported your sister running into traffic. She was struck by a car," Officer Marshall said. "The alleged abductor left the scene. We are tracing that license number now."

"When you trace the vehicle, I think you'll be surprised."

"Is this someone you know?"

"I met him once. Elmore Riley. Goes by Tuck. Call Lena Johnson, FBI agent, Minneapolis."

"FBI?"

"She won't give you any answers but she might buy you lunch."

#

Wednesday evening. Hudson Hospital

By evening every living relative within a day's drive made it to the hospital. All of her aunts and uncles and cousins, even cousin Maddie's husband Rick came. Molly made a mental list and counted fifteen. Molly could read the fear on their faces but she could also see a resolute calm, a foundation of stability. She had seen it before, years ago when she was the victim. At the age of six she couldn't put it into words but, she felt it, and she saw it in the way they treated each other and the way they prayed and laughed and lived. They had faith and she felt it.

The clock on the wall was past 11:00 pm when Libby came out of surgery. The coffee pot had been filled and drained and filled again.

"Hi, I'm Dr. Torgerson. Libby's in recovery. She did fine. She has two plates in her left leg and three pins in her wrist. She's fortunate. No evidence of internal injuries or bleeding in her brain. She has a concussion but no skull fracture. She's a tough kid."

"Do you have any idea how long she might be in the hospital?" Olivia asked.

"Assuming she doesn't have any complications, probably four or five days."

Aunt Luella asked a few medically related questions and the doctor retreated to the recovery room. An air of relief flooded the room. Libby was going to make it.

By the time Libby was moved into a hospital room, most of the family had left. Olivia planted herself into a recliner in the room and wept. All of the emotions from the past twelve hours poured out. Her shoulders shook and she made no effort to stop the tears.

Molly stood beside the bed and held Libby's right hand. Libby opened her eyes slightly and closed them again.

"Can I have some water?" She sounded weak and tired.

She licked her dry lips and accepted the straw in her water glass. She took three long gulps. Libby squeezed Molly's hand and went back to sleep.

#

Thursday morning. Oak Grove, Wisconsin.

Molly didn't know what to expect. She packed a bag with a change of clothes, extra jacket, warm boots, hats and gloves and checked her map. She reviewed the route. Cornucopia was further than she anticipated. North on state highway 35 to Superior and then east on highway 2. From her home in Oak Grove it was almost a three-hour drive in good weather.

It was Thanksgiving Day, snow was predicted. After Libby's accident the family changed plans. Everyone was hopeful, Libby could be discharged from the hospital on Saturday. They planned to get together on the weekend. Molly knew they had plenty of reasons to be thankful.

She wrote a note and left it on the kitchen table. If everything went well, she would be home tomorrow with some answers.

#

Dutch Van Tassel spent Wednesday filing reports. He listed the details and reviewed them several times. It was hard to report the truth. It was even more difficult to remember the lies and tell the same story twice. *Vehicle number 23 left at regional headquarters of Morse Industries. Vehicle was later reported missing.* He filled in the details to make it sound reasonable.

"I want you to file this after lunch." He handed the report to one of his assistants in his office. "I'll be gone for the rest of the day."

"If someone needs you, can I say where you'll be?"

"I have unfinished business in Cornucopia."

#

Thursday morning.

Margaret Axtel felt more paranoid than usual. She liked to drink her morning coffee in her pottery studio. The sun came in the east window and she could watch the traffic go by on the highway.

Just like Bobby, she counted things. She was deaf and her only option was watching what went on around her. She counted cars and watched people. The first time she saw the metallic blue Chevy Silverado pickup and the silver airstream go by she didn't pay much attention. The second time she made a note. The fourth time it went by she got out her double barrel shotgun and put it behind the kitchen door.

Chapter 43

People buy into the leader before they
buy into the vision. – John Maxwell

Molly made it Cornucopia in record time. Her watch said
12:37 when she pulled into a parking spot on the edge of
town. She walked into the Siskiwit Bay Coffee shop and
found a spot to sit. She ordered a black coffee and a chicken
salad sandwich. There was a young man working the counter. In Molly's opinion he looked trustworthy.

"Do you know where Margaret Axtel lives?" She asked.

"Yep. She's about a half mile back on the highway." He
talked while he made a cappuccino for another customer.
"What's up with Manic Margaret?"

"I don't know. Why?"

"You're the second person to ask today."

"Really?"

"Grizzly Adams. He had a glass eye and a gray ponytail. He and Margaret appeared to be cut from the same pattern."

There's only one person to match that description. "When was he here?"

"Couple hours ago."

"Anything else I should know about Margaret Axtel?"

"Do you know sign language?"

"Should I?"

"Doesn't matter. Margaret doesn't either. Bring this." He handed her a small chalkboard and a stick of chalk. "Write your name and something nice. You have to park along the main road and take a path over a short footbridge to the house otherwise it's a two-mile drive on back roads to get to her driveway on the other side of the creek. When you cross the bridge hold it up for her to see."

I don't like bridges. "What if I don't?" She asked.

"Two men went missing last year. Never found. Rumor has it, Crazy Margaret killed them and buried them in her cellar."

Molly swallowed hard. She left her sandwich and half of her coffee untouched on the table. She zipped her coat and pulled her cap down over her ears and left her car in the parking lot of the Siskiwit Bay Coffee house. Molly walked on the shoulder of the road heading toward crazy

325

Margaret's house. The half-mile walk gave her time to think.

"Why did you tell her that?" one of the girls behind the counter asked. "About the missing men."

"Manic Margaret is my second cousin's aunt. A legend in the area is good for business."

From the side of the road a fieldstone walkway curved through the trees and over a small foot bridge crossing a deep ditch, ending at the porch of an old house. Through the window Molly could see a woman staring back at her.

Molly took the chalk and wrote her name *Molly Seymour-I need help.* She stepped toward the door holding the chalk board in front of her. There was no response from the house. Molly walked slowly toward the front door. Ten feet away, Molly saw the door slowly open. The business end of a double barrel shotgun edged out from the gap and moved up and down. Molly stood still. She pointed to herself and to the name on the slate.

She waited for a sign from the door, a signal that she was welcome. Nothing. Seagulls squawked in the distance. A car passed behind her on the highway. Her boots crunched on the dusting of ice pellets along the path.

Using her hand, she wiped away the words on the board and wrote, *Margaret Axtel-Friends.* Molly turned the sign around. No response. Margaret yelled something unintelligible but Molly didn't understand. More of the shotgun appeared in the doorway. Molly felt like running. She was getting nowhere and she was cold.

Once more she wiped the slate clean. On a whim she wrote one more thing and held it up for Margaret to see. The door swung open. Molly could see a late-middle aged woman with long gray streaked hair, gathered into a long braid reaching her waist. Her hands were dirty from clay and they clutched an ancient double-barreled shotgun with hammers pulled back, ready to fire. She set the butt of the shotgun down on the floor and waved Molly toward the house. At the door Margaret took the slate and chalk and drew a circle around the words and pointed to herself. *Molly Hatchet.*

Where do I start? Molly moved slowly, not sure what to expect. Margaret motioned for her to sit. Molly took off her coat and sat down with her chalkboard on her lap. *Bobby Smith, do you know him?*

Margaret nodded yes.

This is going to take forever. Molly tried to think of a way to streamline the process. Hoping to find something of interest she wrote: *Can I see your studio?*

Margaret seemed to brighten considerably. She put aside the shotgun and motioned for Molly to follow her. The biggest room was her main ceramics studio. Stacks of glazed pots, plates, vases and a hundred other things were jumbled on shelves awaiting firing. Large dishes arranged on pedestals were ready for use as bird baths.

From the first room they entered her living quarters. It appeared Margaret lived in a single room. A single bed was covered with rumpled blankets next to a small kitchen table and kitchen nook. Half of a dried sandwich sat on a cutting board. A stained coffee percolator was on the stove top. On the other side of the living quarters was another door. A padlock prevented their entrance to the other room. Margaret made no moves toward the room. There was dust on the door knob, it hadn't been opened recently.

Margaret motioned for her to follow back into the front studio. Across the room was another door, closed and locked. The door handle was clean. Molly started toward the door and Margaret grabbed her shotgun and stepped in her way. *She's hiding something.* Molly stepped back and pointed at the door. She took her chalk and wrote *Bobby's room?* She pointed at the room. Margaret waved the end of the shotgun toward the chair. As Molly went to sit down she heard a noise from the locked room.

"Who's in there?" Molly yelled. She heard thumping but no voice. She looked directly at Margaret and said, "Open the door." Margaret read her lips. Using the end of her shotgun, Margaret directed her toward the door.

Molly unlatched the door and pulled it open. Seated in the middle of the room was an old man. Each leg and each arm were zip-tied to the chair. Around his face was an elastic bandage wrapped tight holding a bunched-up rag in his mouth. A big swollen bruise hovered above his bad eye. Molly could see embarrassment in his good eye.

"Dag, what are you doing here?" Molly started toward him but hesitated at the menacing wave of the gun. She took her chalk board and wrote: *My friend*. Margaret appeared to consider her options. Finally, she put the gun down and nodded.

Molly unwrapped the Ace bandage from his face and removed the gag. "She's the real Molly Hatchet." Dag said.

"I figured it out. But what happened to you?"

"Cut these ties and we'll talk."

After Dag was cut free, he massaged his wrists and ankles, trying to restore sensation and circulation. The ties left deep pressure creases in his skin. He put his hands in the air, as a sign of submission to Margaret. Molly read the lines of suspicion in her face but Margaret made no moves of aggression.

Dag picked up his jacket and pulled some folded papers from his inside pocket. He handed them to Molly and said. "Margaret is a distant cousin to Professor Smith."

"Did she hit you in the head?" Molly smiled.

"See that big ceramic bowl?" Dag pointed toward a pile of bowls, dishes and other handmade objects. "I misjudged her. I was distracted and she hit me in the side of the head. When I woke up she had me tied to this chair."

"She doesn't trust you."

"She isn't taking her medications, either."

"One room is locked. She hasn't been in there recently," Molly said, "If Bobby Smith had information hidden, it's probably in there."

"Don't look now but she's got another visitor." Dag looked out the front window, down the walk. A tan colored Ford Taurus pulled up and parked along the side of the road. A tall man with a short camo coat and a black and red plaid Stormy Kromer cap got out of the car and started walking toward the house.

Margaret ignored her house guests and went to the front door. She cracked open the door and waved the double barrel shotgun. The man stopped thirty yards from the house and reached into his coat. Margaret raised her shotgun and pointed in his direction.

Bang! The man dove to the side and crouched behind a tree. *Bang!*

Molly heard the first bullet hit the house. The door frame splintered with the second shot and bullet fragments ricocheted, hitting Margaret in the right upper arm. She dropped the shotgun and fell to the floor. Blood dripped onto the rug from the wound near her shoulder.

Dag and Molly dove out of sight below the level of the windows. Dag picked up the shotgun. The mechanism was so rusted it wouldn't open. It's only use was a double-barreled club. He tossed it aside. Waving it at the intruder would only invite more gunfire.

Margaret tried to talk but her speech was garbled and hard to understand. Molly tried to calm her but she pushed Molly aside and crawled out of the gallery and into the back, living space. Molly followed.

Margaret reached into a small kitchen drawer under her toaster and pulled out a key ring. She waved her hand at Molly and Dag to follow. Margaret unlocked the dusty door and the three of them crawled inside and pushed the door shut behind them.

Molly could see no other way out. They were trapped.

Chapter 44

The best kept secrets are those in plain sight.

– George Banister

Wednesday afternoon, Cornucopia, Wisconsin.

Dutch Van Tassel and a pilot flew into Duluth International airport in a twin-engine prop plane. The private pilot was an off-grid contact used for clandestine operations and paid out of a slush fund. Officially Dutch was on vacation driving to Alabama on a golf vacation with some friends. It was good to be on vacation because he had plenty to think about during his drive along the south shore of Lake Superior.

Dutch entered the GPS coordinates for Cornucopia, Wisconsin and turned east onto Highway 2 after he came off the Bong bridge from Duluth into Wisconsin. The light brown Ford Taurus was rented under a false identity. The fake moustache and glasses disguised his face. He wore a Duluth Bulldogs cap pulled down low enough to shade his eyes.

Since Robert Smith was recruited, Dutch kept files on all of his contacts. After his disappearance in Charlotte, questions were raised, officially and unofficially. No one believed he was capable of disappearing on his own. The FBI didn't do it. There was no evidence of any other government agency involvement. He didn't believe the mob would do it.

Van Tassel didn't think Kalishnov had any direct involvement. There were foreign agents operating on American soil, but the US Government kept tabs on most of them. Only those operating in deep cover would dare abduct a US citizen from a hospital unless the target had something very valuable. Valuable enough to risk exposure. Bobby Smith wasn't that type of target.

Tuck Riley was another matter. The official report was illegal use of a government vehicle with intent to commit a crime; motivation unknown. The suburban along with the body was moved to his home and the vehicle wiped for prints other than those of Riley and Libby Seymour. Someone would discover his body within the next twenty- four hours.

Margaret Axtel was an enigma. All of their files indicated she was deaf, eccentric and paranoid, two standard deviations from the mean. But Smith had maintained some level of contact with her over the past few years. There was nothing to indicate a romantic relationship between them, but it appeared to be more than a simple distant family connection. Dutch made a mental list of all the reasons Smith would visit Axtel and nothing made any sense except the possibility she was hiding something. Or Smith was hiding something and Axtel was the guard dog. Either way, a visit to Margaret Axtel seemed like a good idea.

As he was driving, he cursed to himself for not looking more like a local. He should have rented a Ford pickup instead of a Taurus. Van Tassel pulled into Wild Willie's bait and liquor store along the highway. They had camo jackets and red-black plaid Stormy-Kromer caps for sale. He bought one of each and a bag of Jack Link's beef jerky. He reached for a diet coke but changed his mind and bought a 12 pack of Grain-Belt beer.

"Goin' turkey huntin'?" The guy behind the counter asked.

"Yes," Dutch mumbled. He looked down, avoiding direct eye contact.

"Watch out for snow," The guy said.

"Snow?"

"Yessiree. Lake effect. Might get a foot or two."

"I'll keep that in mind. Thanks." Dutch reached for the door.

"Oh...one more thing, in case you didn't know. It's deer huntin' season. You better wear blaze orange or someone's likely to blow your head off." He smiled. "Especially if they see you wearing your argyle socks and Gucci loafers. The boys up in Cornucopia don't like argyle socks." He laughed and spit out a soggy wad of chewing tobacco into a paper cup as he leaned over the counter to get a better look at Dutch's shiny shoes as he walked out the bait store. A long line of spit ran into his whiskers and he wiped it with the back of his hand as the tan colored Taurus turned east onto the highway. Dutch Van Tassel would never be a local.

His GPS announced his arrival at his destination in one-half mile. He slowed his driving and became more aware of his surroundings. He saw the fire number for the house: 27277. It was set back from the highway. There was a dirt and ice-covered parking area and a path to the house. Dutch went up the road, into town and turned around. As he came to Margaret's studio he was suddenly aware of a carved wooden sign nailed to a tree near the walk. It said *Molly* and had an image of a small axe stuck into a stump or log. *Molly Hatchet.*

As he walked toward the house, the door parted slightly. Dutch saw the double barrel shotgun pointing in his direction.

He grabbed his 9mm Beretta and fired-twice. He saw the door frame splinter and heard a scream and a thud. The sound a body makes before it dies.

#

Margaret tossed the dusty padlock aside as they entered the room. She pushed it shut behind her and latched the door from the inside. Molly looked around. There was a computer on the desk, a laser printer on a shelf and stereo equipment, high quality stuff, not something used by a deaf person.

Behind the computer were several dusty books and an empty beer can. Molly turned on the computer but it was password protected. She rebooted the computer in safe-mode and tried to bypass the encryption but was unable access the files.

Together Molly and Dag moved a bookshelf to reinforce the door. He took a mental inventory of the contents of the room; books, sports memorabilia, classic rock and roll vinyl albums, a phonograph player, a rollaway cot, a few blankets and not much else.

Molly found a corkscrew and a few old wine corks but didn't see any bottles or glasses. She found a clean t-shirt in a chest of drawers and using a scissors, she cut it into strips and bandaged Margaret's arm. The wound appeared to be more superficial than originally thought. Margaret was using the arm so it was unlikely the bone was broken.

Molly peered under the bed, hoping to find stashed weapons, baseball bats or anything to be used in self-defense. She found nothing.

"Dag, do you know who's shooting at us?" Molly asked.

"Unfortunately, I do," Dag said. "When I reviewed the files I received, I discovered Dutch Van Tassel has a history of private security consulting for Mork Industries and several other firms around Chicago."

"So, you're saying we have the FBI shooting at us?"

"Not officially."

Molly's mouth went dry. She wanted a drink of water and the kitchen was across the gallery. Any attempt to go across the room would be seen from the outside. If Dutch was jumpy enough to fire two quick shots into the house, he probably wouldn't hold back if he saw movement.

There was only one small window in their room, facing out the back of the house. She looked through the woods toward Lake Superior. She saw no threat in that direction. Behind the house the hill dropped away suddenly. Any attacker coming from that direction would be coming uphill, a poor strategic option.

"How would Dutch know we were here?" She asked.

"He didn't. He's here for the same reason we are. Margaret Axtel has something and he's looking for it."

"What are we looking for?" Molly asked. She walked around the room looking at photos, signed baseballs and Led Zeppelin concert posters. Her toe hit the edge of a slightly upturned floor board. She tripped and fell.

"Hey look at this," she said. She pointed to an area where the bookcase had rested. Looking carefully at the oak parquet flooring, she saw one edge was slightly raised. Molly followed the edge and realized there was a seam in the floor creating a larger square about 3x3 feet. "Is this a trapdoor?"

The grit of normal life had accumulated in the lines between other flooring blocks but not along the trapdoor. It had been opened recently. Carefully probing around the edge, she found a small loose piece. She pried it up, revealing a recessed steel ring.

Dag bent down and grabbed the ring. The flooring squeaked from the tight fit but the door swung up and rested against the wall. Just below the floor on a shelf sat two flashlights. Dag reached in and flipped the switch. The batteries were good. He handed the other to Molly.

Margaret watched their activities but made no motions to stop them. She tapped Molly on the shoulder and pointed down the hole. Then she pointed to the ceiling light and made a motion as if pulling a string. Molly understood.

She was the first one down the ladder into the subterranean recess. It was dark and Molly didn't like it but it was better than getting shot by Dutch Van Tassel.

Chapter 43

Age appears best in four forms: old wood to burn, old
wine to drink, old friends to trust and old books to read.
– Francis Bacon

When Dutch saw the shotgun aimed in his direction, he
reacted as he was trained. He fired twice and took cover.
From the shelter of the trees he watched the house. Margaret Axtel was the only person visible initially but after the
shots he saw two more people in the house. He had no
backup and retreating to the airport didn't accomplish his
objective. He had to find out if Smith had compromising
information that would put Van Tassel and *Catch-22* at
risk. He already lost the element of surprise. Dutch considered his options. A direct assault on the house was foolish.
They were armed with a shotgun and at close range it was
more damaging than his Beretta, but he had better

firepower in the car trunk. He decided to maintain his position until night and move in. The plan was simple: smoke them out and take them down, one by one.

#

Molly stepped from the ladder onto an uneven flagstone cellar floor. It was dry, and the sandy grit crunched under her feet. In the beam of her flashlight she saw the reflective glint of glass, hundreds of bottles of wine stacked sideways in angled wooden alcoves. In the center of the room was a beaded chain hanging from a single light bulb in the ceiling of the cellar. Molly pulled the chain. The light came on, flickered and went out. She tested the bulb and found it was loose. A quick turn and the room was lit.

The room was rectangular. She estimated it to be twelve or more feet wide and probably half again as long. Along two walls were wine racks reaching from floor to ceiling. Nearly half of the shelves were filled with wine. In the center of the room was a small cabinet, table height with a notebook, a candle and pencil resting on the top. Several coins were stacked on the table, Morgan silver dollars. Molly opened the door to the free-standing cabinet and found high quality wine glasses of differing styles for different varietals. There was very fine layer of dust on the bottles and the countertop.

Dag joined her in the wine cellar. His good eye adjusted to the dim light. "This is out of character for Margaret Axtel. She doesn't fit in with the Napa crowd. I'm certain your professor Smith is behind this."

He picked up a bottle and read the label; *1999 Harlan Estate Cabernet*. Another read; *1995 Opus One Napa Valley Bordeaux Blend*. "This isn't your typical Tuesday night spaghetti wine." He put the bottle back in place.

Molly climbed up the ladder to check on Margaret. She was resting on the bed, alive but subdued. The gunshot took the fight out of her. Molly returned to the wine cellar. "There must be something more important than wine down here." She took her flashlight and tried to look behind bottles and shelves. Against the wall was a framed painting of a 1945 Chateau Lafite Rothschild on a rustic table with a platter of cheese and grapes. Molly bumped the edge of the painting. It was hinged on one side and swung out from the wall.

"I think I found what we're looking for," Molly said. She swung the painting aside and recessed into the concrete wall was a safe with four red glowing LED lights showing on the front. She ran her fingers over the embossed plate- *Sicherheits*. "What do you think?" She stepped to the side as Dag inspected the safe.

"German made, high quality. No spot for a key." He stepped back and looked at the four LED lights in sequence. "This is an audio lock. You need to match a tone for each light in order to open the lock."

"It's the clue from his cap," Molly said. "The musical chord that Phineas played at my aunt's place."

"Can you sing in perfect pitch?" Dag asked.

"He could have used a guitar tuner app on his phone. A convenient way to open the safe."

"Sounds too simple, unless there's an automatic lockout for a failed sequence," Dag said. "No one goes to this much trouble unless they're hiding something important."

"Have you ever seen this before?" Molly asked.

"Once, with a drug dealer in Columbia. The lock was wired to a detonator and we didn't know it. If you didn't have the exact tones in order and duration and volume, the bomb went off."

"What happened?"

"One of my guys died."

Molly's mouth went dry. "I need a drink." She picked out the Opus One and opened the cork. The wine flowed out of the bottle like liquid velvet in the dim light. She admired the color. She swirled the wine and took a sip. She imagined Jesus at the last supper and thought to herself this could be her last supper as well. Opus One was a good choice for her final drink.

Absentmindedly she dipped her finger into the wine and rubbed it around the rim. A clear ethereal tone rang out from the glass. One of the LED lights flickered from red to amber and back to red.

"Dag, I have it."

"What?"

"Watch the lights." She dipped her finger into the wine and gently applied pressure to the rim of the class. The glass rang again and the third light flickered from red to amber. She pushed harder to make the tone louder but nothing else changed. She stopped and the light went back to red.

Suddenly the room went dark. There was no light from the room above. The sun had set and there was only a faint glow in the sky showing through the small window in the room where Margaret lay asleep on Bobby Smith's cot.

"He cut the power," Dag said.

"But the LED lights are still glowing."

"That means the safe has a battery backup power source. We probably have fifteen minutes before we lose power, maybe less."

Molly used her flashlight to find the candles. She lit as many as she could find. Seven small flames held their ground against the blackness of the wine cellar.

"Open some more wine," she said to Dag. She got out four more cabernet glasses and set them side by side on the countertop. She poured some more in her own glass and took a drink to steady her hand. *I hope this works.*

As she started to pour the other four glasses she heard a loud crash in the house above. She could hear shards of glass striking ceramic pots and furniture.

"You have ten minutes," said a voice from outside. Another shotgun blast and a second window shattered.

#

Dutch watched the house for activity. After huddling in the cold behind the trees he began to shiver. His feet were cold. *The boys in Cornucopia don't like argyle socks.* He retreated to his car to warm himself. With the engine going he maneuvered the car so he had a better view of the front of the house and a safer defensive position, if attacked. His dash clock showed 5:13. The sun had set and the November night was hovering and about to descend on him. There was a wind from the north and light snowflakes were forming. He realized why the boys in Cornucopia didn't wear Gucci loafers.

When Dutch was warmed enough, he got out of the car and popped open the trunk. He organized his assault; two smoke grenades, tear gas, night vision goggles and a sawed-off shotgun with OO buckshot. He could cut a body in half with his eyes shut.

When his eyes adjusted to the night, he crept around the east side of the house and found the electric panel. Prying open the cover he ripped out the main breaker. The house went black. He returned to his observation post near the front of the house and watched. It was quiet. No lights flickering, no candles, no flashlights or silhouettes of people moving in the night.

Returning to the car he retrieved his shotgun and walked through the trees to the front of the house. He found a loose stone surrounding a rustic flower bed and heaved it through one of the front windows. He listened for a response. Nothing.

"You have ten minutes," he yelled through the window. To make sure they understood, he fired the shotgun through another window and stepped back into the woods.

Dutch checked his watch and set a timer for 8 minutes.

Chapter 44

God loves a good sandwich. – John W Ingalls

Bobby Smith was disoriented when they pushed him into
the back of the delivery truck. He was no longer dizzy but
the lingering effects of the drugs made him tired. He
couldn't concentrate. He lay on the floor of the truck making use of some plastic covered hospital pillows. At one
point the truck came to a stop and he realized he had been
sleeping. He didn't know where he was or who had him,
but he was alive. For now.

The truck pulled into McDonalds. Bobby tried to see
through the window to get his bearings.

"Stay down." The man in the driver's seat looked at him
through the rearview mirror.

"Where am I?" Bobby asked.

"Doesn't matter. Not staying here. What do you want?"

"What?"

"Food. What do you want?"

"I don't care... hamburger and fries." Bobby added, "and something to drink." He slumped back to his bed on the floor and dozed off. Sometime later he awoke. The hamburger in a bag was on the floor beside him, cold and the drink was warm. They were moving again. He felt better and sat up, leaning against the stacks of laundry. There was no seat in the back, this was a comfortable as he was going to get.

"Where are you taking me?" Bobby asked.

"If we told you, we'd have to kill you." The two men laughed but offered no more information. Bobby didn't want to aggravate his situation. He didn't know if they were friends or enemies or something in between. So far, he wasn't shot or dumped into the river or had his legs broken. There was hope.

Twice during the night, the two men switched as driver and passenger. They stopped for gas and Bobby got on his knees to looked through the cab and out the windshield. Several cars had Tennessee license plates. He didn't know where in Tennessee but he figured he was heading west.

Just as the eastern sky was beginning to lighten, the truck pulled into a big metal building and the motorized door closed behind them. The men opened the back of the panel truck and helped him out. They pointed out a bath-room if he needed it. When he came out there was someone else to meet him.

The new driver opened the side door to a Winnebago RV and pointed inside. Bobby stepped in and they drove off. There were no books or magazines to read and the scenery was a boring blur out the dirty side window. He had nothing else to do, so he made himself a good sand-wich from the groceries in the small refrigerator and popped open the top of a ginger-ale.

#

Thursday evening, Cornucopia

Molly was good at identifying musical notes, but it helped if she had a reference and she wasn't being threat-ened with death. In her mind she played middle C. She took the first glass and ran her finger around the rim. The tone was clear, but it wasn't an E. *Too low.* She added more wine, just a bit. Dipping her finger, she tried again.

"The light turned amber," Dag said.

"Give me more wine," Molly said. Dag opened another bottle. She drizzled in some Opus One and tested the sound.

"Green light."

"Which one?"

"Last one."

The cold night air from the broken windows found the open trap door and started to pool in the wine cellar. Three of the candles blew out. Dag scrambled to relight them. He bumped the wine glasses and knocked three of them over. Wine spilled onto the table and ran into a puddle on the floor. Two glasses broke.

"Dag! I need light and more wine." Molly pushed the shards of glass aside and pulled out three more glasses. They were different shapes.

"I can't find the cork screw." Dag said. He was trying to block the breeze from blowing out the candles.

"I don't care what you do. We've already lost a couple minutes. Whatever's in that safe may be the only thing saving us." Molly tried to quiet her mind and hear the music, the notes that could save their lives.

Dag grabbed a $500 bottle of wine. Gritting his teeth, he swung the bottle down sharply on the edge of the shelf and broke off the neck of the bottle. Wine and splinters of glass hit him on the arm and chest. More than half of the wine remained in the bottle. He handed it to Molly.

She tried the first glass again. The first light went green. When she stopped making the tone, the light remained green for about ten seconds and then went red again. She poured more wine into a new glass and tested it. If the first glass was *E,* she now needed *G.* She poured wine in and out of the glass until it sounded right. Another light went green.

"I think I have two of them," she said. Taking the third glass she tried to pour more wine. "Ouch!"

She pulled her hand back and shined her flashlight on it. Blood oozed out of the side of her little finger. *Not squirting. Good.*

She ignored the bleeding and poured more wine into glass number three. *C...I need B flat.* She poured out some wine. *Too much.* She added a bit more. Her hand was shaking. *Too much again.* She drank it down, just a sip. She could taste her blood in the wine. Running her finger around the rim, light number two flickered green and then amber. She added a couple more sips back in. *Green light. One more.*

"How much time do we have?"

"Not enough. I'm guessing four minutes." Dag didn't sound too certain.

Molly poured the fourth glass. *I need a D.* She couldn't compare glasses to determine the correct amount because they were different sizes. She dipped her finger and tried again. *Green light.*

"I'm ready. I think I have them all." Molly made certain there wasn't anything in her way and arranged them from lowest to highest note. "Let's hope it isn't wired to a bomb."

She dipped her finger and began with *E. The first light turned green.* Second glass. *Fourth light turned green.* Third glass. *Second light.* Fourth glass. *Third light.* Then suddenly all of them turned amber and stayed amber.

"We're locked out. Right notes, wrong sequence." Molly sat down to rest. "The sequence is inverted. That's why he wrote it upside down on his cap."

They waited. Dag checked his watch. "Two minutes left."

There was noise upstairs. A loud clunk followed by a hissing noise. Molly could smell smoke and a haze collected above the trap door, drifting into the wine cellar.

"Smoke screen," Dag said, "Keep working." If he was worried about what was to follow he didn't reveal it to Molly.

Suddenly the lights all switched from amber to red. "I think it's OK. Must be a three-minute reset." Molly took a deep breath. *Think Molly. Stay calm. She* dipped her finger. *E-B♭-G-D...*

All lights turned green...red...green. The door clicked and swung open.

Chapter 45

Do not go gentle into that good night.
Old age should burn and rage at the close of day;
Rage, rage against the dying of the light.
– Dylan Thomas

Thursday evening, Hudson Hospital.

"CODE BLUE 237-CODE BLUE 237"

"Somebody help! Please help!" Olivia yelled from the door of Libby's hospital room.

Libby heard the words over the hospital intercom as she slipped away. The pain was excruciating and sudden. Like a knife stabbing into a tire, letting all the air out at once. Suddenly she found herself floating or hovering over the bed. She didn't recognize her own body lying crumpled, like dirty laundry, in the bed. Libby felt light and free. She had never felt this way before. She could hear her mother sobbing and praying by the bedside. Libby tried to comfort her but when she reached out to touch her mom, her hand was a vapor. She felt nothing. No pain. No sadness. Nothing. Time stood still. There was no time, everything just was.

Libby watched the doctors come rushing into the room. She tried to stop them. She tried to tell them she was OK but they wouldn't listen. They pushed her mom out of the way and ripped her hospital gown off. She saw herself lying naked in the bed with strangers hovering and pounding and poking on her body. *Poor girl.* Libby felt detached. She knew it was her on the bed but at the same time she couldn't believe it or didn't want to believe she was dead. One doctor shoved a tube down her throat, another listened for heart sounds and breathing.

"Breath sounds on the right, nothing on the left," she heard. "Pull the tube back."

The person at her head pulled the tube back a tiny bit. "Still nothing. She has a tension pneumothorax on the left." The doctor grabbed a scalpel from the crash cart. Feeling along her side, he made a stab between the ribs and the air came rushing out. He pushed a tube through the hole into her chest and connected it to a bubbling water seal device on the floor. They wrapped tape around and around the tube and crisscrossed it on her chest over the stab wound which was dripping blood onto the sheets.

"Start compressions," he said. The nurse put her hands on Libby's bare chest and started pushing and counting 1 and 2 and... Libby tried grabbing their arms. She yelled *I'm fine* but no one heard her. Then she saw a blip on the heart monitor, then another.

In one big whoosh she was sucked back into her body. And the pain began. She coughed and gagged and desperately tried grabbing at the tube down her throat. The doctor tied her hands down. *Mom help me!* But she couldn't talk. *I want to see Molly before I die.* Her struggles weakened and slumped into the bed as the nurse pushed morphine into her IV.

#

Thursday night.

Molly carefully opened the door of the vault. She reached in and pulled out the first thing she touched. A stack of hundred-dollar bills. She dropped it onto the floor. There were dozens of bundles of cash, rare coins and bars of gold. Molly pushed it all aside. Money wasn't the reason she was here. In the weak beam of her flashlight she saw it, a zip drive. *No one locks a zip drive filled with Neil Diamond songs in a vault.* She grabbed it and shoved it into her bra, out of sight.

Then she found a notebook with the words *Catch-22* written on the cover. Small, with a pink cover, like a school girl's diary. She opened the pages and said to Dag, "This is filled with football games. Winners and losers."

"Why would anyone keep a notebook on old football games in a vault?" Dag asked

"He has the winners and losers and the point spread, but these games haven't been played yet. NFL playoffs and the Super Bowl."

"Bring it to me, nice and slow." Molly and Dag turned to see a dark silhouette of a man leaning into the trapdoor.

"What if I burn it?" Molly reached toward the candle.

"Go ahead. I'll kill the old lady, then I'll nail this door down and set the house on fire. You decide." Dutch reached down through the trapdoor and took the notebook. "What else did you find?"

"Money, coins..."

"You first. Up the ladder." He pointed to Dag. "Hands in front where I can see you." He kept a flashlight aimed into Dag's face as he climbed the ladder.

As Dag was climbing out of the hole, Dutch hit him with a taser and he collapsed onto the floor, paralyzed. Dutch took big plastic zip ties and bound his hands together behind his back. Molly heard Dutch grunt as he dragged Dag away from the door.

"Alright missy, you next."

"Don't taser me," Molly said. "I'll cooperate."

"Don't worry, I have plans for you."

Molly came up the ladder with a light shining in her eyes. She hesitated as she came into the room expecting to be hit. She wasn't.

"You go in front. If you try anything, he dies."

Molly nodded her head. Her knees felt weak and shaky. She hadn't eaten anything for hours. She walked out the door toward Van Tassel's car.

"In case you get any ideas..." Dutch took out a bottle of pepper spray and hit Dag in the face.

Dag jerked his head back. Immediately he started coughing and gagging. Tears and snot ran down his face and dripped off his beard. He staggered and fell to his knees. His breath came in gasps and wheezes. "I can't see." He shook his head side to side. "I'm blind."

"Get in the driver's seat," Dutch said to Molly.

Dutch opened the rear driver's side door and pushed Dag into the car. He walked around and got in the back seat across from Molly. "Turn right and drive."

"What about Margaret?" Molly asked.

Dutch didn't answer. In the rearview mirror Molly saw an orange glow forming in the windows of the house. She tried to see through her tears and reached to wipe her eyes.

357

"Keep both hands on the steering wheel where I can see them."

"You killed her!" Molly yelled. "You'll rot in hell for this."

"Every time you flap your lip, the old man gets another dose." He pulled out his pepper spray and hit Dag with another short blast. Molly could hear him gasping and wheezing.

They drove in relative silence except for Dag's coughing and sputtering. When Molly reached the east side of Superior, Van Tassel directed her to continue on Highway 2 and cross the bridge into Duluth.

"Up the hill, go to the airport." He said nothing further. Molly obeyed. They drove past a police car parked along the highway and Molly considered doing something drastic to get his attention. Then they were past and out of sight. It was too late.

Dutch tapped his cell phone and called ahead to the pilot. She listened to his side of the conversation. "What do you mean they won't comply? Did you show your FBI credentials?"

He listened for a minute. "I need direct access from the vehicle to the plane. Radio the airport in Superior and explain the situation. I'll meet you there."

He turned off his phone. "Turn around. We're going back."

Forty-five minutes later the de Havilland twin otter plane landed and taxied to the end of the runway where Dutch, Molly, and Dag were waiting.

Dag was the first one onto the plane. He was forced to sit in the sideways facing seat behind the pilot. Once in place, his feet were tied together. Molly was next. Dutch bound her hands together behind her back and pushed her into the seat next to Dag.

"You'll never get away with this," she said. As Dutch was binding her feet together she spit in his face.

"Listen you little brat. Since you like to spit, I'll give you a good reason to spit." He slapped her and sprayed her face with a short blast of pepper spray.

She blinked and cried. Her eyelids swelled shut and tears flooded her face. The burning was intense. Her nose dripped onto her shirt. She was blind.

"Don't close your eyes. Blink fast." Dag whispered.

The plane taxied and the engines roared. She felt them lift off the ground. They were airborne. The plane ride was rough and cold. Within an hour the burning in her eyes subsided and Molly could see, but it was blurry. She cringed knowing how Dag had endured it more than once. Her wrists hurt. There was a sharp bolt sticking out of the back of her seat jabbing her hands. She felt wetness and wondered if it was blood.

Her legs and back cramped. She wanted to stand but she couldn't. She tried to move her arms but they were tight behind her. She leaned forward as far as she could and her back felt better. The bolt caught on the wrist bindings. She pulled and felt it rub but it didn't move. She rubbed again and felt the plastic tie grate over the threads of the bolt.

She looked toward the cockpit. Dutch and the pilot had headphones on. They weren't concerned about the passengers in business class. Molly repeated the motions. She counted the rubs, *10-15-20*. The zip-tie was fraying.

More than two and a half hours elapsed since take-off from Superior airport. The plane was loud. The monotonous droning gave her a headache. Her bindings were nearly free but she had no plan beyond that. Dag slumped beside her. Only the gurgling snot still running from his nose let her know he was still alive.

Dutch pulled off his headphones and got up from his seat. He came to the back of the plane and got into a jumpsuit. As he strapped on a parachute one of the cords swung and hit her in the face. It stung her cheek. She jerked to the side and the ties around her wrist caught on the bolt. She felt the plastic break and the numbness gradually worked out of her fingers. She dared not move her arms for fear her freedom would be revealed.

When Dutch was done, the pilot came back. It was obvious the plane was on autopilot. She heard the conversation between them.

"We'll be at the drop zone in ten minutes. Cattle ranch. No power lines."

"How much fuel?"

"Thirty minutes, tops."

Dutch checked his altimeter. "3000 feet," he said to the pilot.

When the pilot strapped on his parachute, Molly felt her blood turn to ice. She played the scenario in her mind. The plane was over North Dakota somewhere along the Canadian border. When the pilot and Dutch jumped they were left to crash when the fuel ran out. By then, Dutch would be across the border, rendezvousing in the night, with another killer. She kept quiet, expecting another dose of pepper spray or a slap in the face. Molly hung her head and looked away. Her hands were free, her ankles were getting loose.

"Happy landing." Dutch Van Tassel took one more look at Dag and Molly, slumped sideways in the seat.

The jump door was opened and bitter cold air rushed in. Molly gasped in the cold air. Suddenly they were alone.

The pilot and Dutch disappeared into the night. She didn't worry about freezing to death. She would be dead in twenty minutes, splattered on a frozen cow pasture.

Molly jerked her foot up and down. She was able to push one shoe off her heel and slip her foot through the binding. Then she yanked the other one free.

"Can you fly?" she yelled to Dag. The noise was overwhelming. She wanted to close the jump door but she feared getting too close and being sucked out.

"I know something about flying, but I can't see." Dag tried opening his good eye. It was swollen shut. "Cut me loose."

Molly frantically dug around under the seat and behind the pilot's seat. She found a dull wire cutter and clipped the hard plastic bindings on Dag's wrists and ankles.

"Help me up." Dag struggled to his feet. He extended his arms, feeling his way along. He came to the narrow opening between the cargo area and the cockpit. He felt his way into the co-pilot seat.

"You should sit over here," Molly yelled as she pushed him toward the pilot's seat.

"No. You have to fly the plane. I'll help you."

Molly climbed into the pilot seat. She was hyperventilating and felt dizzy. Her hands were wet with sweat. She had no idea what to do.

"Put the helmet on," Dag yelled. He did the same. They had communication without yelling.

"I can hear you," she said, "Now what?"

"Find the transponder and turn it to 7700 and call MAY-DAY."

Molly fumbled with the dial. She was afraid to touch anything. The instrument panel was a confusing array of buttons and dials. She recognized some things but didn't know what to do.

"Any station, MAY-DAY, MAY-DAY, MAY-DAY!"

The radio crackled to life. The noise startled her. "This is air traffic control, Minot. Identify yourself."

"I need help." Molly's mind raced. "The pilot jumped out of the plane and I don't know how to fly." She tried to breath slow and think clearly.

"What is your location?"

"I don't know."

"GPS coordinates, look on the instrument panel."

Molly found the GPS and read off the numbers.

"Good, I have you on radar at 2800 feet altitude. You're about 180 miles east of us."

"The fuel light is blinking. I'm running out of fuel." Molly tried to keep her voice even. She wanted to scream.

"Set your heading to 240 degrees."

"Dag, tell me what to do."

"It looks like a compass. Straight ahead to your left."

"I found it."

"What does it say."

"We're going toward 270 degrees."

"Adjust the numbers to 240."

Molly adjusted the setting. She stiffened in her seat as the plane began to bank to the left.

"We're going at 240 degrees," Molly said to the tower. "What next?"

"The nearest county airport is fifty miles. Do you have enough fuel?"

Molly felt one of the engines sputter but keep on running. "No...I don't know, we're almost out."

"Listen close. You're going to have to fly the plane yourself. I'm going to talk you through it. Can the other person help you?"

Molly shot a quick glance at her co-pilot. "He's blind in one eye and he can't see out of the other."

There was a pause from the tower. "Find the throttle and slow your speed down to 120 knots. Now find the auto-pilot switch and turn it off. Before you do, make sure you have your hands on the controls."

Dag explained where the throttle was. She pulled it back slightly and felt the plane slow. She took a big breath and clicked the autopilot off. A sick feeling rose in her stomach as the plane pitched and dipped. Dag grabbed the co-pilot controls and steadied her hand.

"OK, now what?" Molly asked.

"The highway patrol has been notified. They are on the highway ten miles ahead of you. You will have to land on the highway."

"I can't see it."

"Look for flashing lights. When you see them turn your heading back to 270 degrees. You'll have to turn with the controls because the autopilot is off."

"I can't see anything! I don't think I can do it." She strained her eyes looking for anything to make sense. Most of her view was inky blackness and the dim glow from the instrument panel.

"Slow down to 100 knots."

"I see it. I see the lights," Molly said. A flicker of hope flashing in the darkness below.

"Good. Try to line up with the lights and slow your speed, you will gradually lose altitude."

"OK, I think we're aimed the right way."

"What does your altimeter read?"

"135 feet, we're dropping!" Suddenly the engines sputtered and went quiet. She felt the plane start to fall. "The engines quit!"

"Put your landing gear down and pull back on the controls and bring the nose of the plane up!"

"What landing gear!?" It was too late.

The tail section barely missed the state patrol car and hit the pavement hard. The body of the plane slammed into the road and bounced. Sparks flew as part of the tail was ripped away from the plane. They skidded for two hundred feet and turned sideways into the ditch before coming to rest.

Molly's head snapped forward then back. Her helmet struck the back of the cockpit and the speakers went dead. Molly took a deep breath and released her seatbelt. *Well, that wasn't so bad.* And then reality hit her.

Chapter 46

Some say the world will end in fire, some say in ice.
– Robert Frost

Friday morning, North Dakota.

Molly's shoulders shook as she wept. The stress of the abduction, the flight and the landing came flooding out. The cold howling wind, lashing through the open door of the aircraft, was a bad memory. The terror of flying a plane into the dark night was over. They were alive and on the ground.

The ambulance was on the scene and ready after receiving the report from traffic control. Unfortunately, CNN affiliate KXMB-TV out of Minot also showed up, but by then, Dag and Molly had been transported to the local hospital, evaluated and transferred to Minot.

Minneapolis.

Lena Johnson was so angry she ate a bacon cheeseburger for lunch, but the bun was gluten free. She looked at
the report and shook her head. Everything she believed
about Dutch Van Tassel was a lie. All of the evidence
pointed toward conspiracy, extortion, murder, arson, theft,
tampering with evidence, failure to return a rental car and
driving without seatbelts.

She made a list of what she knew and what she suspected. Dutch Van Tassel and the pilot disappeared and
probably crossed the border into Canada. Bobby Smith
vanished without a trace from the hospital in Charlotte.
Molly Seymour and Dag survived a harrowing plane landing on a highway in North Dakota.

Catch-22 was the link, but what was the key to explain
it?

"Agent Johnson, we're ready."

Lena climbed into the back seat of the black suburban.
The driver headed out to a municipal airfield in Maple
Grove, northwest of Minneapolis. A charter plane was
ready to take her to Minot, North Dakota. She wanted to
interview Dag and Molly in the hospital before anyone else
did.

Friday, Hudson Hospital

Libby improved quickly. The doctors discontinued the ET tube, so she could breathe on her own. As the sedative wore off, she was more alert. Her throat was raw, and her voice was hoarse, but she was glad to be alive.

She wondered about her experience. It seemed surreal, but so vivid in her mind. She wondered if it was a dream or a hallucination. For now, it didn't matter. She was back.

"Mom, will you hand me the TV remote?"

"How are you feeling?" Olivia handed her the remote and watched her grimace as she reached out.

"It hurts." She didn't feel like talking. Having the TV turned on, distracted her and everyone else from asking every ten minutes, how she felt.

Libby turned on the television, clicking through the home shopping network, ESPN, and half dozen others. She found nothing of interest and handed the remote back to her mom. "Here, watch what you want."

"Do you mind if I watch CNN?" Olivia asked.

Libby shrugged. Anything was better than nothing.

There was the usual political banter. No conclusions, no victories, it was always the same. Then the story changed.

We have an amazing story from North Dakota. Molly Mae Seymour, a 21-year-old college student from the Minneapolis-St. Paul area was abducted at gunpoint from northern Wisconsin, and taken in a twin-engine airplane out of Superior, Wisconsin. But the captors skydived out of the plane as it was running out of fuel. Molly along with Mr. Dag Rasmussen were tied up in the plane. Molly was able to free herself and her fellow captor, who was blind. She successfully flew the plane and landed on a highway at night as the plane ran out of fuel. The passengers, Molly Seymour and Dag Rasmussen were transported to a hospital in Minot, North Dakota. She is being treated for hypothermia and non-life-threatening injuries. Both the FBI and the FAA are involved in the investigation.

I'm Ole Torkelsen for CNN affiliate KXMB out of Minot, North Dakota.

A Penrose Christian University ID photo of Molly was put into the upper right corner of the scene as film footage panned the landing site. The plane was tilted sideways on the side of the road with a section of the tail missing. The nighttime image appeared more gruesome with a half-dozen blood red flashing emergency lights and pelting sleet.

Libby was speechless.

Olivia said, "What has that girl gotten into now?"

Lena Johnson landed at Minot Regional airport. The waiting police officer transported her directly to the hospital.

"We've secured the hospital. No one is allowed contact with the survivors except immediate family, unless I clear them." Sheriff Andrewsen appeared confident with his control of the situation.

Lena thanked him and helped herself into the passenger seat of the waiting squad car. He flipped on the emergency lights and sped to the hospital.

At the hospital she showed her credentials to the officer guarding the patient rooms and went into Dag's room first. He was sitting in a chair in the corner of the room listening to the television.

"Mr. Rasmussen, we meet again." Lena announced as she walked into the room. He clicked off the TV and turned his head toward her. Dag dabbed the ointment in his good eye and blinked. "Agent Johnson." Lena thought his voice lacked enthusiasm.

"Were you expecting someone else?" Lena asked.

"I didn't expect to be here. Anything is a bonus."

"Dag, I'm not sure we're on good terms but we need to work together. I need you to trust me."

"Like the Flying Dutchman?"

371

"I'm not him. He blindsided all of us." Lena looked down at the floor as she spoke.

"I need some guarantees," Dag said.

"Like what?"

"The girl's a heroine. She saved my life. Give her the credit she deserves. Second, I have a witness. Someone on the inside who can give you the details. All of them. You need to guarantee immunity or no deals."

"Who?"

"Not yet."

"Anything else?

"I need someone to get my truck and camper in Cornucopia."

"That's all?"

Dag got a pen and paper from the stand beside the hospital bed. He wrote *R.G. Wilkins, Justice Department, DC.* He folded the paper and handed it to her. "You can ignore all the suits in Washington but don't ignore Wilkins. He's the deal maker."

"Why would a Washington insider talk to me?"

"He won't." Dag took another paper and wrote. *Ramon Allones Cohiba Cubans. Box of 10.* "Get these Cuban cigars and wrap seven of them inside a piece of paper with your number. Nothing else. Don't send any other brand. Send it to his office. He'll call."

"Why only seven?"

"The other three are for me."

As she walked out of Dag's room she turned and said, "I was wrong about you."

"Is that an apology?" His good eye was starting to get its laser focus back. He stared at Lena.

"No, but it's a start." She turned right in the hallway. Three rooms down she stopped and knocked on Molly's door.

"Hi, I'm Lena Johnson, FBI. Can I ask you some questions?"

Molly's hair was still wet from a shower but she was dressed and looked surprisingly good to Lena. She could see Molly's eyes were puffy and red. There was a bruise across her face and swelling on the forehead. She had bandages on her arms but she was smiling. Not what she expected from a plane crash survivor.

"Mr. Rasmussen told me you saved his life," Lena said.

"It was a miracle anyone survived. We're here by the grace of God. That's all."

"That's not what they're saying on TV."

"You can't trust everything you hear on TV." Molly sipped some ice water through a straw.

They talked for over an hour. At times Molly seemed friendly and chatty, like old friends at a coffee shop. Lena reviewed her three pages of notes. There was enough information to send Dutch Van Tassel to prison for life.

Molly started to tear up. "I need to know something. When we left Cornucopia, Dutch set fire to Margaret's house. I want to know what happened."

Lena made a couple phone calls. After ten minutes she smiled. "Good news. Someone driving by reported the fire. They got her out, alive. She's in the hospital in Duluth."

"And her house?"

"Not good from what they tell me." Lena decided it was time to go. "Is there anything else you want to tell me before I leave?"

Molly hesitated.

Chapter 47

I've made it a rule never to smoke more than one cigar
at a time. – Mark Twain

Mid December, Oak Grove, Wisconsin.

Libby healed like a champ and was home from the hospital within a week. By mid-December she was getting
around with crutches. She had a nagging pain in her side
where the chest tube was placed but it was tolerable, and
she never complained.

Molly moved back home and worked herself into a routine. She and her mother never mentioned the wedding.
Her wedding dress hung in the closet, ready for the next el-
igible bachelor. Molly knew it was over and strangely she

felt no remorse. She didn't waste time trying to analyze why she had no regrets, she had bigger fish to fry.

The zip drive was password protected but using a self-designed cryptogram algorithm software she solved it without breaking a sweat. She was shocked to find a detailed blueprint for the Cossack Weapon; the weapon she designed as a sixteen-year-old college freshman. Even more startling were the utilization plans. Refined and mass-produced by Mork Industries, these simple but devastating weapons were being used to target politicians, athletes, business executives, and foreign ambassadors.

Molly found lists of bank accounts, money transfers, phone numbers, corrupt federal agents, dirty cops, contacts and a host of other things she never dreamed existed. She didn't want to know how Bobby Smith got this information but having it gave her tremendous leverage or put a very high price on her head.

There was only one person she trusted with this data - Dag. Telling her family would put them at risk. After her experience with Dutch Van Tassel, she didn't trust Agent Johnson. Even if she could be trusted, what about her superiors? Molly didn't want to crash any more airplanes in the dark.

Molly made three copies of the data. Sharing it and keeping it safe would be the tricky part.

"Mom, I'm going up to Namukwa, to Aunt Luella's place today. I'm meeting a couple of the cousins. I'll be back tomorrow night."

"OK. But don't get into trouble like you did the last time."

"It's over Mom, don't worry." As Molly gave her a hug goodbye she noticed a streak of gray hair. Molly pulled back just a bit and took a closer look. *It's probably my fault.*

#

Lena's cell phone vibrated as she came into her office on Monday morning. The message was simple; a phone number with a D.C. area code. She closed her office door and returned the call.

"Wilkins."

"I'm agent Lena Johnson, FBI. I was told you like Cuban cigars."

"Dag sent you. Don't talk on the phone. Wednesday, Starbucks, 15th and Franklin, 7am."

She heard the phone go dead. *Starbucks, 15th and Franklin?* She entered the address into Google Maps. *Washington DC? In forty-eight hours?*

There wasn't money in the budget for a midlevel agent to jet around the country for clandestine cappuccinos. She was concerned others in her division may be involved. It would have to be on her own dime with a good excuse. *I can't use appendicitis again, maybe root canal or malaria.*

Two days later. Washington DC, Starbucks, 15th and Franklin.

Lena took the red eye flight out of Minneapolis and landed in DC around 2 am. She slept on a bench at the airport until 5:30 then caught a taxi to 15th and Franklin. The coffee shop was busy with commuters getting their morning caffeine fix. In the corner was a short bald man with a cup of coffee and a bagel. His black wool coat was open at the front and Lena could see his Washington Redskins silk tie. He had a folded copy of the Wall Street Journal on the table and a Cuban cigar was sitting next to his coffee.

She bought a tall cup of Colombian with a shot of espresso and a poppy seed muffin. "Is this seat taken?" she asked.

"Do you like cigars?"

"No, but I know an old Dane who does."

He picked up his coffee and jerked his head toward the door. Lena followed. When they got to the street he said. "The walls have ears. In D.C. everyone is listening."

She followed him for two blocks. They chatted about the weather, the price of gasoline and the latest movies being released for Christmas. At the end of the block Wilkins turned and went into a 24-hour theater. They got seats in the back-right corner. Lena feared falling asleep. He gave her a small microphone to clip to her collar and an ear bud, so they could talk in low voices and still hear each other.

Wilkins started. "Dag and I worked out the cigar signal years ago. Three or less was serious but not urgent. Seven is the highest number. You've got one hour."

Lena spent the last forty-eight hours trying to condense everything into a coherent package. She started with Dutch and ended with the plane crash in North Dakota two weeks ago. She checked her watch, thirty-eight minutes.

There was a long pause. Lena wondered if Wilkins was more interested in the movie than what she said. Finally, he answered. "Who's the witness?"

"It has to be Smith. I can't think of anyone else on the inside willing to talk."

"And you have proof?"

"Enough to indict Van Tassel."

"Not enough for me. I need hard evidence of this *Catch-22* thing before I start pulling strings."

"The girl has something she isn't telling me."

"Is she protecting someone?"

"I don't think so. Dag claims he will produce hard evidence if you guarantee protection for the witness."

"I need facts before I act, not after." He stood to go. The meeting was over.

As they walked out of the theater into the morning air, Lena gave him a note with a phone number.

"What's this?"

"A secure number. Call Dag tomorrow."

"Where is he?"

"Volunteering at a food shelf in Namukwa, Wisconsin."

#

Thursday. Namukwa food shelf.

Dag closed the door behind him in the back room of the food shelf as he answered his phone. "Do you think Johnson's involved?" he asked.

Wilkins said, "Midwest Lutherans are all the same."

"What does that mean?"

"She's a poor liar. She's clean."

"Good. I'll send the basics by email. Same offsite server and address as before?"

"Same. I'll send the documents Fedex to a safe house you designate."

"Arrange a face-to-face. If this is as big as you say, the Justice Department is going to be busy. So what do you think of the Redskins this year? People in D.C. are already talking Super Bowl."

"I wouldn't bet on them."

"Why?"

"Wait until you see what I'm sending."

After Dag hung up the phone he sent three encrypted files to Wilkins. There were enough names and numbers to prompt a congressional investigation. He made one more phone call.

"Yeah?"

"Keep him under wraps. Meeting arranged. Saturday before Christmas. Blue Heron Café, 2 pm. Grand Avenue, St. Paul."

He ended the call and took a deep breath. *When this is over, I'm going to retire...again.*

Chapter 48

Poets have been mysteriously silent
on the subject of cheese. – G. K. Chesterton

Saturday before Christmas, Grand Avenue.

Grand Avenue was bustling with people on the last shopping weekend before Christmas. Every store and restaurant had signs and specials. Christmas carolers in small and large groups marched up and down the sidewalks belting out traditional songs. Lena Johnson parked on the far western end of Grand and counted no less than five different Santa's posing for pictures, ho-ho-hoeing in front of stores or ringing monotonous bells beside red kettles.

She walked seven blocks east until she came to the Blue Heron Café and checked her watch, 1:37. Meeting was at 2 pm. She noticed the black suburban with dark tinted windows, three blocks from the café. She wasn't alone. Another was parked a block past the café. She reached under her coat and adjusted her 9mm Glock.

At ten minutes before the hour, she saw Wilkins exit the far vehicle and enter the front of the restaurant. The guy in the ski jacket and Vikings stocking cap at the front of the store gave him an imperceptible nod. Another man in a suit and long black trench coat got out of a rental car next to the suburban and followed Wilkins inside. Lena followed.

The Santa across the street from the Blue Heron put on a pair of sunglasses. The bright afternoon sun reflecting off the snow hurt his good eye. He rang the bell casually and thanked the shoppers who donated. Two blocks east he watched a group of carolers sing Jingle Bells for the fifth time. Everything was in order.

Lena ignored the hostess and walked to Wilkin's table. Wilkins took off his black calfskin gloves and cracked his knuckles. "The deal's off," he said. He glanced at the lawyer to his left.

"The NFL doesn't want a trial. If this goes, public it would mean civil war. The player's union would sue every television network claiming injuries, ratings would plummet, the credibility of the NFL and every other major sports industry would be in question. No one could claim any recent playoff or Super Bowl games were legitimate."

Wilkins added, "There's enough circumstantial evidence to suspect several multinational businesses with ties to Russia and organized crime in New York, Chicago and Europe, but if we open Pandora's box we don't know what could happen."

Agent Johnson put both hands to her head and rubbed her temples. "You're going to turn your back and walk away?"

"We didn't say this would be ignored. We feel it's best to handle this quietly. Without publicity."

"The truth needs to come out," Lena said.

"American's can't handle the truth," Wilkins said.

Across the street, the one-eyed Santa continued ringing his bell. He looked up and down the street. Everything was ready. *Where's the sign?*

The waitress stood back by the kitchen door watching the table carefully. The woman at the table rubbed her temples and looked down. It was time to take the order.

"Are we ready to order?" The waitress asked.

One man waved her away, the other said, "Coffee, black."

Lena Johnson looked up at the waitress. She had her short dark hair pulled back and held in place with a pink bandana. She wore black rimmed glasses and had faded brown dots on her cheeks made to look like freckles.

"I'll have the steak sandwich, medium rare," Lena said. *She's a tofu girl. Something's wrong.*

"Thank you, I'll take care of that as soon as possible." Instead of returning to the kitchen, the waitress walked slowly around the salad bar and out the front door. Once outside, she took the bandana and glasses off and walked quickly toward the Christmas carolers two blocks to the east.

The one-eyed Santa watched Molly leave. There was a black Cadillac with dark windows and Illinois plates moving slowly down the street, west to east. Two windows were down and the men were studying the crowds.

Dag raised a walkie-talkie to his mouth and said, "Something's wrong. We're not alone. Abort."

"In the crowd. That's him." The driver honked and gestured at the people crossing the street in the crosswalk.

A horse drawn carriage, carrying holiday revelers, approached from the east. It was nearly to the black Cadillac. When the horse was close, Dag kicked over the red kettle. The steel cover clanked and rolled into the street in front of the horses. Coins scattered everywhere. The horses bolted sending one wheel of the carriage into the left front fender of the car. Dag heard the driver swear as he opened the door. A mob of people descended on the coins and cash lying in the street.

He looked to his left. Two blocks down Molly crossed over to the group of singers. Jingle Bells erupted for the seventeenth time. Two people exited the back of the group heading away from the crowd.

The Cadillac driver yelled and pressed the horn. Two men from the opposite side of the car jumped out and ran down the street. They reached inside their coats and took out handguns.

Molly and the man, ran down the street and ducked into the garage and into the garden shed. She closed the door behind her and pulled the cabinet. It swung away from the wall on hinges.

"Go," she said and pushed him into the darkness. She followed and pulled the cabinet back in place. She felt for the hook in the dark and clipped it in place.

"I forgot the flashlight." Molly removed the hook and started to push the door open.

"They ran in here." She heard the sound of shoes scuffing on concrete. Trash cans were toppled. Glass shattered. One of the trash cans clattered against the cabinet where she stood. Molly held her breath, afraid to move. If she wavered, they were dead.

"Hey, this is private property." Molly recognized the voice.

"Get lost, Santa Claus." While the men were distracted, Molly hooked the door. They would find their way in the dark.

The only light was the faint streak, leaking into the tunnel from Henkel's garden shed. "I can't do this." She felt goosebumps form on her arms and legs. Little hairs prickled on the back of her neck, along the hangman's noose tattoo. Her breath came in jerks. She slumped to the floor, her hands and knees felt the cold wet tunnel. "I'm afraid of the dark."

He didn't answer. She couldn't see him. She heard his scuffling and breathing somewhere behind her. She held her hand up in front of her eyes. It was invisible. There was more swearing and yelling and banging on the other side of the door. *There's a way, only one way.* She stood up and reached out with her right hand trying to find the wall of the crypt. It was cold and unmoving like a homeless man she found, dead and frozen behind the Gospel Mission.

Turning her back on the sliver of light coming from the garage she said, "This way, follow me."

Feeling along the damp concrete and stone wall with their right hands they inched into the labyrinth. Molly tried to remember the forks and side tunnels. *I think there were three.* Slowly she put one foot in front of the other, feeling for steps. She heard rodents squeaking in the darkness and felt the warm body of a rat bump against her foot. She kicked into the darkness and yelled. The scurrying stopped for a few seconds and then resumed.

Damp, dusty cobwebs hit her face and she stopped to wipe them away. Then she tripped. "We're at the first steps. It should go up and then turn to the right."

"OK, I'm behind you."

Molly felt his hand on her shoulder. She counted thirteen steps up, a flat landing, turn to the right and seven more steps. "Move with me to the left wall. There is another tunnel to the right after the first steps. I don't know where it goes." They shuffled in the darkness. One of them kicked an empty bottle in the darkness. It clattered against the wall and bounced down the steps. A rat screeched around the corner. They heard the fluttering in the air around their heads. Bats. Molly bit her lip and swallowed the scream before it got out.

One hundred twenty-three steps, turn right. She felt her toes bump into another set of steps. *Should be seventeen steps, no turns.* She counted them as they went. *Fifteen. Did I go the wrong way? No. Keep going. Turn right. Another fork coming up. There it is. Thirty-seven paces. Dead end.*

She felt with her hand. It was a door. *I hope it's the right door.* There were no latches, no knobs, no hooks and no light leaking into the cavern.

Knock-knock pause, knock-knock-knock, pause, knock. She waited...nothing. Two-three-one was the signal. She did it again. Listening carefully, Molly heard scraping and the door swung open.

The old woman squinted as she peered into the dark tunnel and motioned them out. She gave Molly a hug and turned to the man. "Mr. Smith, I presume?"

#

Gladys had a pot of tea ready and matzo ball soup. As they rested and ate, Gladys gave instructions.

"Mr. Smith, there's a closet in the guest room. You should find a UPS uniform just your size. Put it on. The UPS truck will be here in thirty minutes. You can trust the driver, his name is Albert. Your new identification and passport and papers are in the envelope. There's enough money until you meet your new contacts."

"I don't deserve this," he said.

"I know," Gladys said. "None of us do. But you're sorry for what you did and you changed."

Gladys went into the bedroom and came out with a box. "This is Otto's old coat. Take it."

"Why are you giving this to me?"

389

"Because he's been dead seventeen years. I'm sick of looking at it." She added, "If you need money, there's three diamonds sewn in the hem."

Molly said. "You told me, you lost your coat."

"I did, but Otto kept his. We nearly starved because he was too stingy to sell the diamonds."

"How can I repay you."

"Spend the rest of your days for good and help someone else."

"I will."

Chapter 51

If I had a flower for every time I thought of you...I could walk through my garden forever. – Alfred Tennyson

Christmas Eve, Namukwa.

"Ho-ho-ho." Santa Dag walked into the room in his undercover Santa suit and set a package under the Christmas tree.

"Dag, after this year, you've become one of the family." Tom raised a flute of champagne in the air. "To Dag."

"Cheers." Everyone else raised their glasses in unison.

Molly stood up in the middle of everyone, to speak. "I want to apologize to everyone for the grief I've caused this year. Mom and Dad, without your love and prayers, I might not be here. I love you." Molly gave her dad a hug and kiss on the cheek, but she held onto her mother until they were cried out.

"I'm sorry about Grandma's wedding dress," she said. "I'll get married someday. I promise."

"It's better to marry the right person than wear the right dress." Olivia started to cry again.

"And Libby. If it wasn't for me, you would have never been kidnapped. Will you forgive me?" It was Libby's turn to cry. Then she hit Molly on the shoulder with her crutch.

"Did you hear about Margaret Axtel?" Molly asked the group. Without waiting for an answer, she said. "Dag tell them.'

"The court awarded her the rightful owner of the money that Molly found in the wine cellar. Her arm is healing well and she's going to build a new house in the spring." Dag sat back down.

"Hooray for Margaret." Everyone seemed delighted.

"And the best news," He added. "Most of the wine was saved, and she gave it all to you!"

After dinner everyone filtered back into the living room and sat around the fireplace. Dag pulled out the package from under the tree. "I have one more thing for this family."

Dag stood by the Christmas tree. "I have made many friends and enemies over the past forty years. Sometimes good comes from it. One international company has been very helpful to me and I want to pass on to you what I have enjoyed."

He opened the package and handed out envelopes to everyone. "This is a charter flight to Greece to see Roy and Lola, and you're all invited, everyone one of you."

#

Nine months later, Icaria, Greece.

"All rise." The Greek Orthodox priest raised his hands and everyone stood to their feet. The small gathering cheered, and clapping broke out as the bride walked around the blooming bougainvillea and stepped over the lazy tabby cat sunning on the terrace. Her dress was simple and elegant. It fluttered in the breeze off the deep blue Aegean. She wore a finely woven crown of olive branches and her dark hair hung loosely, past her shoulders. An old man hooked her arm into his as they shuffled along. They came to a stop before the priest.

"Who gives this bride to be married to this man?"

"We do." A short woman with long gray hair, stood and walked to the other side of the bride. The old man and the old woman linked hands behind the back of the bride as the priest read and spoke and prayed. After kisses and hugs, they joined the hands of the bride and groom together and returned to their seats.

393

"Lilja Pappas, do you take this man to be your husband?"

"I do."

"Nick Pappadopolis, do you take Lilja to be your bride?"

"I do." He slipped a golden ring with three glittering diamonds onto her left hand.

"I now pronounce you husband and wife." Nick embraced Lilja. He dipped her so low, her long hair brushed the terrace, as they kissed. Two doves were released from a small wooden bird cage. They fluttered over the terrace and landed in the olive trees behind the Paradeisus Inn.

At the side of the terrace, a long, narrow, well-worn wooden table was covered with linen. Handmade ceramic vases held bunches of fresh cut flowers, gathered from around the island. Big platters of meats, cheeses, olives and crusty bread were brought out from the kitchen. Tall carafes of local wine and glasses were placed within easy reach of the guests.

They laughed and danced and ate until they could eat no more, then they danced again. Molly found a quiet corner and sat alone for a few minutes. She looked at her family, her aunts and uncles and cousins. They were all there, just like it was fifteen years ago. She was happy.

"Are you accustomed to your new name yet?" She asked the groom.

"Nick Pappadopolis is a far cry from Bobby Smith," he said. "You know, I wouldn't be here if it wasn't for your kindness and forgiveness. I can't thank you enough."

"My grandpa and grandma are so happy for you and Lilja. It will be a good life for you here in Icaria."

"What are your plans?" Nick asked.

"I dropped out of creative writing in college. It's too dangerous." They laughed. "I entered a master's program in cryptology and should be done in six months. I've been heavily recruited by several organizations. I think Dag and Agent Johnson had something to do with that."

#

"Please sit down. We've got something to tell you." Roy and Lola motioned for their children and grandchildren to sit. There was Tom and Luella, Richard and Vera, Emma and Phineas and Molly's parents, Olivia and Harry. Her cousins listened attentively as their grandparents addressed them. Molly saw Maddie, Zoe, Theo, Mary Beatrice and Daisy. Her little sister Libby sat beside Olivia.

"It's time for us to come home," Lola said. "We feel good and we're as healthy as old people can be, but like elephants, we want to come home to die."

"When?"

"We're leaving on the plane with you," Roy said. "We've transferred everything we have here to Nick and Lilja."

"Where are you going to live?" Luella asked.

"With you."

#

The music and eating and partying never stopped. Sometime after midnight Molly took her sandals off to rest her feet. She sat on the stone bench to stare at the moonlight reflecting off the sea. Much had happened over the past couple years, most of it, unexpected. She felt a small seed of contentment beginning to sprout. She wasn't going to predict the future, she would just take it as it came.

There was movement beside her. She lookup to see a young man approach and sit beside her on the bench. He handed her a glass of wine.

"Hi, I'm Orion." His voice was steady and pleasant. He smiled at her.

"Like the stars?" She asked. He nodded.

Molly smiled back. She saw his thick hair, decadent and unruly. His eyes were as black as the sky beyond the stars. She reached up and took the wine. Her hand brushed his, lightly.

"I'm Molly," she said, "Molly Hatchet."

Epilogue

How did it get so late, so soon? – Dr. Seuss

Roy and Lola said goodbye to everyone on the island. It was a long goodbye. Fifteen years of laughter, dominoes and homemade wine weren't easily dismissed. But time was good to them. When they left the Paradeisus Inn and took the water taxi to Naxos, they knew it was the last time. Roy wanted to sit on the deck and listen to the loon's eerie call over Lake Namukwa one more time before they closed the lid over him. Lola accused him of being dramatic but they both knew the truth. They were living on borrowed time and had been for years.

Nick and Lilja Pappadopolis were the new owners of the Inn. Lilja knew all the nuances of the old place and Nick was a good pupil. He made the transition from hardened gambler to innkeeper without problem. The lifestyle suited him fine. He loved the people and they loved him right back. Everyone shared their bounty and no one went without. But he missed Chicago Cubs baseball.

Nick was in his forties but Lilja was more than twelve years younger. Before the end of their first year of marriage, she conceived and had a little boy. They named him Yorrie.

Dag tried retiring again but he got into trouble. He went on a singles cruise for retired people and got into an argument with another passenger. He threw the guy overboard. Dag was arrested and kicked off the ship in Jamaica. He knew some of the officials in the country, from his drug war days. They let him off as long as he didn't come back to Jamaica and start trouble. When he got back to the states, he retired from retirement and a started new business: Pinkerton's Private Eye. He worked out of the basement of 1710 Summit Avenue. His view wasn't very good but he had a really interesting back door into the office, and his landlady made him matzo ball soup twice a week and green tea every afternoon.

Libby healed up just fine. She started running as a way to rehab her leg and discovered she liked running. She went to state competition for cross-country running and placed third.

Molly finished her master's program in cryptology in December, the same year her grandparents moved back to Namukwa, Wisconsin. After her graduation she felt uneasy and troubled. When she needed time to think she liked to hang out at the Chattering Squirrel Coffee Shop. It was a sunny Friday morning as she opened her laptop and typed in the password for free wifi. Her Costa Rican blend coffee was steaming in the mug beside her on the small table.

The headlines grabbed her attention and she forgot about checking her email.

CNN, The Washington Post, ABC, USA Today, even Fox News...each had some version of the same story. The President and his advisors were stunned and confused about "Sonic Attacks" in China. Diplomats were being re-called and China pledged to investigate.

The chatter in the coffee shop faded into the background. Her coffee went cold.

She wanted to tell her story but no one would believe her. It had started with her freshman paper, then Bobby Smith, Tuck Riley, Mork Industries, the FBI, the Russians and now it was in the hands of political elite around the world. Where would it end?

This time she needed more than just a mug of black coffee and a chair in the corner of the coffee shop. Molly bought a round-trip ticket to Italy and rented a small apartment in Riva del Garda for two weeks. She drank espresso in the mornings and chianti in the evenings with linguini and gelato. She slept late, read books on the piazza and took long walks by the lake.

She discovered an antique store specializing in old books. She loved to browse the stacks of books in Libri Antiquaria. She bought three books and retired to her table by the lake. In the second book she found it. A note in the margin.

Bonus Material

There's no friend as loyal as a book – Ernest Hemingway

August, Riva del Garda, Trentino, Italy.

Molly sat in the closest shade she could find and sipped a macchiato. Her pistachio gelato was melting fast in the afternoon heat and she sucked it through a straw as it puddled in the corner of her dish.

She pulled three books out of her handbag and set them on the table. The second book had a small scribbled note in the margin and a signature. It looked old, at least old enough to pique her interest, so she wanted to follow up with the store owner and ask some questions. The brisk wind from the lake, the same wind which called the wind surfers, fluttered her pages and caused one loose page to dance across the grass. She retrieved it and tucked the book away for another afternoon. Molly picked up her handbag and walked across the cobblestone piazza to the old bookstore for her last visit before returning to America.

Libri Antiquaria bookshop was one of her favorite hangouts when she visited Riva del Garda. It was her third time to the hamlet on the north shore of Lago de Garda.

Her first was during a study-abroad semester with Penrose Christian University and the second was with a friend, touring Europe for the summer, living in youth hostels and train stations. This time she was alone, trying to figure out her life. After her failed wedding engagement and the plane crash she looked at life differently. Not a complete turnaround but enough of a change to make her think and Riva del Lago was a good place to do it.

She loved the slower pace of life. An afternoon by the lake was an eternity compressed into an afternoon, sipping a dry rosato or cappuccino. *Meriggiare* was the word the locals used to describe the simple escape from the hot afternoon sun, into the cool inviting shade. Since coming to Lago di Garda, it was her new favorite word, ranking near the top of the list with vino, linguini, and gelato.

The book store opened on a side street two blocks up from the lake shore and three blocks from the clock tower. It was small and if you hurried you missed the entrance. The narrow door was dark stained wood, carved in medieval patterns typical for the southern Austrian-northern Italian area known as Alto-Adige. The door was heavy and it took extra effort to push it open. Enough effort that Molly wasn't sure if the door was locked or unlocked.

The door creaked open and the smell of history leaked into the streets. There was a dark mustiness of sequestered knowledge hidden in the nooks and shelves behind the heavy door. She breathed deeply, inhaling the stories of centuries past.

"Buena sera."

Molly turned toward the voice. A short old man with a bald head and a bristling fringe of gray hair peered between stacks of books set on the counter. His round glasses were perched halfway between the front and back end of his nose. The thick lens amplified the size of his eyes giving Molly a fleeting image of a bullfrog hiding in the dark. She imagined him to be a modern monk protecting the wisdom of the ages.

"Ciao...parlo Inglese?" Molly knew enough Italian to order spaghetti, wine and maybe tiramisu but anything more was a challenge.

"Yes...I speak English. How can I help you?" He asked. "My name is Giuseppe."

"Like Pinocchio?" she asked.

"No. That's Geppetto."

"Of course. I'm sorry." Molly blushed.

"That's okay. I'm pleased that you found my store." Giuseppe said. "I think I recognize you. Were you here about two years ago, with a friend?"

"Yes, I was. You have a good memory." She said.

"My memory is beginning to fail, but young beautiful American women in here is almost as rare as the books. It is hard for me to forget you," Giuseppe smiled. "If I recall correctly, you like historical mysteries, biographies, journals and such. Yes?"

"Yes. I like history, especially stories about unsolved mysteries, or lost treasure, things like that." Molly moved between the stacks looking for books written in English. She remembered the book store from her previous visit.

"Most of our books are in Italian, some are in French but we have a large selection in English. Some dating back more than two hundred years." Giuseppe waved his arm and directed her to the back corner of the store. "We also have reprints of books dated from before the 1700's. The originals are obviously very rare."

Molly followed him to the back corner of the bookstore. She was surprised by the depth of the book shop, stretching from a tiny street front to a large back end, encompassing several rooms. The books stacks were tall and she couldn't see over or around them. When the short frog-eyed bookstore proprietor left her, she became absorbed in her search. Twenty minutes lapsed into thirty and then an hour. She decided to wait and ask about the note and the signature after she browsed a while.

She heard a bell tinkle as the front door opened and closed.

*

Giovanni Maldonado adjusted his sunglasses as he opened the passenger door of the red Ferrari. It was hot outside and his lens fogged, moving from the air-conditioned interior to the muggy air outside. He tilted them atop of his head and blinked.

"Cinque minuti." He said to the driver as he closed the door. His polished leather shoes made staccato taps as he walked across the cobblestone piazza and turned the corner. His dark eyes surveyed his surroundings. The park benches facing Lago di Garda were filled with young lovers and old men. Pigeons flocked and fluttered on the pavement, searching for crumbs. He reached under his jacket and rechecked his BerettaU22 Neos.

Giovanni walked quickly toward his destination, Libri Antiquaria, two streets east of his parking spot. He came to the corner of Via Cuomo and Via Vitale and paused. He stopped by the next corner and checked his path. *No one following. He would have it in his hands in three minutes.*

The bell above the door tinkled as he entered. The bug-eyed proprietor stared at him through the pile of books on the counter. Giovanni paused and listened. He heard nothing else. He saw no movement.

"Are you alone?" Giovanni asked. Giuseppe started straight ahead and nodded his head once, up and down. "Do you have it?"

The book store owner stood on his tip-toes and pulled out a book from the stack on the highest shelf, out of reach from the normal customers. The cover was a faded green canvas and the top edge was tattered and frayed. He ran his fingers over the cover. The title was faded but he could still feel a slight indentation from the old printing press.

"Ten thousand euro. We agreed. The final payment. Where is it?" He held the old book so tight his fingers blanched.

Giovanni took an envelope from his inside jacket pocket and set it onto the table. "Le libra," he said and reached out to take it from the old man. "You get the rest when we confirm the book's authenticity." Giovanni grabbed the book and opened the cover. There was one loose page. The owner backed away until he was pressed against the shelves in the corner behind the counter. He had nowhere to turn.

"Where is the other? Two. You said two pages." The tone of Giovanni's voice raised. "Where are they?"

"Where's the money? Then you get the other page." Giuseppe's voice faltered. "We agreed."

"You're pawns." Giovanni pulled out his Beretta and leveled the muzzle. "Pawns get sacrificed to win the game." Two quick spits came from the .22 caliber handgun. Giovanni grabbed the book and left. The doorbell tinkled as he shut the door.

#

Molly huddled in the corner of the back room. Her heart pounded in her chest. She heard the brief argument from the front but ignored it. Italians were passionate people, they waved their hands and raised their voices in the simplest discussions. It always sounded as if they were arguing. But the gunshots weren't normal. Two quick firecracker noises and the doorbell tinkled again. Then all was quiet except for the gasp and groan from the front.

Molly's heart pounded and she took quick shallow breaths. She counted to fifty, waiting to see if the gunman would return. *He's gone.* She crept through the stacks until she could see into the front part of the store. Nothing moved. She turned the last corner and saw Giuseppe crumpled in the corner, blood stains on the left shoulder and left side of his upper chest. His breathing was rapid and shallow. Molly didn't know if he was conscious. She reached his side and touched his face. Blood ran from his nose and the corner of his mouth. He coughed and blood sprayed out, onto Molly's arm.

"Giuseppe?" She asked as she turned his head. His glasses were thrown to the floor from the fall against the book shelf. He blinked several times.

"My glasses." He said. He fumbled about with his right arm, searching.

She found them and he pushed them into place on his nose. His eyes came into focus as he looked at Molly. He rolled to his left side and reached with his right arm and touched a worn, dark brown book at the end of the row on the bottom shelf. He pulled it out and gave it to her.

"He took the wrong book." He pressed into her hands. "Don't let him get it. You will know what to do."

"Police." She stood and reached for the telephone on the wall. "What is the number?"

"No carabinieri." He said, "It's too late. Go. Go out the back…" His breathing gurgled.

"Who wants this? What is it?" Molly asked. She held the book before his eyes.

"No…I can't…" He gave one final cough. "Magari…"

About the Author

John W Ingalls MD is a rural family physician in northwestern Wisconsin. He lives in the same area settled by his great-great-great grandparents, Lansford and Laura Ingalls who are grandparents to the famed and beloved author, Laura Ingalls Wilder.

Dr. Ingalls graduated from Webster High School, Webster Wisconsin in 1976. Following three years in the US Army, he attended the University of Minnesota, graduating with a BS degree in biology. In 1985 he and his family moved to Madison, Wisconsin where he attended the University of Wisconsin and returned to his home town to practice medicine where he remains today.

Married to his wife, Tammy they enjoy all things related to the great outdoors, extensive travel, fine dining, and time spent with close friends. Together they have four wonderful daughters, Leah, Anna, Abigail and Billie Kay. Each of the girls are married to gracious and loving husbands and they are now raising their own families and writing their own stories.